ADAM CANFIELD
THE LAST REPORTER

ADAM CANFIELD
THE LAST REPORTER

MICHAEL WINERIP

CANDLEWICK PRESS

Copyright © 2009 by Michael Winerip

From "Dear Levi: Letters from the Overland Trail"
by Elvira Woodruff, copyright © 1994 by Elvira Woodruff.
Used by permission of Alfred A. Knopf, an imprint of Random
House Children's Books, a division of Random House, Inc.

"The River Otter" by Janeen R. Adil was originally published
in *Ladybug* magazine. Used by permission of the author.

Stagecoach image copyright © 2009 by Vallentin Vassileff/Shutterstock Images.

Otter image copyright © 2009 by Supreme Graphics/Shutterstock Images.

First edition 2009

Library of Congress Cataloging-in-Publication Data

Winerip, Michael, date.
Adam Canfield, the last reporter / Michael Winerip. — 1st ed.
p. cm.
Summary: When the school board shuts down the student newspaper,
the Ameche Brothers, two budding entrepreneurs with a knack for refurbishing
junk but a shaky command of journalistic ethics, step in to help.
ISBN 978-0-7636-2342-5
[1. Newspapers — Fiction. 2. Journalism — Fiction. 3. Middle schools — Fiction.
4. Schools — Fiction. 5. Interpersonal relations — Fiction.]   I. Title.
PZ7.W72494Adc 2009
[Fic] — dc22   2009007347

09 10 11 12 13 14 BVG 10 9 8 7 6 5 4 3 2 1

Printed in Berryville, VA, U.S.A.

This book was typeset in Slimbach.

Candlewick Press
99 Dover Street
Somerville, Massachusetts 02144

visit us at www.candlewick.com

For Libby and Mike, Tilda and Harold

chapter 1

Who *Are* These Ameche Brothers?

"Adam, are you there?" Jennifer banged on the van. "I know you are!" she shouted. She cupped her hands around her eyes and stood on tiptoe to see through the tinted windows. He *was* in there, his legs stretched out on the floor by the backseat, motionless.

Her legs had goose bumps. The wind was blowing off the river, and it seemed more like early March than early May. "Come on, Adam. . . . You can't do this. You knew I was coming over!" She banged on the van several more times. "We've been planning this for a week . . . *Adam!*" She peered in again. Not a twitch.

Jennifer was standing in Adam's driveway, scream-ing at his locked van. *"Adam Canfield, you birdbrain, you know we have to see the Ameche brothers! Wake up! AAAAAAAAAA-dam!"*

"Jennifer, sweetie. Stop." It was Adam's mother, standing at the front-porch door. "You're dealing with an Olympic-class sleeper. You've got to pull out the big guns." She stretched her arm toward the van and pressed her key, unlocking the doors. "Go hard," she called.

Jennifer slid the side door open. She grabbed Adam's ankle and shook it. Nothing. She did it again.

"Come on," she said. "I know you're awake."

"I'm not. Go away."

"How come you're talking if you're not awake?" she said.

There was a long pause.

"Only my lips are awake."

Jennifer climbed up onto the middle seat of the van. She was on her knees, facing the back, elbows resting on the seat top, staring down at Adam on the floor. She made a hocking sound.

"Adam Canfield, if you don't wake up right now — and I mean all of you, not just your lips — I will spit this loogie right on your head. One . . ."

She made a hocking sound again. He was sure she was bluffing. Jennifer's manners were way too good for her to spit on her coeditor.

"Two . . ." A double hocking sound. No way she could hold all that loogie in without gagging. She was definitely bluffing. He wished he could take a peek to be sure, but then it would be hard to argue that he was asleep.

"Three."

He felt something wet.

"Gross!" he screamed, sitting bolt upright and using his sleeve to wipe the side of his face.

She held up a water bottle and let a few drops fall. "Faked you out."

"You are a terrible person," Adam said. "I wasn't hurting a fly, taking a little Sunday afternoon nap. . . ."

"A nap?" Jennifer said. "You take naps in your van?"

"Lots of people sleep in the car," said Adam.

"Not when it's parked in the driveway."

Did he have to explain himself every second? On a chilly afternoon with lots of sun, the van was the coziest place he knew. He'd been minding his own business, playing Bubble Struggle on the computer

3

for maybe two hours at most, when his parents started making a big thing about how he was wasting his life on "stupid" computer games and then staying up past midnight to finish his homework. Somehow that calm discussion had turned into a yelling match. So he'd stomped out of the family room to prove his point, ducked out the back door by the boiler room, and circled toward the front of the house, trying to think of a plan. There was the van, looking warm and friendly. He'd climbed in for a minute.

"Close the door," he said to Jennifer. "It's freezing out."

"Your mom says you've been conked out for more than two hours."

His mom knew he was in the van? What was she, the FBI? Just for one second, couldn't she be like other moms and feel terrible because he'd run away?

"I had the strangest dream," Adam said. "I dreamed that we had no school tomorrow because they came out with a new flavor of Brown-Sugar Wallops."

Jennifer just stared at him.

"Your hair's different," he said.

She smiled. She'd put it in braids, and she wiggled her head back and forth to bounce them.

"They look like the flying swings at Tri-River Adventure Park," he said. "I love that ride."

"I guess that's a compliment," she said. "We've got to go. I told the Ameche brothers we'd be there by now. I need you to take this seriously, Adam. I really think they're our best chance to save the *Slash.*"

"Right," said Adam. He was thinking of the long list of people who had tried to save the *Slash* — their school newspaper at Harris Elementary/Middle School — and how all of them had failed.

Mrs. Quigley, the acting principal, hadn't been able to save the *Slash,* and she loved Adam and Jennifer.

Mr. Brooks, his favorite teacher, hadn't been able to save the *Slash.*

A letter from the National Scholastic Press Association on official stationery defending freedom of the press hadn't been able to save the *Slash.*

A story in the *New York Times* that praised the *Slash* hadn't saved the *Slash.*

How were the Ameche brothers going to save the *Slash*? They were just kids. Adam had said all of this to Jennifer more than once, but the girl would not quit.

"You're the one who's dreaming," he said.

"Got to live your dreams," said Jennifer, jumping out of the van. Adam did not move; he seemed

5

to be struggling with a large lump in his pocket. He finally pulled out a plastic grocery bag with a smooth, rock-hard white sphere inside, almost as big as a tennis ball.

"My God, what is that?" asked Jennifer. "It looks like a giant eyeball."

Adam took it from the bag and stuffed it into his mouth. His eyes bulged from opening his jaw so wide. After a lot of loud slurping, he popped the ball back into the bag with his tongue.

"Want a suck of my jawbreaker?" he said. "It's delicious."

Adam and Jennifer biked together, racing much of the way.

"Passing on the left!" he yelled, streaking by her.

"Au revoir, mon chéri," she called when she overtook him.

The e-mail from the Ameche brothers had said they lived in the West End, which was on the other side of the downtown area. It was a pretty long ride, twenty minutes even biking hard, but Adam loved this time of year, when he could bike everywhere. His bike was his freedom. He loved riding to the West

End and often wished he lived there. It was a beachy neighborhood by the river that had once been a summer community of little cottages. Over the years, city people had moved out to live there full-time, winterizing the cottages, adding porches and decks and second and third floors.

Houses in the West End were crowded in so close that backyards were just narrow strips. Most houses did not have garages or driveways, so the streets and alleys were crammed with parked cars.

That's what Adam loved: everything was more squeezed together than in River Path or River Bluffs, where he and Jennifer lived. Every block had restaurants and bars and delis and pizzerias. And real shops: a butcher, a florist, a tailor, along with ice-cream and hardware stores and even a baseball-card store. And people were always walking around, even late at night. Kids in the West End had no trouble getting up wiffle ball or touch-football games or finding other kids to kick around a Hacky Sack. To Adam, the West End seemed like one big sleepover.

All the West End streets and alleys were named for months or states. February Path. Minnesota Walk. The Ameche brothers' e-mail said they lived on May Way West, in the middle of the block.

"That must be it," Jennifer said. "The e-mail said to look for a basketball hoop painted in zebra stripes with a neon-orange backboard."

Adam perked up. Zebra stripes? Neon-orange backboard?

Who were these Ameche brothers?

The house had stairs leading down to a basement and up to a front porch. "To the cave or the mountains?" asked Adam.

"Neither," said Jennifer. "They said to follow the yellow wire along the side of the house to the back. They said their headquarters is out back."

"Headquarters?" repeated Adam.

Who *were* these Ameche brothers?

The coeditors walked around the side, along a concrete path, to a high fence in back. Adam reached over the gate and undid the latch.

It was stunning to take in so much clutter at once: old motors, engine parts, used tires, gardening tools, a ripped hockey net, half a kayak paddle, several buckets of muddy golf balls, three broken fishing poles, a power mower with no wheels, a deflated blow-up raft, divers' wet suits, assorted boots. The yard was mostly cement, and along the back fence were stacks of orange plastic storage containers that reached past the top.

Adam noticed that it smelled a little bad. The odor seemed to come from the garden, which was against the house, but it wasn't like most gardens Adam had seen. There were three tiers of soil climbing upward like stairs, each bordered by long wooden beams. If Adam wasn't mistaken, they were filled with tomato plants. Adam could see little bones sticking out of the soil. And there seemed to be — could it be? — lots of bird doo?

"Maybe this is a mistake," said Jennifer. "I think we should go."

"No," said Adam. "This is great. How did you find these guys again?"

"I told you ten times — online," Jennifer whispered. She'd been trying to think of some way they could raise money to put out the *Slash* all by themselves, now that the paper had been closed down by the school board for causing too much trouble. She'd found the Ameches' ad on TremblesList, under "Business Start-Ups/Kids." The listing said that they were kids themselves, experts at starting up businesses for fellow kids. They said that they'd started a bunch of businesses, including a computer-repair business, a motorbike-repair business, a motor-scooter repair business, a model-airplane repair business, a cookie sales business, a golf-ball sales business, a lemonade-stand franchise business, an iPod music-download business, a toy-repair business, a spaghetti-sauce business, a tomato-paste business, a ketchup business, a pickled-tomato business, a tomato-soup business, a diced-tomato business, a stewed-tomato business, and a fresh-tomato business.

When Jennifer wrote, they'd messaged back saying that they'd never started a newspaper but would be happy to try one.

"I thought it would be nicer," Jennifer said. "More official-looking. We should go."

"What do you mean?" said Adam. "This *is* nice. That has to be their headquarters over there." He nodded toward a wooden storage shed that took up the entire width of the yard, maybe ten feet across. The yellow wire they'd been following went right inside it.

"What if they're Internet predators like they tell us about in Health and Careers class?" Jennifer whispered. "Maybe they're not even kids. Maybe they're two fat old guys with bad teeth who lure kids into their junky backyard and then . . . Oh, my God, we should go."

"Junky?" said Adam "What do you mean? No way. Two fat old guys with bad teeth wouldn't paint their rim with zebra stripes. They'd never have a neon-orange backboard. My reporter's instinct tells me we're onto something big here."

"I'm getting out," said Jennifer.

"No you're not," said Adam. "You're way too good a person to leave me at the mercy of two fat old guys with bad teeth. You could never live with yourself if something terrible happened to me while I was here *alone.*"

"But you can live with yourself if it turns out that you are leading *me* straight into a fat old perv trap?"

"I'm not as good a person as you," said Adam.

"Deep down inside you are."

"That's a long way to go," he said, and before she could say more, he knocked on the shed door.

There was no response, so he knocked twice more. Adam and Jennifer could hear talking inside, then saw a curtain over the shed window move slightly, and heard someone say, "It's not Ma."

"Then open it."

"Fans, our next two guests have arrived. Please say hello to . . ."

Two boys who were talking into their computer with microphone headsets were now staring at Adam and Jennifer. One of them was pointing a webcam on the top of his screen at them.

"Welcome to the *Ameche Brothers' Talk Till You Drop, All-Live Except the Recorded Parts* webcast, with Don and Alan Ameche serving your needs 24/7. Would you like to tell us your names, or are you fugitives from the law?"

Adam and Jennifer looked at each other. "Are you really broadcasting?" asked Jennifer. "Are people watching?"

"Globally speaking, two billion people have Internet hookups," said the bigger Ameche. "So don't get nervous." He motioned for them to sit on a couple of plastic crates that were squeezed in beside the Ameches. Adam glanced around. The shed was as jam-packed as the backyard, but mostly with gardening stuff: bags of potting soil, peat moss and fertilizer, gloves, spades, a pitchfork, a rake, a couple of saws. And there were stacks and stacks of used paint cans.

The bigger Ameche picked up an empty seed packet from the floor, crumpled it in his hand, then held his closed fist in front of the webcam and squeezed it all around, making crinkling noises. "I have a hundred-dollar bill in my hand at this very

12

moment that I'm ready to give away to the e-mailer with the best question for our guests this afternoon."

"Oops," said the smaller Ameche. "It's 4:17. Time for the weather report." He looked at Adam. "Would you mind doing the weather report for us?"

"He doesn't know anything about the weather," said Jennifer.

"Sure he does," said the bigger Ameche brother. "Just step outside. That's right. What do you see?"

"Well," said Adam, "not much. The sky's blue, the sun's out, and it feels kind of cold."

"Perfect," said the larger Ameche. "That's better than the lady on News 12 Accu-Weather." He turned toward the webcam. "Our *Talk Till You Drop* meteorologist has checked the Doppler radar readings here at the Ameche May Way West studios on the banks of the Tremble River in the heart of beautiful Tremble County and reports blue skies, plenty of sunshine, and temperatures — Wait a minute. . . . What's that? Oh, please, no. . . . Did you say . . . *funnel cloud*? That cloud's getting closer. . . . Oh, my God, I've never seen it get so dark, so fast. . . . *A twister!*"

The bigger Ameche grabbed a blue plastic tarp that was covering a pile of bags of soil under the table and tossed it over the computer, the webcam, his head, and his brother's head. "I hope you folks at home can see what we're up against here as this monstrous tornado bears down on us. I can't make out my fingers in front of my face. . . . And my brother? Alan, are you there? Alan? Oh, little Alan, I hardly knew you. . . . I have to apologize to all our loyal fans out there in cyberspace, but we're heading for cover. This is Don Ameche, signing off. . . ."

Adam and Jennifer looked at each other. Adam poked his head out of the shed just to be sure. The sky'd never looked bluer. He stepped back in. Both Ameches were still under the tarp. All Adam could see was two bumps in the tarp where their heads were.

"They look ridiculous," Jennifer whispered.

Adam wished he'd thought of it.

"Hey," said Adam. "Excuse me, I just . . ."

"Shhh," said one of the head bumps. "Just one second and the website will go remote. I'm upload-ing some video of the tornado from *The Wizard of Oz*. It'll make a nice wrap-up. . . ."

They finally tossed the tarp off, then brushed pot-ting soil from their hair and clothes.

"Boy," said Adam, "that's a lot of work. You must be worn out." He went into his pocket and pulled out the plastic bag with his giant jawbreaker. "Want a suck?" he said. "Great energy pick-me-up. Has one hundred percent of the daily sugar dose recommended by the National Council of Candy Manufacturers."

"That's gross," said Jennifer. "It's bad enough that *you* do it. Now you're going to share your germs with them?"

"What are you talking about?" said Adam. "Give me your water bottle." He took the jawbreaker out of the bag. "OK if the floor gets a little wet?" he asked.

"No problem," said the bigger Ameche. "We need to wet down the peat moss; the dust's bad for the computers."

Adam doused the jawbreaker with water and handed it to the bigger Ameche, who took a long, slurpy suck, then cleaned it off and gave his brother a turn.

"Too bad the webcast's on remote," said Don Ameche. "This would have been a terrific guest segment."

"What's your viewership?" asked Jennifer.

"Pretty much nobody," said Alan Ameche.

"That's not true," said Don Ameche. "We get a couple of hits a month. An occasional e-mail."

As if on cue, there was the sound of an e-mail arriving.

15

Alan glanced at the screen. "That doesn't really count," he said. "I can tell without reading it. It's that annoying third grader who tries to win the hundred-dollar prize every time."

"We think she's a wack job," said Don. "Very grandiose. She claims to be the world's greatest third-grade reporter."

Adam and Jennifer looked at each other but didn't say a word.

"Anyone ever win the hundred-dollar prize?" asked Adam.

"You kidding?" said Don. "Does it look like we have a hundred dollars?"

"OK," said Jennifer. "We should go. It was nice visiting with you."

"Wait," said Don. "We've had other e-mails. Not that long ago, either. From this girl who wants us to help her start a newspaper."

"She seemed pretty smart," said Alan. "Her spelling was good."

"Yeah," said Don. "I'm pretty sure she's no wack job."

"That's me," said Jennifer. "But we don't need to bother you. I can see it would be a waste of time. We need a business manager and webmaster to raise money so we can put out our newspaper — which, by the way, is based on this old-fashioned idea that it's important to stick to facts, something I can see you're not familiar with. We need money, not empty seed packets."

"Hey, wait," said Don. "We make lots—"

"And I'll tell you one more thing," said Jennifer. "That third-grade wack job? Phoebe is no wack job. A little difficult maybe, a bit high-strung. But she really may be the world's greatest third-grade reporter. And I think it's cruel that you'd lie to people that way — especially a third grader, sitting at home in front of her little computer trying so hard to win a prize that's just a big joke to you."

"Jennifer," said Adam, "please. I think the Ameches can help us. It's just a goof."

"Great," said Jennifer. "Then you and the brothers work it out. You don't need me. A little responsibility would be good for you, Adam Canfield. I'm going. I've got real stuff to do." And she stomped out, knocking over paint cans and stirring up a cloud of peat-moss dust as she went.

chapter 2

A Business Concern

Adam apologized to the Ameche brothers for Jennifer. He told them what a great person she was. He said that once they got to know her, they'd think she was terrific, too, and then he started explaining why they'd come. He hadn't gotten very far when there was a bunch of noise outside, in the yard. They could hear things being knocked around.

"*Shhh,*" said Don. He pulled the curtain away from the shed window a tiny bit and peeked out. "Oh, geez, it's Ma," he said. "She's back from Busy Bee already. Quick, grab a bag of soil and pretend you're helping us with the tomatoes."

They were too late. Mrs. Ameche was at the door. "Ameche brothers," she said. "I see the same weeds in my tomatoes that were there at nine this morning when I left. I don't see any evidence of fresh topsoil. I don't see any fresh bird poop.

"I will not stand for this," she continued. "You love it when I win the Big Tomato. You love the prestige of being state champ. You stick it on every jar of tomato product you move out of here, but I don't see you working for it."

"Aw, Ma," said Don. "We were just getting to the soil."

"Eight hours to lift a bag of topsoil?" said Mrs. Ameche, shaking her head.

"If you must know, Ma, we were setting up an important business deal here," said Don.

"We're negotiating to join a big media company," said Alan.

"Really?" said their mom. Then she turned to Adam, "You're a big media company? You don't look it, unless . . . You're not one of the Murdoch kids, are you? And if that's a yes, why would you waste your time with the Ameche brothers?"

"I don't think I am wasting my time," said Adam. "I'm coeditor of the *Slash*. We're the student newspaper of Harris Elementary/Middle School. Well, I *was* coeditor of the *Slash*."

"You lost your job?" said Mrs. Ameche. "The Ameche brothers are negotiating with an unemployed coeditor? Typical."

"Actually, I lost my newspaper," said Adam. "I'm still coeditor, but our newspaper got shut down."

Mrs. Ameche nodded. "Bad time for newspapers," she said. "Who was that black girl running out of here? She a media company, too? She looked upset. Ameche brothers, you didn't say anything prejudiced, did you?"

"Aw, come on, Ma," said Don.

"You think we're like Uncle Louie?" said Alan.

"Thank God, no," said Mrs. Ameche. "I raised you better than that. So what is going on here? Certainly nothing to do with taking care of my tomatoes."

"Well, if you must know, Ma," said Don, "not much is going on."

"Because someone interrupted the negotiations," said Alan. "You wouldn't have any idea who, Ma?"

"Sorry," said Mrs. Ameche. "My apologies, Ameche brothers. You two have been so busy, you probably haven't had a moment to listen to the weather report this afternoon. I heard they're predicting some pretty violent storms. Anybody heard the weather report?"

All three boys looked at her, but Mrs. Ameche turned her attention to Adam. "Well, let's hear it, young man. So you're no Murdoch. That's all right. Neither are the Ameche brothers. You got a name?"

It took quite a while for Adam to tell. He gave them some of the history of the *Slash*, including the name ("Harris Elementary *slash* Middle School, get it?"). He also described several of the best stories they'd done in the past year. And even though the Ameche brothers went to a different middle school, they'd actually heard about one of the stories, the one that saved the basketball hoops.

"Jennifer and I discovered that the zoning board had a secret plan to get rid of all the hoops, and we did a big front-page story," said Adam. "That's what got everybody working so hard to save the hoops."

"We signed a petition for the hoops," said Mrs. Ameche. "That was your story?"

Adam nodded. "I really like your hoop," he said. "I wish I had zebra stripes."

"Ma's an artist," said Don. "She does portraits at the Busy Bee flea market. Her record is four in an hour."

"Please, that's pushing it," said Mrs. Ameche. "Nearly killed me. Drained all my artistic juices. I like having at least a half hour for each painting. You need time to get the eyes right." She gave Adam a business card. It said DONATELLA AMECHE/PORTRAITS-WHILE-YOU-SHOP/SATISFACTION GUARANTEED.

"So why'd they shut you down if you did such great stories?" asked Mrs. Ameche. "Sounds like they should have given you some big award."

"That was the problem," said Adam. "The stories got a little too great." He told them about the final edition of the *Slash*, the March/April issue. He described how they'd done a big investigation about the Bolands' attempt to take over the poor section of town, the Willows, by pressuring people to leave so that the Bolands could build million-dollar mini-estates. "After that," Adam said, "the Bolands got so teed off, they made the school shut down the *Slash*."

"You took on the Bolands?" Mrs. Ameche let out a low whistle. "You're talking about the Bolands who own Bolandvision Cable and Boland News 12 and the *Citizen-Gazette-Herald-Advertiser* and Boland Realtors, Inc.? Those Bolands?"

"Those Bolands," said Adam.

"Didn't hear about that story," said Mrs. Ameche. "But I could understand how that could get you shut down. Powerful people. They like their version of the news. You upset the Bolands, they could squish you good."

"Like a bug," said Adam.

Mrs. Ameche wanted to know how a kid paper like the *Slash* got such big stories, and Adam said it was a lot of ways. Sometimes they'd just notice a problem and get suspicious and start nosing around. And sometimes they'd get a call from a top-secret source who gave them an inside tip, and then they'd start nosing around some more. "We just dig, dig, dig until we get to the bottom of things," he said.

"Oh," said Mrs. Ameche. "Dig, dig, dig, is it? You hear that, Ameche brothers? Does that remind you of anything you were supposed to do, do, do to the weeds in my garden, garden, garden?"

"Oh, Ma, we were going to do it," said Don. "Just give us a break."

"Just one stinking break, Ma," said Alan. "That's all we're asking."

Adam was getting a bad feeling about Mrs. Ameche. She should be nicer to the Ameche brothers. They seemed like really neat kids. *She* seemed like a slave driver.

Mrs. Ameche was not done, not by a long shot. "So what on God's earth brings you to the Ameche brothers?" she asked. "You expect them to help you with the Bolands? You sure you got the right Ameche brothers?"

"Ma," said Don.

"Come on, Ma," said Alan.

"To be truthful: money," said Adam. "We need to raise money so we can afford to put out the paper by ourselves. So we can pay to have it printed without using school money. So we can put together a website for the paper. So we can be free from the school and nobody can shut us down again if they don't like something we write. We need it to be like a grown-up paper — sell ads to raise money. And we need help because, Jennifer and I, we don't know anything about business. That's why Jennifer answered the Ameche brothers' ad about being experts on starting businesses for kids."

"That reminds me," said Mrs. Ameche. "Ameche brothers, my apologies, I owe you money. We sold a ton of your golf balls today, and someone bought a rubber raft and a fishing pole, and that guy finally

24

came to pick up that rebuilt model-airplane engine. I wrote it all down. Here . . . I owe you eighty-seven dollars each. Plus, I got two more computer jobs for you. I wrote down their cell numbers."

Adam's eyes bugged out. The Ameche brothers did know how to make money! His reporter's instinct was as good as ever. Jennifer would be *so* sorry she left; he could already hear her begging for forgiveness.

"OK, Ameche brothers, tomatoes. You've got work to do. I don't want to hear any excuses. Weed patrol, march."

"Please, Ma," said Don, "just let us talk to Adam about the newspaper stuff, then we'll do the garden work. We promise."

"We really promise, Ma," said Alan. "We honest to God promise. Cross my heart and hope to die, Ma."

"Cross mine, too, Ma," said Don. "Hope to die, Ma."

"Promise, huh? Cross your hearts, huh?" Mrs. Ameche didn't look impressed. "Well, Ameche brothers, you would definitely be dead if that crossing promise was enforceable. The deal was, you didn't have to go to the flea market so long as you did the garden work—cross your hearts. Now we have

25

a new deal: you don't have to do the garden work so you can form this media company—cross your hearts. Adam, would you trust the Ameche brothers for one single second?"

Adam did not hesitate. "They seem good," he said. "They must be doing something right. I mean eighty-seven dollars each—that's big money."

Mrs. Ameche smiled. "Oh, Adam," she said, "you are a traitor to common sense." She said she'd be willing to go along with it on one condition. Once they finished the media company, Adam had to help with the tomatoes. "If you're going to be partners with the Ameche brothers, Mr. Slash"—and here Mrs. Ameche made a slashing motion with her finger—"then we need to find out what kind of work ethic you've got. Make sure you're not afraid to get a little bird doo on your hands. Hopefully, you'll be a positive influence on these heart-crossing, low-life Ameche brothers."

"Ma," said Don.

"Come on, Ma," said Alan.

They waited a few minutes, then Adam peeked out around the curtain. "She's gone," he said.

"You sure?" said Don.

"How do you know?" said Alan.

"I can't see her anywhere," said Adam. "And I can see the whole yard."

"You sure she's not hiding behind the crates?" said Don.

"Sure," said Adam. "She's not there. I can see."

"Doesn't mean a thing," said Don.

"Sometimes she climbs up on the shed roof and listens," said Alan. "You'd better check."

Adam walked outside and looked on the roof. Mrs. Ameche was not there. He came back in and sat down on a crate. "She's tough," Adam said.

"Yeah," said Don, "she keeps us on our toes."

"She gets inside your head," Alan said. "Ma's pretty wily."

"You want something to drink?" Don asked. The computers were sitting on a plywood board that was held up on one side by a two-drawer filing cabinet. On the other side, Adam now realized as Don opened the door, was a mini-refrigerator.

"Zap cola?" asked Don.

"Five times the caffeine of regular cola," said Alan, popping open a frosty. "We keep it on special order at C-Town."

"I'm good," said Adam. "I got the jawbreaker in

case I'm running down. Look, I've really got to go. We'd better do the tomatoes. We can talk while we get it done."

The three boys began dragging out bags of soil and peat moss and stacking them by the shed door.

"I've got a question," said Adam. "You said you didn't have money. That's why Jennifer got so mad. But your mom just gave you a ton of money."

"Ooh," said Don. "You really don't get business."

"He doesn't get how it works," said Alan.

"Don't worry," said Don. "We'll teach you."

"You've got to spend money to make money," said Alan.

"Golden rule of business," said Don.

"Invest in your future," said Alan.

"Grow your business," said Don.

"Basic microeconomics," said Alan.

"That money," said Don. "It's spent."

"You see that power mower out there?" asked Alan.

"The one with no wheels?" said Adam.

Don and Alan each held up their eighty-seven dollars. "Wheels," they said.

"We can sell that thing for maybe three hundred dollars once we get wheels," said Don.

Adam grinned. He felt a surge of happiness. These Ameche brothers, they really were the ones for this job. It seemed like they could make money on anything. They definitely might be able to save the *Slash*.

"Let's do the tomatoes," said Adam. "I've got a ton of homework." His World History teacher, Mr. Brooks, was making them memorize a speech for the World War II unit. It was ridiculous. Adam loved Mr. Brooks, but memorize a speech? Why memorize when in one second, you could Google? Adam got stuck with something from some guy named Winston Churchpail who was like the king of England during World War II. Adam could not imagine naming a kid Winston, especially with a last name like Churchpail. What were his mother and father thinking? Mr. Brooks said they had to learn at least two whole paragraphs, and Adam knew how he was going to pick them: the two shortest.

The Ameches and Adam bustled around, crawling beneath the table, reaching up on shelves and in the far corners, pulling out a bag of lime, garden gloves, hand rakes, spades, a pitchfork.

"I think that's it," said Don.

"Let's do it," said Alan.

"What about the bird doo?" said Adam. "Where do we get that?"

"Very funny," said Don.

"Joking makes time go fast," said Alan.

"I don't think I was," said Adam. "I didn't see any. Where do you get it?"

"Birds," said Don.

"Definitely birds," said Alan.

chapter 3
Room 306

They were all back in room 306 for the first time since the newspaper had been shut down in April.

Things, however, were far from perfect.

The vital links that made it a newspaper were gone.

The phones had been disconnected.

The computer terminals had been removed.

The fax machine had been confiscated.

Still, it felt like theirs. Eddie the janitor had been so kind—he hadn't cleaned up a thing. Old stories, old photos, and old notebooks were strewn everywhere. Sammy's conversion tables for calculating his groundbreaking yummy-yummy rating system for the bacon-egg-and-cheese sandwiches were right where he'd left them, spread all over the floor in a back corner of the room. The survey sheets for Adam's legendary science-fair investigation were on the desk where he and Shadow had spent so much time plotting the graphs. The Iceberger Crossing sign was on the same couch where Phoebe, world's greatest third-grade reporter, had fallen asleep in the midst of researching her landmark story that saved the three-hundred-year-old climbing tree.

All in all, it was every bit as messy and dusty and gross as it had been on that now-famous afternoon when Mrs. Boland had made her surprise visit and announced she'd never seen such a pigsty.

"It looks great," said Phoebe.

"I know how much you missed it," said Jennifer. "Me, too."

Jennifer had told the acting principal, Mrs. Quigley, that *Slash* staff members were determined to keep the paper going on their own. And immediately, Mrs. Quigley had said that as far as she was concerned, they could use room 306 for their meetings until the end of the year. She told Jennifer that if school officials found out, they might fire her on the spot. But Mrs. Quigley didn't care; she was only a fill-in principal and was leaving at the end of June anyway. "Let them sack me early," she said. "It would be good for my golf game."

Adam and Jennifer knew that Mrs. Quigley had done everything possible to save the *Slash*, but too many powerful people were against them.

"There's no way I can get your phones and computers back," she said. "But I can provide you with a little sustenance now and then."

"Any support would be great," Jennifer said.

Before Adam and Jennifer could tell everyone their plans for saving the *Slash*, Phoebe spotted a big box under the old picnic table they used for story conferences.

"Jennifer, call 911!" yelled Phoebe. "We had a lockdown drill today. If we see any suspicious packages, we're supposed to tell a grown-up immediately and run for cover."

"I think it's OK," said Jennifer.

"The *Slash* has ticked off so many powerful grown-ups," said Phoebe, "a million people would love to blow us up. Call 911!"

"Stay calm, Phoebe," said Jennifer. She took a

pen and carefully cut a slit along the top of the carton. She pushed her hand through the incision and felt around. There was a crinkling sound.

"Don't!" Phoebe yelled. "Did you hear that? *Ticking!* It could be a roadside bomb! Take cover, everyone!" She rolled under a nearby desk and tucked herself into a tight ball, the way they'd practiced at the lockdown drill.

The rest of them stared at Phoebe but did not budge, looking back to Jennifer.

Jennifer reached in, pulled out a flat, round object, examined it carefully, removed the cellophane, then went over to the nearby desk, leaned down, and handed Phoebe a Mrs. Radin's Famous Homemade Super-Chunk Buckets O' Chocolate Moisty Deluxe chocolate-chip cookie.

Sustenance from Mrs. Quigley.

Adam started off by telling everyone about the Ameche brothers. Not all about the Ameche brothers. There was way too much to tell. He certainly didn't go into the tomatoes or the bird doo or their May Way West studios or their exciting weather forecasting habits. He just emphasized that they were really good at making money and mentioned a few of their businesses.

He was afraid that if he said too much, he'd stir up Jennifer again.

After their Sunday visit, it had taken Adam three days to convince his coeditor that the Ameche brothers really were good at making money and that she needed to give them another chance. He kept telling her the story about the eighty-seven dollars and the four power-mower wheels, but he must have been telling it wrong, because she just stared at him.

"Jennifer, everyone knows you've got to spend money to make money," Adam had said.

"What are you talking about?" she said.

"It's basic marketplace principles," said Adam. "Grow your business. Invest in your future. The golden rule."

"Geez," said Jennifer. "All that time alone with the Ameche brothers — it really turned you stupid."

But she finally calmed down. Maybe Adam's discussion of Ameche microeconomics had sunk in.

Or maybe it was because they had no choice. Their next best plan was Phoebe's idea to sell homemade beaded bracelets and necklaces; so far, she'd made twelve dollars.

Jennifer had talked to the print shop. The owner said he could print them five hundred copies of the

Slash — their usual press run — for one thousand dollars. Then, of course, they'd have to hand it out themselves in front of Harris; school officials wouldn't let them send it home in every kid's knapsack anymore, since it was no longer the official paper of Harris Elementary/Middle.

So that was the plan — the Ameche brothers to the rescue. The *Slash* staff was juiced. To them, it seemed like free money from heaven. And the Ameche brothers even promised to create a website that would have all the articles from each issue, along with the staff's e-mail addresses so readers could get hold of reporters, plus regular updates of the news.

The Ameches would raise the money by selling ads. And those ads would appear in both the paper and web version of the *Slash*. "Advertisers like that," said Adam. "It's called double platforming."

"It's called what?" said Jennifer.

"Double platforming," said Adam. "We put their ads in two different places, which gives them more bang for the buck. Plus, the Ameche brothers are a built-in four-legged call."

"Four-legged what?" asked Jennifer.

"You know, two salesman making a house call."

"Why are you talking like that?" said Jennifer.

"Just basic ad lingo," said Adam. "I picked it up from the Ameche brothers. Don't worry — you'll catch on."

"I hope not," said Jennifer. "Ideally they'd sell ten hundred-dollar ads. But if they have trouble with that, they might sell smaller ads for maybe twenty-five dollars. And we'll pay the Ameches for selling the ads, depending on how many they sell."

"They could sell ten ads for one hundred dollars," said Shadow. "Or they could sell forty ads for twenty-five dollars."

"That's right, Shadow," said Jennifer. "And it doesn't have to be just businesses. It could be parents who'd buy ads, like they do for the Harris yearbook—"

"Or they can sell one ad for one thousand dollars," said Shadow. "Or they can sell twenty ads for twenty-five dollars, and five ads for one hundred dollars . . ."

"That's the idea," said Jennifer.

"Or they could sell one ad for two hundred and fifty dollars and one for one hundred dollars and twenty-six for twenty-five dollars," said Shadow. "Or they could sell one ad for five hundred dollars . . ."

"We get it," said Phoebe. "Duh. We're not some

kind of idiots, you know. They could sell one ad for nine hundred and ninety-nine dollars and ninety-nine cents and one for one cent."

"They could?" said Shadow. "Can you sell one ad for one cent? Or are you some kind of idiot?"

"Enough," said Jennifer. "Stop. You two have to learn to get along. Being on our own is not going to be easy. We need everyone pulling together if we're going to keep the *Slash* alive."

"The Ameche brothers will figure it out; that's their job," said Jennifer. "And Adam and I will be working with them. Now I've done a little research. I Googled *journalism ethics* and got 59.2 million hits. There's a lot to it. We have to be careful. There has to be a wall between the news side and our business side. It's not your job to raise money. It's your job to get the news, and we can't mix up the two. You guys can't be asking people you're interviewing to give us money for ads. Like that story Adam and I did last month, on Reverend Shorty and the people in the Willows being forced to move away. We can't be going to Reverend Shorty and asking his church to give money for an ad in the *Slash*. That would be like he was paying to get his story in. That would be like we only tell the stories of people who pay us. No one would trust us if they felt they could buy a story in the *Slash*. If anyone talks to you about wanting to buy an ad, you get in touch with me or Adam and we'll hook them up with the Ameche brothers. OK?"

"Even parents?" asked a boy.

"Even parents," said Adam. "Like Jennifer's mom is great, but she's this big PTA honcho. We've got to be careful that she doesn't start asking us to do nice stories about the PTA just because we ask the PTA for money."

"My mom wouldn't do that," said Jennifer.

"It was just an example," said Adam. "I was just trying to make the point—"

"It wasn't a very good example," said Jennifer.

"Anyway," said Adam, "you get the idea. Like Jennifer said—and Jennifer is the one who's done all the research on this—I mean, 59.2 million hits. We've got to keep a wall between the news side and the business side. Jennifer showed me. All the ethics websites say it."

"We're going to build a wall?" said Shadow. "Bricks make really good walls. Very strong. You can huff and puff, but you can't blow them down. Is the acting principal going to let us build a brick wall in 306?"

"You *are* some kind of idiot," said Phoebe. "It's a

symbolic wall. It's not made out of bricks. It's made out of ideas, symbolically speaking."

"A wall is not made of ideas," said Shadow. "Stories are made of ideas. Call 911, Jennifer."

"Stop," said Jennifer. "You two—I feel like your mom. Please. You have no idea how hard this will be doing this on our own."

"Let's please stay calm," said Adam. "The Ameche brothers won't be working out of 306, anyway. Their headquarters is in the West End. That should help us keep things nice and separate."

"Ameche brothers . . ." said Phoebe. "Ameche brothers . . . That name is familiar. Any relation to the *Ameche Brothers' Talk Till You Drop All-Live Except the Recorded Parts* webcast?"

Adam nodded.

"That's a great show," said Phoebe.

They needed story ideas. Jennifer told them she really hoped they'd have an issue ready to go to press by the end of school. "That's only seven weeks," she said. "And of course, it will depend on how the Ameche brothers do, if they can raise the money. But we want to show these people who shut us down. The Bolands. Dr. Bleepin. All the assistants and associates and deputy superintendents who wouldn't stand up for us. The school board. We are still here. We will not go away. We will print the truth!"

The coeditors had been so focused on figuring out how to pay for the *Slash,* they hadn't been working much on story ideas. "Well, come on," said Jennifer. "What are kids talking about? What's the big news?"

"You're not going to like this," said Sammy, the *Slash*'s undercover food critic. "I know how much everybody hates those state tests. But every class, that's all anyone's talking about this week. The scores are out, and we did great."

Phoebe said that in her before school/after school mandatory/voluntary prep class for the state tests, they were having an old-fashioned ice-cream social to celebrate the third-grade scores. "We're going to wear real plastic straw hats," she said.

"You know, I wasn't thinking about it," said Jennifer. "But we had a pizza party in English class to celebrate. And my mom, she said that the PTA was planning something for the school—she said Harris never had such a jump in scores."

"Sounds like a story," said Adam. "I'll do it." Adam wanted to do some good news. The truth was, he was worn out investigating everything and everybody. The science fair. Devillio. The Willows.

The *Slash* being shut down. Finally, a happy, easy story. "We'll talk about how much the scores went up in each grade," he said. "We'll get all the results. Sammy, we'll need your help on graphics — like you did for your mashed-potato investigation. We'll have bar graphs and pie charts and ice-cream cakes that show the numbers going up."

"And we should write about teachers, too," said Phoebe. "The teachers must be way better, since the scores went up. And we should write about how much harder everyone worked than ever before. How great before school/after school mandatory/voluntary was. And how everyone's getting smarter. I hope everybody knows what this means: We are the smartest kids in the history of this school."

They got quiet. Kids looked around at each other. Them? The smartest ever? Many were thinking of older brothers and sisters and how smart *they* were. Adam was thinking of this older boy, Franky Cutty, who was at the high school now and was the most impressive big kid he'd ever met.

Smarter than that?

"We're number one," chanted Phoebe. "We're number one."

"I guess it's possible," Adam said softly.

Sammy said his undercover food critic column was going to rate chocolate milk at restaurants around Tremble. Several staffers thought that was a bad idea — there wasn't enough to it. Someone suggested that he might do chocolate milk and hot chocolate and chocolate milk shakes combined, since they're part of the same family of liquids, but Sammy was quite adamant that there was more than enough to fill a column on chocolate milk alone.

"I used to think the same thing," he said. "But then, I don't know, maybe a month ago, I ordered a chocolate milk at the West River Diner. It was a real letdown. The chocolate syrup was thick on the bottom and had not been properly stirred in. There was no bubbly chocolate foam on top. The glass had been completely filled, meaning you couldn't put a straw in and blow bubbles without spilling on the table.

"They didn't even give me a straw. I had to ask twice. I know it's hard to believe, but I swear I'm not making it up. And that wasn't the worst. I tasted it. . . ." Here Sammy paused.

"What?" said a photographer. "What?"

"Warm."

A few shuddered. "Warm milk?" said a typist. "Gross."

"Room temperature," said Sammy.

It made Adam so uncomfortable that he pulled out his jawbreaker and gave it a couple of quick sucks.

"You know," said Sammy, "this isn't just some big joke: rate the chocolate milks — which one gets 4 yummy-yummies? Oh, big deal, rah-rah. This story is a service to every kid in this community. We need to define the standards for chocolate milk here in Tremble. Draw the line. Who will do it if we don't? There's a lot of backsliding, precisely because too many people say it's only chocolate milk. We've got to stop that kind of thinking. Every part of the meal — I don't care if it's the mashed potatoes or the bacon on the bacon-egg-and-cheese or the chocolate milk — it should be a little masterpiece. This stuff matters!"

They were quiet. He'd gotten to them. It was the most they'd ever heard Sammy talk at once. They knew that he liked food, but until now, they'd never realized how deep it went. That was the wonderful thing about a newspaper. This was why they had to save the *Slash*. People had these passions you didn't even know about, and the *Slash* gave them a chance to express them.

"Fantastic, Sammy," said Adam. "I'm convinced."

44

"Me, too," said Jennifer. "Plus, it's spring. Weather's getting warm. Hot chocolate's not on readers' minds. They're thinking of nice cold, foamy chocolate milk. They're thinking of taking a big icy swallow, then putting their straw in and making bubbles so the glass still looks filled to the top. And the *Slash*'s undercover food critic will tell them where it's done right."

"I'll do my best," said Sammy.

Jennifer reminded them that they'd need a story on the Bolands and the school board shutting down the *Slash*.

Then Phoebe raised her hand. She announced that she had the greatest idea ever, which did not surprise Adam. The fact was, it was true; Phoebe did these amazing stories. Her profile of Eddie the janitor had led them to the $75,000 in stolen money; her feature on the dental society's smile contest exposed phony grown-ups; her articles on a new state policy had saved the climbing tree.

Phoebe was definitely legendary, but it was exhausting working with the world's greatest third-grade reporter. Even when the stories were well written. Adam and Jennifer had to hold her little third-grade hand every step of the way — symbolically speaking, as Phoebe would say. "Yes, Phoebe, you did a good job." "Yes, Phoebe, it was the best story in the history of the world." "Yes, Phoebe, the entire planet loves you."

"What's the idea?" said Adam, bracing himself.

"I want to do an advice column," she said. "We'll call it 'Ask Phoebe.'"

An advice column? thought Adam. "An advice column?" said Adam. "You're in third grade! What do you know? You're not big enough to give advice."

"Well, I used to think that, too," said Phoebe. "But then I was working on my memoir—"

"Memoir!" said Adam. "Memoir! A memoir is a story of your life written when you're old and famous and have done a lot of important stuff. Like George Washington or Abraham Lincoln or Mother Teresa. You can't write a memoir. You're in third grade."

"No, no, no," said Phoebe. "You're thinking of the *old* meaning of memoir. The new meaning has much more democracy in it. Anyone can write a memoir under the new rules, even if they've never done anything. And it doesn't even have to be totally true, as long as it seems like it *could* be true. My teacher had us write a memoir of our lives up until now. So I'm just going to keep going and make it into a book."

"Well, that makes sense," said Jennifer. "So you're just starting, like, a diary, and when you get grown-up and have done a bunch of important stuff, you'll finish it."

"Oh, no," said Phoebe. "I think it'll be done by fourth grade at the latest. I already have more than a hundred pages."

Adam didn't know if he had the energy to stand in front of this onrushing locomotive named Ask Phoebe and absorb the crash. Advice from Phoebe? Who could possibly be less qualified? Was there anyone on this earth who had less perspective than Phoebe? What did Phoebe know about the pressures of being in middle school? What did Phoebe know about sports? What did Phoebe know about boy/girl stuff? What did Phoebe know about the ins and outs, the ups and downs, of life itself?

What did Phoebe know, period?

Nothing!

But if there was one thing Adam had learned from being Phoebe's coeditor for nearly a year, it was that you don't try to fight Phoebe on the big principles. Get her on the small stuff.

"Tell me this, Ask Phoebe. How are you going to get people to send you questions?" Adam paused. He was pretty sure he had her. "We don't have a website yet, and probably won't until the next issue of the *Slash* comes out. We can't have you writing a column just for your little third-grade friends. Remember, we're the *Slash,* the newspaper of Harris Elementary SLASH"—and here Adam made a *slash* sign in the air for emphasis—"Middle School. How is anyone else going to know about Ask Phoebe? How will they find you?"

"Dear *Slash* Coeditor," said Phoebe. "Thank you for your question. For your information, I already printed up flyers on the *Slash* copy machine to hand out at school so kids know where to send letters or e-mail questions. I already have a slogan: *Need answers in a hurry? Ask Phoebe and don't worry!*"

Then she handed Adam a flyer.

This could not be happening. She had used the *Slash* copy machine? The only reason it was even working was because Adam had fixed it. Phoebe refused to lift one finger to help. Unfairness was piling on unfairness. Adam was positive: It did not make one single bit of sense. A third grader writing an advice column?

"Anyone else have any other questions for Ask Phoebe?" asked Phoebe.

Adam wanted to ask Phoebe how much time he could get in juvenile detention hall for punching a third grader real hard in the stomach a hundred straight times. No way she was getting away with this.

"No way!" Adam exploded. "You are an outrage. You are . . ."

Phoebe's eyes widened and she turned toward Jennifer, blinking really fast like some sort of damsel in distress.

"Don't," said Adam, "Don't try crying your way out of this."

"Let's all relax a minute," Jennifer said. "Adam. . . . Please . . . I understand why you're so upset, but I have to admit — and I know it's a weakness — I love advice columns. I read Dear Abby and Ask Amy all the time. It's kind of cool, the way so many people write in, pour out their problems and no one knows it's them — they're just, like, Heartbroken in Kansas City or Missing Him in Mississippi."

"That's great," said Adam. "I'm happy for you. Just one problem — Dear Abby is not in third grade."

"I know," said Jennifer. "It's a good point. But why don't we do this. Phoebe, you can put out the flyers and then write a sample column with questions and answers and if the coeditors like it, we'll print it."

"But if we don't," shouted Adam, "WE WON'T!"

"Geesh," said Phoebe, staring right at Adam. "Ask Phoebe has some advice for you: Try not to get so worked up over little things. That kind of stress is not good." Then Phoebe smiled and said, "See?"

The staff began to pile out of 306.

"Take it easy, Sammy," Jennifer said. "Great stuff on the chocolate milk. Thanks for standing up for what you believe."

Sammy nodded. "You got to do what you got to do," he said.

Adam was leaving with Sammy, but Jennifer asked him to hang around for a minute.

After the door closed, Jennifer said, "I've got something big. I didn't want to say it with everybody around."

"Do we have to do this now?" said Adam. "I've got to memorize this speech for Mr. Brooks."

"This will just take a second," said Jennifer. "It's big."

"Something on the Bolands?" asked Adam.

"Nope," she said. "It's about the student government election coming up."

Adam had no interest in student government. All smoke and mirrors and nothing to it, as far as he was concerned. Every spring they'd elect new officers for the next school year. All the grown-ups at school would make such a big fuss. Kids would get so worked up — making special buttons and posters and leaflets to hand out. And the promises they'd make. Soda machines. Candy machines. An ice cream parlor in the cafeteria. A shooting range on the roof. McDonald's for lunch. A new skateboard park. Right. Never happened. The advisers wouldn't let them do anything fun. They'd wind up having a car wash and bake sale and raise money for a new fax machine for the main office. As far as Adam was concerned, student government was just grown-up dictators behind the scenes pushing around powerless kids.

"They're buying the election," said Jennifer.

"Who?" said Adam. What he was thinking was, Who'd want it?

"Stub Keenan," said Jennifer. "People are saying it's the dirtiest student council election ever."

"Stub Keenan?" said Adam. "He's, like, one of

the most popular kids at Harris. Why would he have to do anything dirty? He'd win easy."

"I don't know," said Jennifer. "But I'm sure they're right."

"Who?" said Adam. "Who's saying?"

Jennifer said she had a secret source. She'd promised not to tell anyone who it was.

Including Adam.

"Jennifer, we're coeditors," he said. "We tell each other everything."

"I know," she said, "but that was the only way I could get the information."

Adam was mad. First Jennifer agreed to that ridiculous Ask Phoebe mess, now this. He'd always shared his sources with Jennifer. Hadn't he given her Mrs. Willard for the Willows story? Hadn't he gone along with her to the Pine Street church and figured out Reverend Shorty's riddle? Hadn't he given her a tour of the climbing tree? Hadn't he rescued her from Mrs. Boland?

"Geez, Jennifer," he said. "Sometimes you need to push these sources back; you don't just go along with what they say. No offense, but you're just too nice. You've got to show them who's boss. I mean, what do we have to go on? People saying it's a dirty election. They say that about every election." Adam shook his head in disgust.

Jennifer unfolded a piece of paper and laid it on a desk in front of Adam. It was a list of names. Then she said, "These kids got two hundred and fifty songs downloaded on their iPods free by promising to vote for Stub Keenan."

chapter 4

Not His Fault

Adam had a middle-school baseball game, but it didn't start until five, so he decided to bike home, eat something, chill out a little, then bike back for the game. His parents wouldn't be home from work yet, and he liked having the house to himself.

Being the most overprogrammed kid in America, he wasn't used to getting out of school when so many kids were walking home. He loved whizzing by them, especially the girls, and rode with no hands in the middle of the street so everyone could see what a well-balanced individual he was. A few kids called his name, and he waved without looking back. He was surprised at how many kids he didn't know. To remind himself how fast he was, he started counting all the kids he was passing. There were two girls, two boys and a girl, and just as he turned onto his street, on his corner, two tall boys, making a grand total of thirty-seven, the biggest margin of victory since Lance Armstrong won the Tour de France by seven minutes and thirty-seven seconds in 1999!

And Adam wasn't even taking steroids. He rode right up onto his front lawn, jumped off the bike before it had totally stopped, and bounded into the house.

"*Canfield wins again!*" he shouted as he burst into the living room to thunderous applause. He had to admit, he was pretty funny. He dropped his backpack by the front door, then went downstairs to the back of the house to the family room to check the computer for messages.

There was something good. A note from Erik Forrest. Mr. Forrest was the world-famous reporter Adam had written about for the last issue of the *Slash*. When the *Slash* was shut down for doing the great story about the schemy Bolands, Mr. Forrest had helped them out. He'd done a front page story in the *New York Times* that described the Bolands trying to bulldoze the Willows. He had even mentioned the *Slash* investigation. The *New York Times*! Adam had been sure that everyone would know forever what a great paper the *Slash* was.

Unfortunately, no one in Tremble except their relatives seemed to care.

The subject field in Forrest's e-mail said: *State Investigation!*

Adam raced through the message, hoping to find something in the e-mail that said, "The *Slash* will be saved!" Not a word of that. So he returned to the top and read the whole e-mail. It said there was some good news; after the story in the *Times,* the state office of fair housing had opened an investigation into the Bolands.

Adam let out a hoot. The Bolands were being investigated! Thanks to the *Slash* — and of course, the *New York Times*! What if they went to prison? What a story!

Mr. Forrest said the *Times* would probably run a news brief.

Adam reread the e-mail to make sure he hadn't missed anything. A news brief? He was amazed — in the next *Slash* it would be on the front page. Adam could already see the headlines:

BOLANDS UNDER INVESTIGATION!
ADAM CANFIELD WINS PULITZER PRIZE!
EVERYONE WANTS HIS AUTOGRAPH!

It was a good lesson. One newspaper's front-page scoop is another newspaper's news brief.

Adam forwarded the e-mail to Jennifer, then headed upstairs to get a snack. As he passed the front door, he slowed, then stopped.

That was weird. Where was it? He went out front. It wasn't on the lawn. Hadn't he left it there? He checked the garage, then the side yard. He stepped out into the street and walked a couple of houses in each direction.

He came back and circled his house one more time.

It was gone.

His bike was gone.

Adam rode his mom's bike to his baseball game. He was dreading what would happen when his parents found out. He knew they'd scream. They'd want to know why he hadn't locked his bike or put it in the garage.

How could it be his fault? The bike was out there for one second, at most. It was in the front yard — an automatic safety zone. Was he supposed to know that some creep would steal it even before Adam could eat his snack?

It had to be one of the kids he'd passed coming home from school. It had to be someone close behind him, since the bike had disappeared so fast. Those two tall boys on the corner?

That night, when he told his parents, they were angry, but it was a quiet angry. "I paid a lot of money for that bike," his dad said, and pounded his fist on the table, though he didn't seem to be pounding at Adam; it seemed more like general pounding.

They called the police, and a detective came over to take down the information. It wasn't anywhere near as big a deal as the time Adam had been mugged for his snow-shoveling money. He was surprised; the police officers who had come to the house after he was mugged wore uniforms, carried guns, and had seemed huge — real muscle guys. This detective wore a suit coat and tie, had a big belly, and was old, like somebody's grandfather.

After the Canfields described the bike — a black-

and-white Electra cruiser—the detective asked for the serial number. Adam's dad didn't have it, but the detective said the people at the bike shop record all the numbers, and they could get it from them.

"You have much luck getting bikes back?" asked Adam's dad.

"Not much," the detective said. "I'm on the job twenty-five years, seen just about everything. Getting one back—maybe once in a blue moon."

Adam's dad said they were going to drive around and see if they could spot it. "Any suggestions?" he asked.

"Check the alleys behind the restaurants in town," the officer said. "Sometimes the kids working at the restaurants steal them."

Adam and his dad spent about an hour driving around. They rode through several neighborhoods, going up and down streets slowly, looking into side yards, and checking out any kids riding by. Adam felt like they were about to find it any minute, and every time someone rode by, he tensed, but they didn't see it.

"Keep your eyes open at school," his dad said.

/ / / / /

Adam checked the bike racks in the morning and right after school but saw no sign of it. He was using his mom's bike now and never left it unlocked.

One morning, as he straightened up after locking the bike, he found himself staring up at Stub Keenan. They knew each other by sight, but that was about it. They did different sports — Stub played football, wrestling, and lacrosse; Adam soccer, basketball, and baseball. They'd been in the same class just once, back in kindergarten. Adam believed you couldn't form too many life-or-death opinions about people based on kindergarten. Stub wasn't even Stub then — he was Roderick. Adam didn't know where the nickname came from, but he could guess why a person named Roderick might need one. The big thing Adam remembered was that Stub had been real good on the monkey bars; he could zip back and forth and hang forever. He wasn't sure whether that would make Stub a good school president.

Adam noticed an iPod wire hanging from Stub's ear; it felt funny knowing a major secret about someone he barely knew — *if* Jennifer was right.

"Big Adam — a girl's bike?" said Stub. "Kinda gay."

"Looking for the kid who stole mine," said Adam.

"Whoa," said Stub.

"My mom's," Adam said, pointing to the bike.

"Hey, we should set up a student patrol to protect kids' bikes. That's a great idea," said Stub. "Maybe we could deputize kids, like crossing guards. Give 'em special badges. I'm running for president, Big Adam — that's something I'd do. If you want to be chief of the patrol, I could get you in on that."

Adam thought, Right, and a parachute jump on the school roof. But he didn't say it. He wondered if Stub was going to offer him a free download.

"Heard the baseball team got scraped," said Stub.

Adam nodded. They'd lost 12–0. He hoped Stub wouldn't ask how he'd done — Adam had struck out twice.

"How'd you do?" Stub asked.

"Nothing great," said Adam.

"GTG," said Stub. "Take one?" He handed Adam a campaign button that said PREZ STUB. "You know Billy Cutty?" asked Stub.

Adam didn't. "Any relation to Franky?"

"Cousins, I think," said Stub.

Franky was a few grades ahead of Adam, in high school now. But Adam knew him when Franky was still at Harris Middle and liked him a lot. He was that rare big kid who actually was nice to younger kids.

Franky loved the *Slash* and said how great it was. Normally big kids wouldn't admit anything like that. Adam hadn't seen Franky for months and wondered what he was up to.

"Billy Cutty's my campaign manager," said Stub. "If you can't find me, Billy's the one. You need anything, or if there's any way we can help—Billy's my guy. You can't miss him—he's usually got a million buttons all over his shirt, and he sits at our campaign table at lunch. Hey, good luck finding your bike, Big Adam. That's a bad deal. Makes you feel like you can't trust anybody. What's it look like?"

Adam described his cruiser, and Stub said, "I'll watch for it."

"Thanks, Stub," said Adam. "Appreciate it."

Mrs. Stanky was Adam's Language Arts teacher. She wasn't his favorite adult, but she was bearable. The last few days she'd been incredibly nice to him, and Adam suspected it was because they'd gotten their scores back on the state test and once again, he'd received a perfect 4+. Second year in a row. Teachers liked kids with high scores; it made them feel like smart teachers.

She was describing their last big writing project of the year. "It's going to be a lot of fun," she said. "Now that the state tests are over, we don't have to worry about the five-paragraph essay anymore. We don't have to follow the writing formula from the state high commission on standards. We're going to do some real writing, like actual grown-up writers. My kids always say it's their favorite thing all year. You're about to see how much fun writing can be."

A girl raised her hand. "Mrs. Stanky, after all we did on the five-paragraph essay — you're saying it's not real writing? No offense, Mrs. Stanky, but how bogus is that?"

Boy, Adam agreed. Mrs. Stanky had spent months drilling the five-paragraph essay formula into their brains for the state test. Topic sentence. Then three examples to back it up: one from literature, one from history, one from popular culture. Then concluding sentence. Repeat for paragaphs two through five. Try not to explode from boredom.

And if ever you tried something different — like writing a paragraph that was one sentence long with dashes in the middle — they'd take off points and send your name to the state high commission.

"Boys and girls, I misspoke," said Mrs. Stanky.

"The five-paragraph essay is real writing. It is important. You need it for the state test. When you get to
high school, you'll need it for the SAT writing sample.
It's just, it has nothing to do with real-life writing.
To the best of my knowledge, you'll never do a
five-paragraph essay in college, or in business or in
newspapers or magazines, or blogs or short stories or
novels or poetry or corporate memos or advertising.
I've read that some big researchers have studied it and
have never been able to find an actual example of a
five-paragaph essay ever being published anywhere.
But you never know. I'm sure someday, some great
researcher like Jane Goodall or Louis Leakey will find
that maybe in a fishing village in Madagascar . . ."

The girl raised her hand again.

"Enough," said Mrs. Stanky. "Let's accentuate
the positive."

She told them that they were going to do a profile
of some student in the school who was really different from them. And it couldn't be someone in their
English class. And they had to interview that kid a
lot, so that they really understood the differences.
And they should follow that person around and go
to his or her home if they could, and meet his or her
parents if that were possible.

And they had to do some real, primary research, she said. They were supposed to go to the library and find a copy of a newspaper for the day that kid was born so that they could see what was going on in Tremble and around the nation and world on that day.

"I'm not talking about Googling that date," said Mrs. Stanky. "No Googling. I will know if that's how you do it. I will take off points if I catch you Googling. That goes for Yahooing, too. You must read the actual newspaper. I've arranged with the librarian at the main branch. There will be a research sheet that you all must sign so I know you've been there."

"One more thing," she said. "Be careful. Say someone is born on December 2nd, 1984 —"

"Is that your birthday, Mrs. Stanky?" said a boy.

"I said *someone*, not me," she said. "So, if you want to find out what happened on December 2nd, 1984, what day's paper do you want?"

"Duh," said a girl. "December 2nd, 1984."

"You sure?" said Mrs. Stanky.

Adam knew what she meant. To find out what happened on December 2nd, they'd have to read the December 3rd newspaper. It took a few minutes for someone to finally say it.

Adam was excited. It did sound fun. He knew who he was going to do, too: Shadow. You couldn't get much more different than Shadow. Plus Adam already knew a lot about Shadow. He'd visited Shadow's after-school job. He knew his boss was Mr. Johnny Stack, who looked out for Shadow; Adam would love the chance to finally meet him. He also knew Shadow lived in foster care and took special ed classes in 107A. He'd never been in 107A. It would be neat to see what went on inside there. Plus he liked spending time with Shadow. Shadow definitely was different.

At lunch, Adam found Jennifer. He pulled the speech he had to memorize for Mr. Brooks out of his backpack and handed it to her. "Test me," he said. "I think I know it."

When he'd finished, Jennifer said, "Not bad. You did good on the stuff about battling Hitler and moving the world forward to the 'broad, sunlit uplands,' I love that. You just forgot the part about the free world sinking into the abyss of a new Dark Age. You want to try one more time?"

"Nah," said Adam. "It's close enough. Guess who I ran into today at the bike rack? Stub Keenan."

"Was he stealing your bike?" she asked.

"No," said Adam. "Actually I was hoping he was giving out free bikes to kids who'd vote for him."

"You'd do it," said Jennifer.

"I might," said Adam.

"Did he offer you a free download?" asked Jennifer.

"He didn't," said Adam. "He was campaigning."

"So how are we going to get that story?" she asked.

Adam didn't know. He didn't think they could just print the list of names unless they had someone telling them on the record — being quoted by name — that these were kids who got the iPod downloads. "I don't suppose your source — who's so secret you can't tell your coeditor — would be quoted saying these are the kids who got downloads?"

Jennifer shook her head. "No way."

"Is there anyone who knows Stub real well, who Stub pissed off so bad he might tell us?"

Jennifer was quiet, then finally said, "Not who'd be named. At least I can't think of anyone."

"You know what's funny," said Adam. "Stub told me his campaign manager is this kid Billy Cutty. The campaign manager must know about the downloads. Well, the thing is — I know his cousin, Franky Cutty — he's this really neat big kid."

Jennifer shrugged.

"It's just a little surprising," said Adam. "I guess good people can have bad cousins."

"Your cousin does," said Jennifer.

"That's probably an insult, isn't it," said Adam. They talked about whether one of them — or maybe both — should ask Stub for a free iPod download to see if it was true, but decided against it. The whole thing could get twisted around, like it was their idea to get something for their vote. It could make Adam and Jennifer look like the bad guys — asking for a freebie. And then Stub could say he'd only done it because they asked.

"It would be our word against Stub's," said Jennifer. "We don't want that." Adam agreed. If it were their word against Stub's, they'd lose. The school board had shut them down for being troublemakers. Most adults didn't look closely into stuff like that; they wouldn't understand that Adam and Jennifer were *good* troublemakers.

Adam could see what they had to do, and was dreading it. "We're going to have to talk to the kids on that list," he said. That would be a mess. Once he or Jennifer started asking kids about free downloads, word would get back to Stub. Then they'd be in a big fight with Stub, and none of the other kids on that list would talk.

How could they ever get someone to admit it?

The bell rang. "Who knows?" said Adam. "Maybe there are stories you can't put in the paper even though they're true." He hated to think that. He'd always believed that if it was true, there was a way.

"We have to," said Jennifer. "The person who gave me the list took a huge risk. We can't let Stub steal the election."

Adam shrugged. He used to think that truth would win out, but since the *Slash* had been shut down for printing the truth about the Bolands, he wasn't so sure. He took his apple and carrots, put them back in his lunch bag, and tossed the bag in the garbage.

"That's good food," Jennifer said.

"I used to bring it home," said Adam. "But my dad got ticked—he really believes in making me a balanced lunch. So, I chuck it out to make him feel good."

/ / / / /

After school, but before baseball practice, Adam went out to the bike rack. His bike — or rather, his mom's — was still there. Several kids were unlocking bikes to head home and Adam noticed a boy he didn't know pulling out a black bike. Adam's eyes riveted on it; he'd swear it was his. It was different, but the same. The bike was a flat black color, not the shiny black-and-white of Adam's bike. There was no chain guard. And in several spots — the post under the handlebars, the back of the seat, the bar supporting the seat — were big decals with lightning bolts that Adam's bike didn't have.

"Hey," said Adam. "Wait."

The kid was starting to push off.

"Could I take a look at that bike for a second?" said Adam.

The kid was pedaling. Adam didn't recognize him. He hadn't gotten a great look at the two boys on the corner that day, but this boy didn't look like them. They were tall; this kid was short and chubby. Adam caught up, got in the way of the boy, and held the bike by the handlebars.

"Can I look at that bike?" asked Adam. "Where'd you get it?"

"Borrowed . . . from a friend," the kid said. "I really need to go." He hopped on and pushed away.

Adam was almost positive. The curve of the handlebars felt so familiar. Somebody must have painted it. And the decals—that was it!—they'd been put everywhere the Electra nameplates would be. The kid had disguised it. Adam could have grabbed the kid; he didn't seem tough—but held back. There wasn't total proof. Adam was going to have to get the serial number from his dad and keep it in his pocket. His dad had showed him where the serial number was, on the bottom, under the pedals. He'd said it was like a fingerpint, branded into the metal, so you couldn't get rid of it, even if it was painted over.

Maybe the kid was telling the truth. Maybe he had borrowed it. But then this kid had to know the boy who stole it. Adam was mad at himself. He watched the kid ride off. He should have asked. He thought of following the kid, but he had baseball practice. The coach might bench him for being late, or worse, make him do laps.

chapter 5
An Ethics Shortage

Adam didn't know where to start for the test story, so he decided to visit Mrs. Quigley, the acting principal. She'd be delighted to talk to him about such good news. He figured that even if she wasn't the exact right person, she usually had an extra plate of Moisty Deluxe cookies sitting around, so it wouldn't be a total waste.

On this afternoon, bless her acting-principal heart, she had cold milk, too. Why did Mrs. Quigley have to be leaving at the end of the school year? It wasn't fair. Adam figured maybe they were getting rid of her because she liked kids too much.

"It's wonderful to see you, Adam," she said. "I really miss the visits from you and Jennifer. I miss being the *Slash* adviser. I miss our story meetings. I miss knowing what's really going on around here. So come on, tell me, how's the *Slash* doing, now that you're free from Dr. Bleepin and the school board and all those grown-ups who believe in censorship?"

Adam told her they had a webmaster and business managers selling ads and raising money to pay to get the *Slash* printed. He didn't mention who; he figured it would be better if she thought they were actual grown-ups with suits and shoes with laces, instead of the Ameche brothers working in a storage shed.

"Can I buy an ad?" asked Mrs. Quigley. "I'd be delighted. Would two hundred dollars help things along? I could give you a check right now."

Oh, would it. If only. "I'm sorry," said Adam. "We can't. Not while you're principal. No offense, but it would be kind of like an ethics violation. I mean, not you, Mrs. Quigley. You're no ethics violation; you're the nicest principal. But if we took—"

Mrs. Quigley nodded. "It would be like I was trying to bribe you to put good news in the *Slash*. You're worried that for my two hundred dollars I'd want you to say, 'Mrs. Quigley, the world's greatest acting principal . . .' You are something, young man. I don't meet many adults as ethical as you."

Adam was embarrassed. He didn't feel too ethical. He knew that if it weren't for Jennifer, his ethics would be way down in the sewer with everyone else's.

"So how can I help?" she asked.

Adam told her they wanted to do a story on the state test scores going up but he wasn't sure where to start. He said everybody was saying how well Harris did, and he was wondering if she could give him the results for each grade and some reasons she thought the school did so well. "I'll tell you the truth, Mrs. Quigley. I hate before school/after school mandatory/voluntary prep for the test," said Adam. "But I guess it worked, right?"

"Well, maybe," said Mrs. Quigley. "If you're taking sample tests and drilling kids day after day so everyone gets so familiar with the test, scores will go up. But there's more to it, Adam."

"I know," said Adam. "We talked about it at the *Slash* meeting, like teachers got better, right?"

"Well, I'm very proud of our teachers," said Mrs. Quigley. "But we didn't get a single new teacher this year. It's the same group as last year when the scores were lower. Adam, can we go off-the-record for a minute?"

Adam nodded. He wasn't worried about Mrs. Quigley. If there was any chance to get it on the record later, she'd do anything to help.

"You need to go see Dr. Duke," said Mrs. Quigley. "I believe her title's Second Associate Deputy Superintendent for Assessment."

Adam's heart sank. The last thing he wanted was to talk to another deputy super-duper. It had been bad enough talking to Dr. Bleepin for the last *Slash.* People who lied for a living were exhausting to interview.

"Cheer up," Mrs. Quigley said. "Dr. Duke is not like Dr. Bleepin. Dr. Duke's a good woman. I've known her forever. She spent twenty years teaching before going into administration. She really understands testing. That's her job. She can give you a full picture of what's going on, not just here at Harris. She's got all the numbers for the county and the state. I promise, you won't be sorry. It's an important story, Adam. It's every bit as important as the one you did on the Bolands. I'll call her and let her know you're coming by."

Adam asked if her office was near Dr. Bleepin's.

"I don't think she'd want to be seen with me if Dr. Bleepin's around," he said. "He'd probably report her to the deputy super police."

"Well, Dr. Duke outranks Dr. Bleepin, but it's a good point," said Mrs. Quigley. "I'll e-mail and see what she says. Maybe you could use my office."

Adam was grateful, but he felt discouraged. Wasn't there ever a story where you could get all the information in one place? Another story that wasn't going to turn out to be as easy as he'd hoped.

"Why so glum?" said Mrs. Quigley. "I know it's complicated, but life is complicated. It's a blessing to see the complications. You and Jennfier have done remarkable things with the *Slash*. That mention in the *New York Times* — amazing. Most people go to their grave never making the front page unless they murder someone.

"It hasn't helped yet," she continued, "but it may — you may get the *Slash* back in this school yet. Not right away, probably not while I'm here, but maybe sooner than you think. I know it's hard. The better you do, the more people expect. I could give you the Harris test scores and a quote about how great we did and stop there. That's what I'd do with most middle-school reporters. That's what I'd do with the *Citizen-Gazette-Herald-Advertiser* or Boland News 12. They live on the surface. Not you — I'd feel like I was cheating you."

She said that she was glad to hear about the business manager and webmaster. "You're going to need a few grown-ups to help out," she said. "My door's always open, you know that. I told you my dad was a newspaperman back east in Boston. He used to say that great reporters comfort the afflicted and afflict the comfortable. You sit with Dr. Duke, you'll learn stuff that will open your eyes. Before you're done, you'll be afflicting people all the way from Harris to the state capital."

Adam thanked her. It was nice to be praised, but an easy story would be better.

"So what do you think?" said Don Ameche.

"Pretty amazing, huh?" said Alan Ameche.

"Right," said Jennifer. "Pretty amazing."

"Definitely pretty . . . um . . . amazing," said Adam. He could feel it — Jennifer was going to explode. Adam liked the Ameche brothers a lot, and God knows, he liked Jennifer, but somehow, he couldn't make them like one another. Whenever Jennifer was around, the exact wrong words came out of the Ameche brothers' mouths.

He and Jennifer had biked to the May Way West studios to find out how ad sales were doing.

But that's not what the Ameche brothers wanted to talk about.

"Look at that action," said Don.

"See—the moment of impact," said Alan. *"Crash."*

"Did you miss it?" said Don. "I get worked up every time I see it. Let me play it back."

"Stop," said Alan. "That's it. . . . I love this."

Adam must have been seeing wrong. He couldn't spot the crash.

"Look," said Don. "See the bumpers touch? . . . There!"

"And look at the guy jamming on his brakes," said Alan.

"See the car rock?" said Don.

"It's a little hard to tell . . . ." said Adam. As he stared at the computer screen, he could feel his butt getting sore from the plastic crate, but that was not what was making him uncomfortable.

Jennifer was way sorer than Adam's butt.

"Look!" said Don. "The guy's jumping out of the car. He's pissed."

"See how he walks around and checks the point of impact?" said Alan. "And the other guy gets out and looks at his bumper."

"Look at them look," said Don. "Look how they're looking. Did you see that look he gave him? And now they're looking at each other look. I thought it was going to be a huge fight."

"What's all the shaking?" asked Adam. The video seemed to have been shot during an earthquake.

"Alan was so excited to find real news," said Don. "He started jumping up and down. He kept yelling, 'Anybody here see what happened?'"

"It made the picture jiggly," said Alan. "I'll do better next time." He stopped the video.

Adam asked what happened next.

"Nothing," said Don.

"Nothing?" said Adam.

"They both got in their cars and drove off," said Alan.

"Didn't they exchange papers or something?" asked Adam. "Or wait for the police? That's what they do on TV. That's usually when the guy and girl fall in love." He took a sideways glance at Jennifer.

No sign of love there.

"I guess it wasn't a big enough accident," said Alan.

"No real damage," said Don. "Plus it was two guys."

Adam kept looking at the screen. He did not want to make eye contact with Jennifer.

"This will be great on the new *Slash* website," said Alan.

"We're going to put it on as soon as we get the site up," said Don.

"Maybe do a link — great car crashes," said Alan.

"And fires," said Don.

"Police chases," said Alan.

"Ambulances," said Don.

Why didn't Jennifer say something?

The three boys were now staring at Jennifer.

"The wall," she whispered.

"The wall?" asked Don.

"The wall?" asked Alan. "They didn't hit a wall. It was bumpers."

"Oh — you want a car crashing into a wall?" said Don. "No problem. . . . I just Google . . . hit *Images* . . . type in *car, crashes, wall*. . . . Look!" There were 291 photos of cars crashing into walls. He clicked the first. The car was halfway into someone's living room. Three firefighters were studying it. "How's that? A wall crash in under ten seconds," said Don. "You want a video? I go to YouTube. . . ."

Adam was getting frantic. Jennifer seemed to be in a trance. She was staring at the storage-shed wall. Adam followed her gaze. There was a big daddy long-legs climbing up. "The spider on the wall?" asked Adam. Was Jennifer afraid of spiders? He couldn't remember.

"The wall," Jennifer repeated.

Maybe she was frozen in terror. Like that time in the climbing tree. Adam looked at the wall again. On a shelf there was an old stuffed duck, covered by cobwebs, with a small pile of peat moss on its head. Jennifer was kind of environmental. Maybe she was mad about that?

"Are we playing 'I'm thinking of'?" said Don. "I know! The saw hanging on the wall?"

"I love guessing games," said Alan. "The 1987 calendar? No?"

"Adam," Jennifer said, her voice a whisper. "Did you tell them about the wall between the news side and the business side? The wall?"

That wall. Thank heavens. It was so much easier if you knew what you were talking about.

The truth was, he may have overlooked mentioning *that* wall to the Ameches.

"Look," said Jennifer. "I don't know if you've ever seen the *Slash*, but we're not big on car crashes. I mean, if a car crashed into the school, that would be a big story for us. Or if some kids from our school were hurt in a car crash, that would be a story. But if you want general car crashes, all you have to do is turn on News 12. The TV news, that's all they have — car crashes, and fires, and people shooting each other, and people being arrested for selling drugs, and other mayhem. That may be how the world seems to you, but I walk out my door and I don't see a lot of that. To me, things generally seem to be in order. We try to go for stuff that really affects a lot of our readers, things they might not know if it wasn't for the *Slash*. Stuff kind of lying under the surface that can cause big problems if you don't shine light on it. Like when the county had a secret plan to take down all the basketball hoops. Or the principal tried to steal seventy-five thousand dollars of the school's money. Or the science fair being unfair. Or the three-hundred-year-old climbing tree almost getting cut down. Or kids from the Willows being forced to move away because the Bolands were buying up their neighborhood."

Adam stared at Jennifer. How did she speak so well? He wondered if the Ameche brothers understood a word of it.

"Please don't take this the wrong way," said Jennifer, "but we can't have you putting whatever video you like on the *Slash* website. Adam and I, we're the news editors. And you—you're the business managers. We do news. You do money. And there needs to be a wall between the two parts of the paper. News on one side of the wall. Business on the other. If you've got something you think should go on the *Slash* website, you need to tell us, and we'll see if we agree. But just because you know how to put something on the site, doesn't mean it's OK."

The Ameche brothers looked at each other. "Um, we didn't mean to break any rules," said Don.

"We didn't know about the wall," said Alan.

"We thought we were giving you like, free, extra news," said Alan. "We had no idea it was a violation. This is the first newspaper business we had."

"In our other businesses, we don't have walls," said Don. "Everyone just works together to make money."

"Yeah, like our golf business. Mom wakes us up in the middle of the night," said Alan. "And helps us get on the wet suits."

"And Uncle Louie corks up our faces," said Don.

"Corks up your faces?" said Jennifer.

"Yeah, so we don't show up in the headlights," said Alan.

"And Grandpa Mike drops us off at the twelfth hole . . ." said Don.

"At White Lake Golf Club . . ." said Alan.

"And stands guard and puts the balls in the buckets," said Don, "while we search the water hazard."

"And Uncle Louie hoses us off afterward," said Alan. "The water hazard's really mucky on the bottom. You get a lot of weeds in your hair."

Adam and Jennifer looked at each other. The Ameche brothers pulled golf balls out of the water hazard at the twelfth hole at White Lake Golf Club? In the middle of the night? *That's* what all those dirty balls in buckets were. That's how their golf-ball business worked. That's how they could sell three-dollar golf balls for seventy-five cents — they got them free.

"Is that legal?" asked Jennifer.

"Nobody cares," said Don.

"It's just old, lost balls golfers hit in the water," said Alan.

"But the golf course is private property," said Jennifer.

"Next time can I come?" asked Adam.

Jennifer said she had to go, but Adam dragged her outside the May Way West studios and begged her to give the Ameches one more chance. "I think they're going to be OK," he said. "We just have to train them on how a newspaper works; I mean, they're business guys; they're a little rough about some stuff, but—"

"A little rough?" said Jennifer. "We could spend the rest of our lives investigating the Ameches. We could assign the entire *Slash* Spotlight Team to do a special issue on the Ameches' five hundred schemiest businesses."

"Jennifer, look, I'm asking you to trust me. I have a good feeling about the Ameches. We just have to teach them. They seem like fast learners—"

"More like fast earners," said Jennifer.

"That's my point," said Adam. "We need fast earners if we're going to get this issue out, and they've already sold a bunch of ads. They told me."

Finally, Jennifer looked at him.

"So let's go back inside," said Adam, "and see how much money—"

"I don't know," said Jennifer. "It feels hopeless to me."

"You know what?" he said. "You really look cute when you're hopeless."

"Oh, shut up, Adam. I think you're part Ameche yourself."

Adam shrugged, but Jennifer did go back inside.

The Ameches were tapping away madly at their computers. "Just working on downloading some video for our next weather report," said Don. "Looks like we're getting a tsunami—"

"Right, right," said Adam. He asked how many ads they'd sold.

"Almost five hundred dollars' worth," said Don, rattling off the businesses that had bought ads: a cell-phone store, a unisex hair salon, a one-hour photo shop, a copy store, Zap cola ("the high-octane beverage"), a pharmacy, a math tutor.

"That's great," said Adam, and Jennifer actually nodded, too. Adam asked when they could get the money. "The print shop wants about half ahead of time, so they can schedule us in."

"Don't have it yet," said Don.

"You giving them thirty days or something?" asked Adam.

Alan shook his head, and Don handed Adam a

list. The coeditors studied it. "Is this a story list?" asked Jennifer.

"It is," said Don.

"It's the stories the advertisers want the *Slash* to write about them," said Don.

"We included phone numbers and e-mails," said Alan. "And we wrote down what they want their stories to say."

"And how big an ad they bought," said Don, "so you'd know how big to make the story."

"Guy spends a hundred bucks for an ad," said Alan, "he expects a nice big story."

Adam's eyes raced down the list. Basically every advertiser wanted the *Slash* to write an article about what a great business they had. The Zap Cola Company had even provided a story it wanted printed in the *Slash* — on the benefits of caffeine as a one-hundred-percent-natural energy booster. An explanatory note on the article said that it had originally appeared in *Sugar Cola Quarterly*, the research journal of the Soft Drink Institute.

Adam was so stunned, he didn't know what to say.

But Jennifer did.

"Good-bye," she said. "I'm out of here. That's it.

You are idiots. You think it's OK for people to buy stories in the *Slash* that will make them look great? All the hard work we've done to be independent and tell the truth will be destroyed in ten seconds. . . . You . . . you . . . you're such *Total Ameches.* You didn't get one single thing I said about the wall. My God, you're going to turn this into the Boland *Citizen-Gazette-Herald-Advertiser.*"

"Isn't that what you want?" said Alan.

"As good as a grown-up paper," said Don.

"You mean *as bad as.*" Jennifer bolted out the door but immediately banged into something so rock solid that she let out a screech and staggered backward.

It was Mrs. Ameche.

"Oh, my God," said Mrs. Ameche. "Sweetie, every time I see you, you're running away from the Ameche brothers. Did they say something prejudiced? I'll kill them if they did."

"Ma," said Don.

"Quit it, Ma," said Alan.

"Ma, you were on the roof, spying," said Don.

Mrs. Ameche rolled her eyes and swore that she'd been on the ground the entire time. She said that she'd just come out to work on her tomato plants and heard the commotion, and if they didn't believe her, they could check her for shingle marks. She made a big deal of rolling up her sleeves and showing them that there were no little pebbly, dotty pockmarks people get when they lie flat on roofs spying. "I'm clean," she said. She turned to Jennifer. "If they're not racists, sweetie, there's a fair chance they're sexist pigs; is that it?"

Jennifer shook her head.

"It's ethics," said Adam. "No offense, but they don't seem to have any. I mean, at first, I really didn't get it either, Mrs. Ameche. I'm not saying I'm this big ethics pro. If it weren't for Jennifer—"

"Ahhh," said Mrs. Ameche. "Ethics. Right from wrong. The Ameche brothers and the Uncle Louie gene." They all looked at her. "Oh, you know," she said, "every family has its bad seed, someone who isn't wired right, always gets in trouble, but has a perfectly logical explanation for why it's OK for *him* to break the rules. It's like they can't ever do the right thing. Their DNA prohibits it. Uncle Louie couldn't stop being Uncle Louie. It runs in families." She gave the Ameche brothers a hard stare.

Someone who always gets in trouble but has a logical explanation? Adam wondered, Was he a bad seed? He glanced at the Ameches; it was the first time he could remember them not having some zippy comeback.

"We're not like Uncle Louie," Don said softly.

"We're not," said Alan, wiping his nose. "We're not going away."

Adam felt embarrassed; he thought the Ameches might—

"Of course not," said Mrs. Ameche. "Because you have a good mother doing her best to keep you on target. Poor Louie. Never knew a mother's love. But I will say this for Louie: He was a model inmate." Mrs. Ameche gently put one hand on each side of Alan's cheeks and pulled his face forward until their noses mooshed, then she kissed him on the forehead and did the same with Don. "I love you boys," she said. "Big Ameche hug." And she gathered them to her and squeezed them good.

"Love you too, Ma," said Don.

"Ma, my circulation's getting squished," said Alan.

Then she ordered all of them into the house for cider and warm churros she'd just taken out of the oven. "We're going to fill your stomachs and have a good discussion on ethics." She smiled at Jennifer. "It's nice to have a girl around," Mrs. Ameche said.

"Don't you worry, Jenny. We'll straighten out all these ethics-less boys. I predict this will be a very good business for the Ameche brothers. Learning how to put out an ethical newspaper — that would be a good talent to take out into the world. You know, as I think about it, maybe we need to put together a sales packet for your *Slash*. Something to show advertisers. You're going to see that the Ameche brothers—once they understand the rules—are great salesmen."

They all marched up the back stairs, Adam last. As Mrs. Ameche disappeared into the house, he heard her say, "Jenny, honey, the boys tell me the *Slash* is doing a story on state test scores going up. It's an outrage! I know why scores are up — they're making that test easier! Do you believe Don got a four on the eighth-grade English? That's the top score! Don? My Don?"

Adam was pissed. He hated grown-ups who acted like everything was harder when they were kids. Mrs. Ameche was probably going to start telling them how she walked a hundred miles to school through the snow.

He was about to say something when he stepped into the kitchen and smelled those warm churros, and then, nothing else really mattered.

chapter 6

Room 107A

Adam was excited. For their English assignment on writing about someone really different, Mrs. Stanky was letting them skip her class. They were supposed to spend the period with the person they were writing about. Mrs. Stanky said if they were really going to do a profile on someone, they needed to observe that person close up. "You want to breathe the air they breathe," she told them, "walk a mile in their shoes. Spend a day in their life. Climb inside their heads. Look deep into their hearts. Discover what makes them tick." She said biographers and historians did this, documentary filmmakers did it, magazine writers and newspaper reporters did it, even MTV, Nick, and Disney did it on some of their shows.

"Is this like reality TV?" asked a girl.

"Not exactly," said Mrs. Stanky. "We're not making up crazy stuff for people to do and then seeing how stupid they look. It's more we're being flies on the wall. Quietly observing."

"Ah, excuse me, Mrs. Stanky, but historians?" said another girl. "I don't think so. Like, how can you spend a day with Abraham Lincoln? No offense, but he's dead."

"True," said Mrs. Stanky. "You can't. But you can read accounts of people who did spend days with him. And then you can walk where he walked. You could visit Gettysburg; visit his house in Springfield, Illinois; visit the White House. In fact, if any of you would rather do a historical figure—"

Adam didn't care about the White House; he wanted to see Room 107A.

Adam leaned on the door to 107A and peeked through the window. The moment he did, the door flew open and he lost his balance and staggered halfway into the room, practically knocking over a boy wearing a helmet and sitting in a wheelchair, who did a nifty 180-degree spin to avoid a crash. By the time Adam came to a full stop, everyone was staring at him.

"You're late," said Shadow, who had yanked open the door the moment one of Adam's molecules brushed against it. "Third period starts at 10:18, and it is now 10:22. It will be 10:23 in seventeen seconds. You said you'd come at the start of third period. This is not the start of third period."

"Good to see you, too," said Adam.

"I know," said Shadow.

The kid in the wheelchair grunted something that Adam couldn't understand. "Huh? I didn't get—"

"That boy is Derek," Shadow explained. "He said, 'Good thing I'm wearing my helmet.'"

Adam stared at the boy, who suddenly let out a squealing laugh.

"Ahhh," said Adam. "Very funny. Shadow, you didn't tell me there's a comedian in your class."

Shadow looked around the room. "There is no comedian in this class. Comedians are on Comedy Central, channel fifty. In this class is just Mr. Willy, the teacher; Miss Patty, the aide; and twelve kids including me. Eleven kids not including me. Thirteen kids including you, but you're just visiting."

Derek grunted something else. Adam looked at Shadow, who translated: "Derek says, 'If there is a comedian, it is definitely not Shadow, though he is funny.'" Then Shadow turned and said, "Shut up, Derek Screw-Up."

Derek grunted something.

"What'd he say?" asked Adam.

"He said 'Shut up yourself, Shadow Fiddle-Faddle.'"

Shadow turned and said, "You shut up yourself first, Derek."

"Gentlemen," said Mr. Willy, "come on. What's our guest going to think?" Mr. Willy welcomed Adam and said they'd been expecting him and were excited about his visit. "We don't get many visitors," he said. He explained that they had a few more minutes of reading, and then they were moving to their work stations. "You're free to walk around the room, Adam, take notes on anything. Mrs. Stanky explained the project to me, and in all the years she's been doing it — you're the first to pick someone from our class."

"He picked me," said Shadow, and shooting a glance at Derek, he added, "He definitely didn't pick anyone else, especially no one who's name starts with *D* for Derek. I'm picked because Adam is coeditor at the *Slash*. With Jennifer, the other coeditor. I'm the *Slash*'s official fact-checker and proofreader. So far, since I started, I found thirteen mistakes that almost got into the paper. Jennifer says, 'Not too shabby.'"

Derek made a long bunch of grunts that went up and down in several places—Adam was pretty sure he recognized a few words, including *Shadow* and *idiot*—but before he could get a full translation, everyone was shooed back to their seats.

Adam pulled out a reporter's notebook and went over to Shadow's group. They were reading *Matilda* by Roald Dahl, a book Adam loved. It was Shadow's turn—he must have been waiting to go until Adam arrived. Shadow gave Adam a little wave, then started reading.

Adam was surprised. This was Special Education, but Shadow was reading a real middle-school book. It was the part in *Matilda* about Miss Trunchbull, the evil principal—a favorite part for Adam, since he knew a lot about evil principals. And though there were some tricky words—*headmistress, exceedingly, apprehension*—Shadow read them all. Adam wrote in his notebook, *Shadow reads well!* He also wrote down a few of those big words as best he could spell them, because he wanted to put them in his profile. Mrs. Stanky said the details make a subject come alive.

Soon, though, Adam was yawning. What was it? He yawned again. Adam could tell that Mr. Willy was trying to cover a yawn, too. Was it Shadow? Actually, Shadow's voice? Listening to it for so long made Adam sleepy. Everything Shadow read sounded the same. His voice didn't go up and down, in and out, like most people's. When Miss Trunchbull boomed and barked, Shadow read it exactly the same as when Matilda whispered and murmured.

"OK, Shadow," said Mr. Willy. "Good job. There were a lot of big words in there."

"Not big for me," said Shadow. "I can read a word with twenty-six letters." He glanced over at Adam and gave him another wave.

Mr. Willy said he had one more thing to talk about before they moved to their work stations. He pointed to a drawing in the book. Adam looked over his shoulder. It was a cartoonish sketch of Miss Trunchbull, hands on her hips, looking really angry.

"What's Miss Trunchbull feeling in this picture?" asked Mr. Willy.

Shadow stared at the picture and at Mr. Willy but didn't say anything.

"Remember how we talked about reading people's feelings from the expressions on their faces? How does Miss Trunchbull feel in this picture? See her eyes? See her eyebrows slanted down. She's . . ."

Shadow studied it again. "The principal runs the school," he said.

"That's right, but is that a feeling, Shadow?" asked Mr. Willy. He told Shadow to open his binder to the page with the list of feelings and find one for Miss Trunchbull in the picture. Shadow looked down the list, looked back at the picture again, and said, "Sad?"

Adam was surprised; this was baby stuff. This should have been so easy for Shadow.

"How do you feel about Adam being here today?" asked Mr. Willy.

"Like Adam's my friend," said Shadow, glancing over and giving Adam a wave.

"And how does having your friend here make you feel?"

"Like I'm his friend, too," said Shadow.

/ / / / /

They were sitting two to a table. Shadow was sharing a table with a boy named Ronald, who was round and had a very thick neck, thick arms, stubby little fingers, squinty eyes, and a sweet, sweet smile. In the center of each table was a huge pile of earphones like the kind they give out on airplanes. They were small, only a couple of inches long, and each was individually wrapped in plastic. On the floor beside each table were a bunch of boxes, neatly stacked. The smallest boxes were orange, the next size up were white, and the largest were plain cardboard cartons.

Mr. Willy explained the rules to everyone while Miss Patty, the aide, walked around giving each of them a large sheet of paper with numbered squares from one to twelve. Mr. Willy said this was a game, but for some of them it was also one of the kinds of jobs they might get in the summer, or when they got out of school, so it was good practice for that, too.

Shadow raised his hand. "I already have a job, working for Mr. Johnny Stack at the Rec, doing what needs doing. I make four dollars an hour, cash on the barrel."

"We know that," said Mr. Willy. "That's wonderful. But not everyone is as far along on their independence goals as you are—"

"Mr. Johnny Stack says independence is my middle name," said Shadow. "That's why July fourth is my favorite holiday. Independence Day."

"Right," said Mr. Willy. "So this will be more of a game for you, Shadow. No more hands—"

Shadow raised his hand. "Except if it's an emergency," he said, and he gave Adam another little wave.

"Right, right," said Mr. Willy. He explained that they were supposed to take a plastic earphone packet, place it on the number one square, take another, place it on the number two square, and keep doing that until they'd filled all twelve squares on their sheets. Then they were supposed to reach down and pick up the smallest box, the orange one, and put the twelve earphones into the box and close up the box. They were supposed to repeat that until they had six orange boxes. When they had six orange boxes, they were supposed to put them into a bigger white box. And when they had ten white boxes, they were supposed to stack them in the large plain cardboard carton.

Mr. Willy held up a stopwatch. "All set? . . . OK. . . . Go!"

Shadow was fastest. He'd grab a handful of earphones, drop one on each numbered square, scoop them up when he filled twelve squares, stuff them in the orange box, then start on the next orange box.

On the other hand, Ronald, his table mate, looked like he was on vacation. He would take one of the earphones wrapped in plastic, place it on the number-one square, then take the next earphone and put it on the number-two square. Pause. Then he'd go back to the first square and make sure the earphone packet was straight, then make sure the second was straight. Pick out a third . . .

Adam sat transfixed. In the time Shadow would finish a carton, Ronald would be lucky to do two orange boxes.

It was as if Ronald had forgotten the purpose of the game. They were supposed to go as fast as possible, but Ronald was being as neat as possible.

At one point, Adam looked up for a moment and noticed that Mr. Willy was watching him watch Shadow and Ronald.

Mr. Willy called time after Shadow finished a carton. "Good job, everyone," he said. He walked around the room. "Looks like Shadow's our champion," said the teacher. "Let's give him a round of applause."

Shadow nodded to acknowledge the applause.

"Speech, speech," called out Ronald.

Shadow just shrugged.

"How does it feel to win?" said Mr. Willy.

"I did sixty orange boxes," said Shadow. "Ten white boxes and one carton. Sixty orange times twelve is seven hundred and twenty. Ten white times seventy-two is seven hundred and twenty. One carton times seven hundred and twenty is seven hundred and twenty."

Ronald clapped again. "That was a good speech," he said. "I love speeches."

The bell rang. The period was over. The kids in 107A stayed in the room, but Adam had to get to his next class. As he put his reporter's notebook in his back pocket and headed toward the door, Derek grunted to him.

Shadow started to translate, but Adam interrupted.

"I will come back, Derek," said Adam. "Thanks. It was nice meeting you, too. And I'm sorry I almost knocked you over."

Shadow looked at Derek, looked at Adam, and said, "It was nice meeting me, too."

Adam nodded. "Always. See you at the *Slash* meeting."

As Adam walked out, Mr. Willy caught up to him. "You know," he said, "if you really want to write a complete story about Shadow, you need to meet Mr. Johnny Stack."

"I know," said Adam. "Shadow talks about him all the time. His boss at the Rec."

"Oh, he's a lot more than that," said Mr. Willy.

chapter 7
Room 306

Adam did not see the bike again. He did see the chubby kid, several days later, in the hallway. This time, Adam had the serial number with him — he carried it everywhere now — but the kid said the bike was gone. "I told you I just borrowed it," he said.

Adam had been checking the bike rack daily; the kid might be telling the truth.

"Who'd you borrow it from?" Adam asked.

"Don't know his whole name," said the boy.

Adam said he'd take half a name.

"Well, it's James," said the boy. "But it wasn't his bike. He told me he borrowed it from another kid."

Adam felt like a jerk; he should have grabbed the bike when he had the chance.

The newspaper staff looked forward to *Slash* meetings. To be at school in a room full of kids with no teacher always felt great—even when Jennifer was bugging them about getting in their overdue stories. To be able to flop on those dirty, iced-tea–stained couches again and sit on top of desks and tables and throw their backpacks anyplace and make loud burping noises and other gassy sounds that weren't burps without having to say "excuse me"—that was about as grown-up as any middle-school kid could get.

Since Mrs. Quigley had secretly allowed them to use 306 again, everything was ratcheted up another level. They felt positively tingly, as if they were on this underground mission to change the world against all odds.

For all they knew, Tremble school security might come crashing through the door at any second and raid the place.

Everything seemed way braver and riskier than usual.

Unfortunately for Adam and Jennifer, this made

meetings harder to control. They were all so psyched, especially Ask Phoebe.

Adam was ready to kill her. She was raising her hand every second, and while he kept shading his eyes as though the light coming through the windows was blinding him from seeing her wiggly hand, Jennifer was a far better human being and called on her.

Big mistake. "I may need three pages for my first Ask Phoebe column," said Ask Phoebe. "So many people need advice. It's unbelievable how confused everyone is. I've had to come up with ten tips on how to stay out of dramas. For the September issue, I'm going to have to do a special column for the new sixth graders on five ways to decide where to sit in the middle-school cafeteria—"

"Phoebe," said Jennifer, "slow down. We're just trying to get the June issue out. Let's not get ahead of ourselves—"

"Christmas will have to be an extra-long column on gift advice. I already have seventy-three websites that can turn your holiday season around. And I never had a clue what a big issue hair is. Everyone's being let down by their volumizing shampoos and fortifying conditioners. And Valentine's Day, oh my gosh, you have to listen to these love letters. Until Ask Phoebe, I never knew that there were so many broken hearts —"

"Ask Phoebe!" yelled Jennifer. "Stop . . . just stop." Jennifer called a time-out. "Calm down, Phoebe. Please, just take a breath and count to ten to yourself . . ."

"That reminds me," said Ask Phoebe. "I'm going to be doing top ten zero trans fat —"

And then Phoebe stopped. She actually stopped. In mid-sentence. Jennifer had given her such a forceful glare that even Phoebe had noticed. The entire staff had noticed. The room went silent. Adam was wowed; it was as if Jennifer had put every last ounce of her face into that glare. Adam wished he had those kind of crowd control skills; all he could ever think of was throwing Phoebe out a window.

In the calmest of voices, Jennifer explained to Ask Phoebe that while it sounded like things were going great, the coeditors would still have to see a sample column before they made up their minds. Jennifer said they had to get on to the news stories; there was lots to do.

Phoebe nodded. "If there's time at the end, can I read a letter out loud to you guys?" she asked.

"If there's time," said Jennifer. "One."

"Just one?" asked Ask Phoebe.

Adam told them the exciting news about the Bolands being under investigation. "We did it," said Adam. "It's our story that got the state to investigate them. The *Slash*! Little us!" They looked around at one another. Little them? Versus the mighty Bolands?

Adam explained that state investigators were looking into whether the Bolands' plan — to buy up all the old houses in the Willows, tear them down, and put up Boland Estates full of new million-dollar mini-mansions — was unfair to poor families who couldn't afford any other place to live in Tremble County.

"The Bolands are going to jail?" asked a photographer.

Adam shook his head. "I wish," he said. "Long way to go." He explained that just because someone is investigated doesn't mean they're guilty, even though in this case he was sure the Bolands were guilty to the stinking core.

Jennifer told them that she had talked it over with her dad, who was a lawyer. "He said investigations of high and mighty people like the Bolands can take a long time because even the investigators and the investigators' bosses can be scared of them."

Another kid asked if this meant the *Slash* would soon become the official newspaper of Harris Elementary/Middle School again.

"I think it could happen," said Jennifer. "But not that soon. It's definitely a little hopeful." She said it showed that even if the school board had shut them down, other grown-ups—the state investigators—had taken their story on the Bolands seriously. And so did the *New York Times*, by publishing a front-page article about it. "It shows that we're not just troublemakers," said Jennifer.

"Well, we are troublemakers," said Adam. "We're just good troublemakers."

All this meant that they still had to raise money to put out the *Slash*. Jennifer explained that she had good news and bad news on that front. "The good news is that Adam and I had a big meeting with the Ameche brothers, and we straightened out a few problems they were having."

"Problems raising money?" asked Sammy.

"Um, no," said Jennifer.

"They were actually too good at raising money," said Adam.

"That's a problem?" asked Sammy.

"Let's just say they needed some ethics training," said Jennifer. "They didn't realize you can't let people tell you what to put in the newspaper just because they buy an ad from you."

"So we met with their boss," said Adam. "And got it squared away."

"This is the Ameche brothers from the *Talk Till You Drop, All-Live Except the Recorded Parts* webcast?" asked Phoebe. "They're, like, really famous. They don't seem like the kind of people who'd have a boss."

"Actually, their mother," said Jennifer.

"Anyway," said Adam, "the good news is now they really know how to sell ads the totally ethical way, so pretty soon we should have money to get the *Slash* printed."

Jennifer lifted a manila envelope and wiggled it in the air. "We've actually created a sales packet," she said, explaining how the Ameche brothers would be showing it to potential advertisers. The packet included the last few issues of the *Slash*, plus the *New York Times* article about the *Slash*'s story on the Bolands, plus a little about Harris Elementary/

Middle School. "We think showing how great the paper is should really help sell ads," she said.

The staff members still wanted to know the bad news.

"Well, most of the money the Ameches raised so far they had to give back," said Adam. He was dying to change the subject, but they would not let him. This was the problem with trying to manage news people—they wanted every single question answered right down to the bone.

"In terms of how much," said Jennifer. "Five hundred dollars."

"Yipes," said Phoebe, "How much do we—"

"A little over sixty-eight dollars," said Jennifer. "But I think it's going to go a lot better now."

They were quiet. It had better go a lot better. They needed to get from sixty-eight dollars to one thousand dollars in four weeks if there was going to be a June issue of the *Slash*.

They discussed the progress of several articles. Adam told them about the test-scores story. He said it sounded from his meeting with Mrs. Quigley as though something fishy was up, but he couldn't tell what yet and he had set up a meeting with one of the deputy super-dooper-pooperintendents of the Tremble schools.

Sammy summarized what he'd found so far on chocolate milk. "I'm about half done," he told them. "And without going into it too much, it's worse than I thought."

They'd heard about Adam's bike being stolen, which started them all talking about stolen bikes. They knew three other kids who'd had theirs stolen, too, so they added a bike-theft article to the story list.

With the end of the year coming, some of the old teachers were retiring, so Jennifer assigned a story on that.

Jennifer and Adam had decided not to tell everyone about Stub Keenan giving out free iPod downloads in exchange for votes—if it was true. They didn't want anything leaking out until they had a plan. They'd gone through Jennifer's top-secret list and there was no one from the *Slash* getting free downloads, but they didn't want to take a chance. Stub was a popular kid. There was a good chance some of the *Slash* staff members were friendly with him.

Jennifer asked in a casual way if anyone had heard anything interesting on the student-council race, and they'd heard the same thing she had — that Stub would win, easy.

"Anyone know his campaign manager, Billy Cutty?" asked Adam.

"Good kid," said a girl. "Funny."

Then why's he working for Stub? Adam thought, but didn't say anything.

It was time to go. This was the last week for most of the kids on spring sports teams. As they reached for their backpacks, Ask Phoebe called out, "Attention, everyone. Attention. This will just take a minute. I want to read one letter." The staff ignored her; most of them were middle-school kids, and even if Phoebe was the world's greatest third-grade reporter, at the end of the day, she was still a measly third grader.

"It's very lovey-dovey!" shouted Ask Phoebe.

"Nasty?" said a boy.

"Is it sexy, sexy?" asked a girl.

Adam was thinking this might be funny. He wanted to know who wrote it.

"No name," said Ask Phoebe. "It's signed 'Confused Middle Schooler.'"

"*Ooooh,*" a bunch of them hooted.

"OK, Phoebe," said Adam. "Don't say I never did anything for you. Read it quick."

"No!" Jennifer blurted out, and they all looked at her. "I mean, we really don't have time for this. I've got tennis."

"Jennifer, relax," said Adam. "We've got a few minutes. It'll only take a second." Usually he was the one being driven insane by Phoebe; usually Jennifer was angry at him for not being more understanding about Phoebe. It was fun watching Jennifer not being more understanding about Phoebe.

"We don't even know if we're going to have an Ask Phoebe column," said Jennifer. "You're the one who wanted to kill the whole thing."

Adam shrugged. "You're the one who loves Dear Abby."

"Until we know," said Jennifer, "we shouldn't—"

"'Dear Ask Phoebe,'" began Phoebe, who was standing on a chair now. "'There's this boy in my grade; I think I might like him. He's cute and smart, he's good in sports, and we spend a lot of time together—'"

"Oooooh."

"Sexy, sexy," repeated the girl.

"'We mostly have fun,'" read Phoebe. "'We laugh a lot, and I think he might like me. Sometimes he even says I look good—'"

"Ooooooh."

"Please stop," said Jennifer.

"Hang on, folks!" shouted Phoebe, who was relishing her moment of fame. "Here comes the heartbreak: 'But we just spend time together for school stuff, and the rest of the time, he treats me like I'm no one. He never gives me nice little gifts. He never asks me if I want to take a walk or go to a movie or get an ice cream. And if I get upset, he's so spacey that unless I come out and tell him, he doesn't even notice that I'm upset. I think he's the spaciest middle-school boy on the planet. Is there some way I can get him to be more mature? Or should I just give up? Signed, Confused Middle Schooler.'"

The room was in mayhem. Everyone grabbed their backpacks and as they filed out, they chanted, "Give up, give up, give up."

The door slammed shut.

Just Adam and Jennifer were left.

Adam shook his head. "We're going to have to give her a column now," he said. "I hate to admit it, but that was funny."

Jennifer didn't say anything.

"Can you imagine writing a letter like that to someone like Phoebe?" Adam said. "What kind of middle-school girl would be that hard up? And why would she want to spend time with a jerk like that? He sounds like a total loser."

"I think he is," Jennifer whispered, and, grabbing her backpack, hurried out.

chapter 8

She'd Have to Get *Back* to Him?

Adam spotted Jennifer in the cafeteria at the end of lunch period and waved, but he just got a blank stare back. He chased her down the hall and grabbed her by the sleeve, but she said she was sorry, she was late, and pulled her arm away. "I'll have to get back to you," she said.

She'd have to get back to him? Jennifer? Since when did Jennifer talk like that?

That night, at home, he checked his buddy list and Jennifer's screen name was lit up, so he instant-messaged her, very polite, no "wuz up" kind of trashy jive mooch. "Can we get together and talk?" he wrote. But all three times, her screen name suddenly disappeared and he got an auto-reply: "Jennifer is away from her computer."

Right.

Every time Adam had tried to get Jennifer's attention these last few days, it seemed like she looked the other way or hurried off in the opposite direction or started talking to someone else.

Adam was no idiot. She must be upset about something, but what in the world could it possibly be? Certainly nothing to do with him. He had racked his brain. He'd squeezed his mind until his brain juices were practically leaking out, and he had to give himself credit; he could not think of one single thing he'd done wrong lately.

As he reviewed the past few days, he realized that Jennifer's annoying attitude seemed to have started after the last *Slash* meeting. In fact, after the Ask Phoebe stuff. It made sense. Sad to say, but Jennifer must be jealous of him. She was so into controlling everything. She had to run the *Slash* meetings so perfectly, right down to her magic, silencing glare—which Adam had to admit was pretty nifty. But then she'd completely lost it when he gave Phoebe the green light to read the Ask Phoebe question. Come on, he was coeditor. Didn't he have rights, too? Jennifer was the one who loved that Dear Blabby stuff so much. Hadn't the *Slash* staff gone wild? Everyone loved it. Jennifer needed to learn how to handle cub reporters like Phoebe. Sure, you have to put them in their place and drive them into the dirt most of the time. But once in a great while you have to give them a chance to shine, so they'll keep coming back for more abuse. It was a fine-tuning thing that Jennifer hadn't mastered yet.

The more he thought about it, the angrier he became. He was sick of people blaming him for their mistakes. Jennifer really needed to grow up.

Their last Geography Challenge meet of the school year was coming up, the final round of the yearlong Countdown to Total Dominance. The team sponsor, Mr. Landmass, had called a practice session after school to review.

"We're in pretty good shape," he said. "I've been to the official certified national website, and all we need is 173,218.7 points in this meet to clinch being one of the top hundred middle-school teams in the country. If we can do that, that's pretty much the zenith —"

"Point in the sky directly above the observer," said a boy.

"Exactly right!" said Mr. Landmass. "We are cooking with gas —"

"Natural gas: the gaseous element of petroleum extracted from oil wells," said another boy.

"Smokin' Joe!" said Mr. Landmass, "And if — I should say *when* we make the top one hundred, Georgraphy Challenge, Inc. sends a sales rep to our school. They have a big ceremony, and they give us all this free Geography Challenge software and a topographic map —"

"Large-scale contour map showing human and physical features," said a girl.

"Spectacular!" said Mr. Landmass. "Would someone please tell me, who let the dogs out? You guys are good to go. Hold on, there's more." He was reading over a sheet now. "It says we get a framed certificate . . . *Newsweek* will include us on its list of Top Geography Schools in America. . . . a plaque . . . an official scholastic achievement medal — OK, nothing to retire on, but you know, good stuff. Plus, being a top one hundred school in anything is great for property values, so that makes your moms and dads jolly, which is all good."

Mr. Landmass asked a boy to hand out a set of work sheets with terms and definitions. "Let's break up into teams of two and review—"

"I'll work with Jennifer," Adam said.

"No," said Jennifer. "I mean, Tracy and I—"

"That's fine," said Mr. Landmass. "Adam and Jennifer are a team. You can move the desks together for more privacy."

Adam grabbed two desks and dragged them to the far corner of the room, away from everyone else.

"So what's up with you?" asked Adam.

"Where does the Empire State Building rank in tallest buildings in the world?" asked Jennifer, eyes glued to Mr. Landmass's handout.

"Jennifer," Adam said, "what's bothering you? You're acting insane."

"Nothing," said Jennifer. "Come on. Answer the question. You heard Mr. Landmass. . . ."

"Oh, right," said Adam, "I forgot. It would be a major tragedy if we didn't get one of those official Geography Challenge certificates." He paused, looking for a smile, even a teeny upturn at the corners maybe, a slight lift in the eyebrow, but Jennifer's face was locked up tight.

"Ninth biggest," she said. "What do France and Burkina Faso have in common?"

"Girls in bikinis?" said Adam.

"Two of the eight countries located on the Prime Meridian," said Jennifer. "Define *mesa*."

"A mesa is nothing but a big butt," said Adam.

"That's *butte*, as in you're a real *beaut*," said Jennifer. "Have you studied these at all? This is for Countdown to Total Dominance."

"Oh, come on, Jennifer. I'll look it over the night before. You know I always come through. . . ."

"Oh, right," said Jennifer. "Mr. Dependable. The farthest western islands in United States territory?"

"Hawaiian Islands," said Adam. "See, I know stuff."

"Aleutian Islands," said Jennifer. "It's unbelievable the stuff you don't know."

Adam grabbed the paper from Jennifer, which made her at least look at him. "Jennifer, please tell me why you're mad," he said. "Ever since the *Slash* meeting, it's like you're on the warpath. You keep avoiding me at every turn. What's wrong? What?"

"Nothing," she said. "It's nothing."

"Are you mad because of Ask Phoebe?"

She looked at him. For the first time, she actually looked at him, and maybe it was just his imagination, but her big brown eyes seemed a tiny bit softer.

"I know I was against Ask Phoebe," said Adam. "And I know it's absolutely crazy that a third grader would have an advice column, but I was surprised, OK? I mean, that question she read — I didn't know the questions would be such goofs —"

"Goofs?" said Jennifer. "Goofs? . . . That's what you think? You . . . you? . . . You! Just forget it, will you?"

"Jennifer, you've got to be more flexible, kind of go with the flow, you know what I mean?" Adam said. "If people are going to write in such dumb questions, it almost doesn't matter what Phoebe writes back; it's a good laugh, and that will help us get readers for the serious stories in the *Slash*. I mean, we can't help it if people are stupid."

"They really are stupid," said Jennifer.

Finally, Jennifer was agreeing with him, although, for some reason, it didn't feel like the really good kind of agreeing. Still, Adam figured he'd at last found a theme to build on. People's infinite stupidity — he and Jennifer could agree on that — and so he went with it. "I mean, I don't know who was more stupid," said Adam. "The girl who wrote the question or that clueless idiot boy she was all lovey-dovey for. *He doesn't send me gifts. He doesn't take me to the movies. Give up, give up, give up.*"

Jennifer looked ashen. "Stop talking," she said, her voice a whisper. "Just stop. Please. Go away."

Go away? What was this? If anything, she owed him an apology for ducking him and acting mean for no good reason. He was about done being patient with her. Why was Jennifer doing this? She had never been like this before. He was just going to have to level with her. She needed to grow up. Someone had to tell her the hard truth.

"Look," he said, "I'm starting to get pissed. I've tried to be patient with you on this. I've racked my brain, and I sure didn't do anything that — I hate to say this, but I think you're just jealous because I did so well handling Phoebe. You know, you don't have to be in control of everything and everybody, Miss I'm in Control of Everything and Everybody. You have to learn to let go sometimes. Jealousy is a very ugly trait."

124

Jennifer smiled, but it wasn't the kind of smile you hope for or could build on. It was really smirky and nasty.

"Adam Canfield, the problem with you—you are so clueless, you don't even know what you do to people. You are unbelievably oblivious. A total spaceman. My mom told me. She said the most dangerous people in the world are the ones who don't know what they don't know and, you . . . you, Adam Canfield—as far as I'm concerned, you are the champion of not knowing what you don't know. You, Adam Canfield, are at the very tippity top of the list of most dangerous people. From now on—"

"Fine," said Adam. "I'm done trying to be nice."

"Fine," said Jennifer.

"Well, fine," said Adam. "And I mean fine. As far as I'm concerned, we're done being . . . From now on . . . no more . . . I'm not going to . . . any kind of special . . . It's not . . . We're just . . . coeditors. That's it."

"Fine," said Jennifer. "Coeditors."

"Fine," said Adam. "OK, then . . . as your coeditor, I'm asking you for the list of people who got iPod downloads. I figured out how I'm going to do the story. If that's OK with you, coeditor."

"Fine with me, coeditor," said Jennifer, and she went into her backpack and pulled out the list and winged it at him.

"Fine," said Adam.

"It is perfectly fine," said Jennifer, who was gathering up her stuff and throwing it in her backpack. She tossed the pack over her back and marched out the door.

"Fine," he said, watching her disappear.

And then, even Adam noticed. Everyone else was gone, except Mr. Landmass, who was looking over papers at his desk.

As Adam rose to leave, Mr. Landmass glanced up. "You should be ready for the big meet," said Mr. Landmass. "I appreciate all the extra time you put in this afternoon. You don't have a game to get to?"

"I'm fine," said Adam. "I'm really fine."

Their schedules were getting easier. Most activities in their overprogrammed lives—Quiz Bowl Gladiator, Math Olympiad, Geography Challenge, before school/after school mandatory/voluntary prep for the state test, baseball, tennis, band, jazz band, marching band, baritone horn lessons, cello lessons — were either over for the year or soon to be. That meant he wouldn't have to be bumping into Jennifer every stinking second, which was fine with him. He was just going to report his stories and not talk to Jennifer. *Write* his stories and not talk to Jennifer. He was going to put his head down and be on his way and definitely not talk to Jennifer unless it was official coeditor business. And then, he was going to try to keep it under twenty seconds.

She was going to be sorry when he nailed her big Stub Keenan iPod download story. Of course Adam was the one who had to do the hard-core investigative reporting. Her secret source? Big deal. Her hush-hush list? What good was it if she couldn't get it into the paper? She wouldn't be the one getting her hands dirty. *Noooo*. He was the one who'd have to hit the hallways of Harris and squeeze the bloody truth out of people. He was the one who'd have to get them to admit their filthy lies. Fine. He'd do it. He, his lonesome self. And when the story ran on the top of the front page of the *Slash* — the first independently funded edition of the *Slash* in the history of Harris Elementary/Middle School, a true kids' newspaper —

Jennifer would be mighty sorry. She'd be begging him to go back to the way it was before. Unfortunately for Jennifer, it would be too late by then.

They'd just be official coeditors. Period.

Adam kept staring at the list of names. He needed to track down some of these kids, ask them face-to-face if they got free downloads to vote for Stub. He knew he had to proceed cautiously. Think it all out. Catch them off-guard. He didn't want them to see him coming—they'd have time to think up a lie. Or they wouldn't answer his questions. No one *had* to speak to a reporter. And why would they want to? Who wanted to admit to a reporter: "Yes, I'm a lowlife who promised to vote for Stub Keenan in exchange for a crappy little two-hundred-and-fifty-song iPod download. Yes, put my name in your newspaper, and you can say I helped Stub rig the election."

Right.

Somehow, Adam had to get a few of them to tell the truth without knowing they were doing it.

He figured the best time to catch people off-guard was in the morning before homeroom. Kids were still half asleep. In Adam's experience, if you could get a kid early enough in the morning, he might give you all his Christmas stuff.

But how did he find these kids? A few on the list he recognized a little from playing ball or clubs, but they'd probably know he was a reporter and be on their guard.

He had to talk to kids on the list whom he didn't know.

How do you find people you don't know?

He didn't want to ask around—too suspicious.

And then he had the beginning of an idea.

Step One. He needed to get a list of all middle-school students at Harris arranged by homeroom. That way he could match the homeroom list against his list of free downloads. He'd know the homeroom for every kid who got a download.

Step Two. He had to figure out what these kids looked like. He didn't know how he'd do Step Two.

So he'd work on Step One and hope his brain would save him when it was time for Step Two.

He needed the master homeroom list and had some ideas about getting it, including sneaking into the main office when no one was around, like he'd done in Mr. Buchanan's room for the science fair story. The only thing was, that was very risky, and he'd rather find an easier way.

He thought there was a good chance he'd be able to get the list just by asking.

"Adam, hello, how are you? You're here awfully early."

It was Mrs. Rose, the secretary in the main office. He'd wanted to get in before there were a lot of people around.

She gave him a soft, friendly smile. It was amazing. So much had changed in six months. When Mrs. Marris was principal, Mrs. Rose had been his mortal enemy. She seemed like a vicious guard dog protecting a wicked troll. The Head, they'd called her, because, looking up at her standing behind the counter, all you could see was her perfectly round, white, permed head, as if she was just a living skull someone had left on the countertop.

But since the evil Marris had been replaced by friendly Mrs. Quigley, Mrs. Rose had turned out to be really very rosy.

"Looking forward to summer?" she asked.

Boy, Adam was. Diving off the raft to swim in the Tremble River. Visiting his grandparents' cottage by the ocean. Wakeboarding 180s. Picking wild blueberries and raspberries and eating them right off the bush. Boogie boarding. Plus he really wanted to learn to surf. Slowing down. Living the unprogrammed life.

He couldn't wait.

"Need to see Mrs. Quigley?" she asked.

He hesitated. He didn't think so. It might make sense to ask Mrs. Quigley. And he would if he needed to. He just felt like he wanted to save up Mrs. Quigley for when he was really in a tight spot. Like a secret weapon. He was going to try to get this out of Mrs. Rose.

"No, I don't think so," said Adam. "I have a question: When they do attendance, do they have lists for each homeroom?"

"Yes," said Mrs. Rose.

"And they have like last name, and first name?"

"Yes, dear," said Mrs. Rose.

"And it's alphabetical?"

Mrs. Rose nodded.

"And so if you had all the homeroom lists, you'd have basically a list of all the kids in the school?" asked Adam.

"Adam, do me a favor," Mrs. Rose said. "I'm very busy. Just tell me how I can help."

Adam said he'd like a copy of all the middle-school homeroom lists if that wasn't too much trouble.

"Does this have something to do with the *Slash*?" asked Mrs. Rose. "Or are you taking over the attendance office, which I must say — strictly off the cuff — might be an improvement?"

Adam wasn't sure if he should tell the truth, but he didn't have a better plan, so he just said yes.

Mrs. Rose was happy to make copies. Just like that. "Knowing your work," she said, "I'm going to trust that you'll put that list to good use. I can trust you, right, Adam?"

Adam was wondering whether sneaking up on kids outside their homerooms to find out if they got free iPod downloads was trustworthy, but he just nodded. It was a good reporter trick: When you're on the verge of getting valuable documents, shut up as much as possible.

"Do you want to come back or wait?" she asked, and Adam said he'd wait. That was another good trick: If a person was in a generous mood about giving away secret information, get it right away. When it comes to secret documents, moods can change.

Adam took a seat. A few teachers came by, collecting messages from their mailboxes. On the other side of the counter, Adam saw Mrs. Quigley rush past, but she didn't notice him.

In five minutes, Mrs. Rose reappeared and handed Adam a plain manila envelope.

"Thanks," said Adam. "You're great."

She seemed to be waiting for him to leave. "Anything else?" she asked.

"Mrs. Rose, if you wanted to know what a kid looked like at the school but you didn't know him, what would you do?"

"Oh, Adam, I'm surprised — a great reporter like you," she said.

"I know from the time I was mugged that some security guys have handhelds with a photo of every kid in the school," said Adam. "Do you have one of those?

"Oh, no, I'm not important enough for that," said Mrs. Rose. "But there's another —"

"You mean like looking on MySpace or Facebook or YouTube?" said Adam. "I thought of that, and it would probably work for the high school, but not that many middle-school kids have profiles —"

"Adam, I don't even know what Youtoot is, but

133

there's a much simpler way. Think. You're in clubs. You play sports. You know how they take your team photo? What do they do with the photos?"

"I don't know, print them?" said Adam.

Mrs. Rose looked at him. "Adam, I'm going to say something to you that my grandchildren say to me — *Duh!* The yearbook?"

Of course, the yearbook; how could he forget? What an idiot. There were tons of photos of kids on sports teams and clubs, and candid shots, too.

"I'm surprised," said Mrs. Rose. "That's an old newspaper trick. Before I came here, a million years ago, I was a secretary at North Tremble High. And we hated when a newspaper called, asking for a copy of a yearbook. Usually it meant that some kid died in a car crash or was killed in a war or was arrested for something, and the paper didn't have any other way of getting a photo." Mrs. Rose had a faraway look. "I remember this one boy — Oh, never mind. Adam, no one died, did they?"

"Oh, no, Mrs. Rose, no one that I know of. That's not why I need it, but thanks."

"Sure," she said. "You take care, honey. And how's that's sweet coeditor of yours? Jennifer. You're such a cute team."

Adam felt his face getting hot. "Fine, I guess," he mumbled.

"You stick with that girl," said Mrs. Rose. "She's special."

"Yeah, fine," mumbled Adam.

And then Mrs. Rose's hand suddenly appeared above the counter to slap her head, which startled Adam, who was used to thinking of her as only the Head. "Oh, God, I'm an idiot," she said. "I forgot." She told Adam that Mrs. Quigley had set up a meeting for him and Jennifer to interview Dr. Duke, the deputy superintendent who was the testing expert. Mrs. Rose disappeared, then quickly returned with a hall pass that had the time. "Don't forget," she said.

"Ah, Mrs. Rose, you don't have to tell Jennifer. I'm doing this story myself."

"Really?" said Mrs. Rose. "Because Mrs. Quigley insisted that Jennifer be invited, too, and she is the principal, so will that be OK?"

Good lord, what could Adam say? The last thing he wanted was to work on a story with that . . . that . . . that . . . Jennifer. His head hurt thinking about it.

"OK?" Mrs. Rose repeated.

"Fine," said Adam. "Really fine. Just fine." He

turned to go. Nothing was easy. So much was out of his control. His vital fluids felt like they were leaking out his feet. His shoulders sagged; he looked draggy. He didn't even have the strength to pull out his jaw-breaker for a sugar suck.

"Adam?" said Mrs. Rose. "I think it's great the way you guys are keeping that paper going on your own. Most kids — most adults even — would give up. A lot of us grown-ups are pulling for you. It's very brave what you're doing. You ask for help if you need it, OK?"

"Fine."

chapter 9

Test Scores Are Either Up or Not Up

The note Mrs. Rose wrote for Adam had given him permission to leave at the start of third period. Unfortunately, a bottle of half-drunk iced tea that was missing inside his backpack for three months had an easy twist-on cap that, on this very morning, decided to turn into an easy twist-off cap. As a result, Adam wound up throwing away a thick gob of sticky papers, which most likely included the hall pass.

By the time they called him to the office, Jennifer was already there, sitting at a table in the conference room with a legal pad that had a thousand questions written out in her big, neat, loopy handwriting.

There was a platter of Moisty Deluxe cookies in the center of the table, a pitcher of milk, and three drinking glasses. "Dr. Duke just called," said Mrs. Rose. "She's left her office and should be here in a minute. Let me know if you need anything."

Jennifer thanked Mrs. Rose, then without glancing at Adam, put her head down to review her questions.

He didn't mind, not one bit — two could play that game, except Adam didn't have any written questions to be busy with. Nor did he have a piece of paper because of the iced tea situation. Fortunately, great reporters live by their wits, and he sneaked a few napkins from the cookie tray to write on.

Sitting there waiting, he smelled something nice, then realized that was Jennifer's honey apricot shampoo, which reminded him of the old days when they used to be . . . well . . . not just official coeditors.

But this was fine; it really was completely fine. He didn't need a soul.

"Sorry," said Dr. Duke, rushing in and flopping a thick leather briefcase on the table. "I apologize. I had this meeting that was supposed to . . . and then this other meeting that wasn't supposed to . . . Oh, forget it, just promise me you'll never become a deputy superintendent of anything; it's one stupid meeting after another. Supposedly, I'm helping educate children, but to be perfectly honest, you two are the first kids I've seen in a decade. How do you explain that? Well, I can't either. You must be Jennifer," she said, and she reached out and shook Adam's hand. "And you're Adam, I presume," and she shook Jennifer's hand.

They stared at her.

"A joke," she said. "Ha, ha?"

They didn't say anything.

"You know, I'm a huge fan of the *Slash,* and I assumed from reading it that you guys had a great sense of humor. I mean, it has a wonderful, swash-buckling quality. I love a newspaper where you can tell who the good guys are and who the bad guys are."

They stared.

"Hello? Anybody home? You are Adam and Jennifer, right? The investigative reporters?"

"Well, yes," said Jennifer. "Sort of. It's just we're not used to deputy superintendents sounding . . . um . . . well . . ."

"Normal," Adam said. "We met this guy, Dr. Bleepin . . ."

"Oh, yes," said Dr. Duke. "That would explain it. Yes, Dr. Bleepin, he is . . . He *really* is . . . He is a Bleepin. . . . Yes, he's totally Bleepin . . . Enough said, or maybe not said. I presume you met him doing the story on naming the street for Martin Luther King Jr.?"

They were staring again. "How'd you know that?" asked Adam.

"I told you: I read the *Slash*," she said. "I love your newspaper. It's the only real newspaper in Tremble County. You certainly can't count that rag, the *Citizen-Gazette-Herald-Advertiser*. They just print what the Bolands want printed. I loved your story on the Bolands trying to buy up the Willows and force poor people out. It would be unbelievable if you could save the Willows. And the story on the science-fair projects—boy, you got Devillio good. And saving the three-hundred-year-old climbing tree from being chopped down? You know, I climbed that tree as a girl. And after your story, I climbed it again. That reporter, Phoebe—she's still in elementary? Amazing."

"Amazing," repeated Adam, trying to envision Dr. Duke up a tree. "It's like you know every word we wrote."

She nodded. "Of course," she said. "Why do you think I'm willing to sit here and explain the testing racket to a couple of middle-school kids? Why do you think Mrs. Quigley bullied me until I said yes? Now there's a Top Ten bully for you, by the way. Don't let her grandma smile and Moisty Deluxe fool you. That little babe Quigley is a steamroller when it comes to getting things done for her school. And she loves you guys. You know what she told me? She said you guys would probably be urban legends, if you didn't live in the suburbs."

Adam couldn't believe it—that was one of his career goals. Urban legend.

"Enough," she said. "We need to get to work." She grabbed her briefcase, twirled several numbers on a lock, opened the latch, and then handed each of them a packet of tables and graphs that looked like a PowerPoint presentation. Adam flipped the pages quickly. It was really professional and grown-up.

"Let's do it," said Jennifer.

"OK," said Dr. Duke. "Just one last question. Do you mind? What's your underground critic, Sammy, really like? He seems to have a genuine commitment to food."

"He does take it very seriously," said Jennifer.

"You should hear him talk about chocolate milk," said Adam.

"I knew it," said Dr. Duke. "You can tell. The way he wrote about bacon-egg-and-cheese — a lot of feeling there."

She led them through the packet page by page. "OK, now page seven — look it over," she said. "The chart. See if you notice anything." It had taken Adam's brain a little while to adjust, but he was following her pretty well now. Mrs. Quigley had told them that Dr. Duke used to be a teacher, and Adam could tell that she must have been a good one, the way she led them so smoothly from point to point, letting one idea build on the next. She started with the scores from Harris students on the state test and showed them how much they'd gone up over last year — about 10 percentage points. Then she showed them the results for all the Tremble schools, and every single school had gone up, most of them, like Harris, around 10 percentage points, too.

And now this chart they were looking at, on page seven, had scores from all over the state, and they'd also gone up, actually even a little more than Harris, about 12 percentage points on average.

"So?" said Dr. Duke. "Possible explanations? We know it's not just Harris Elementary/Middle School. We know it's not just Tremble. We know it's not even just the Tri-River Region. Why are scores up for almost every school in the state?"

The answers they came up with were the same ones they'd discussed at the *Slash* meeting. Smarter kids. Better teachers. More before school/after school mandatory/voluntary prep for the test.

"OK," said Dr. Duke. "But I think you're leaving out the biggest one. Think. When Mr. Devillio gives back a unit test, what do you do with it?"

"Take it home and get it signed," said Jennifer.

Adam hadn't thought of it until now: How many tests that needed signing had he thrown into the garbage because of his ridiculous iced-tea situation?

"And what do your parents say if you get a good score?" asked Dr. Duke.

"Well, my mom says, great job," said Jennifer. "But when I get a hundred, my dad asks if a lot of kids got a hundred or just me."

"Ah, yes," said Dr. Duke. "Exactly. I had a dad like that. And why does he ask that?"

"Well, because sometimes you're the only one

who got a hundred, and that's a big deal," said Jennifer. "But sometimes a lot of kids get hundreds, 'cause the test is just easy."

"Bingo!" said Dr. Duke. "I think that's the answer we're looking for."

Adam was lost. Jennifer getting a hundred was the answer? He got a lot of hundreds; why wasn't he the answer? He must have been confused about the question. That stupid iced tea; it was hard taking notes in pen on napkins. They ripped a lot.

"Oh, my God," said Jennifer, "I didn't even think of it—you mean the reason everyone's scores went up is they made the state tests easier this year?"

Dr. Duke nodded. "I think that's it," she said.

"Why would they make the state test easy?" asked Adam. "Don't they like to torture kids?"

"Well, I certainly did when I was a teacher," said Dr. Duke. "But think for a minute. How did everyone around Harris feel about the test scores this year?"

"Really happy," said Jennifer. "Practically every class had a party."

"So the kids are happy and the teachers are happy," said Dr. Duke. "And that makes the parents happy, which makes the principals happy—and the superintendents and the mayors and the governor, they're all happy, and especially the state educa-tion commissioner. He's happiest of all because he's the number-one education boss and it looks like his state testing program is making everyone smarter. And when they have big education meetings in Washington, D.C., with the president, the state edu-cation commissioner gets to show off his high test scores in front of all the other state commissioners, which makes those guys wish they had high test scores, too, and that makes them tempted to —"

"Make their tests easier," said Jennifer.

"Exactly," said Dr. Duke. "And the newspapers and TV do big stories about how test scores are going up and everyone's getting so smart and how great the schools are. It's like that old guy used to say on TV, 'Is everybody happy?'"

Adam was quiet. That was the original story he thought he was doing: Good news! Scores up! Everybody's happy! Why was stuff like this always happening to him?

He still wasn't sure he bought it.

Yes, it was true that he scored a perfect 4+ on the state test this year, but he did last year, too. Was Dr. Duke saying that this year's wasn't a real 4+; it was a cheapie?

He never told anyone he was a 4+, never bragged about it, but deep inside, he kind of liked it. When a grown-up or kid somehow discovered that Adam was a four-plusser, they'd look at him differently, as if he had secret powers.

He loved getting that surprised look.

Now this Dr. Duke was saying it was because the test was easy.

"Isn't the state test pretty much the same every year?" Adam asked.

"Oh, no," said Dr. Duke. "They make new ones every year. If they used the same test, teachers and principals and deputy superintendents would be too tempted to cheat. You'd be sitting in those before school/after school mandatory/voluntaries memorizing the test. There's so much pressure on everyone to do better. Did you know we get cash bonuses if you kids get higher test scores? Thousands of dollars. And the newspapers do big stories. And people want to move to towns with high scores and houses are worth more in suburbs with high scores. Adam, I know this may be a little hard for you to see because you're . . . well, you're a four-plusser and almost all tests are easy for you. That's why Mrs. Quigley—"

"You know he's a four-plusser?" Jennifer said.

"Of course," said Dr. Duke. "Testing's my business. Who do you think has to put together the list of four-plussers that they print in the newspaper? Yours truly, Tremble County Schools' Ph.D. psychometrician."

Adam couldn't tell if Dr. Duke was that, or if she was out of her mind. How could all these people she mentioned possibly be in on this big scheme? The whole world was plotting to make the test easy? She was talking about millions and millions of people.

"Do you really think everyone's in on it?" he asked.

"No, no, no," Dr. Duke said. "If I'm right, there are very few people in on this, mainly our illustrious state education commissioner and his band of merry testers. For all the rest, it's just plain old human nature to welcome good news. The world's a tough place, and if someone tells you test scores are up—people want to believe. Everyone who takes these tests, starting with the littlest third graders and straight up to the president, would rather be happy. Have you ever heard anyone complain about test scores going up?"

Mrs. Ameche! thought Adam.

"Well, we do know one person," said Jennifer. "But she's . . . kind of different."

147

"You'd have to be," Dr. Duke said.

Jennifer was making so many notes, her arm was flipping back and forth across her notebook page like a windshield wiper. She told Dr. Duke that she had so much she wanted to quote. "For a testing expert like you to say this, it's amazing," Jennifer said. "Can I just check this one quote? I'm not sure I have it right."

"Oh, no," said Dr. Duke. "Wait, wait, wait. Stop writing. I thought Mrs. Quigley told you. I can't be quoted. They'd fire me. In real life, they shoot the person who says the emperor has no clothes. Mrs. Quigley didn't tell you? Please, listen. I don't have any problem with you using the numbers in the packet. That's all available on the state website, public information; I just put it together in an understandable way. I don't want you saying they're from me, but you don't have to—I'll show you where I pulled stuff off the site.

"Anyway," she went on. "You don't need to quote me. What you really want is a teacher, someone who's been giving the state test and has seen what I'm talking about."

Adam knew it! He knew it! This woman was no psychomagician; she was just plain psycho. Was there anybody on this planet willing to be quoted telling a reporter the truth? No! They'd tell you anything *off-the-record.* In Social Studies they were always talking about all this free speech our founding fathers stuck in the Constitution. Adam wanted to know where exactly it had gone to. Why was the hardest part of every single, stinking story — the Stub Keenan iPod download was the same rotten deal — finding someone who'd be willing to tell you the truth and put their name behind it?

This Dr. Duke, she seemed so cool and jokey, but she was just another typical deputy supernothing. Adam was mad, really mad, and he didn't feel like hiding it. "This is great," he said. "But would you please tell me what teacher will talk to us? Just a name, one name is all I'm asking. I can tell you what's going to happen. No offense, they'll all be just like you: scared to talk." He stared hard, right into her deputy super-eyes.

He was surprised; her eyes seemed a little moist deluxe.

"I'm so sorry," Dr. Duke said softly. "I thought—"

Jennifer interrupted.

"Dr. Duke," she said, "don't feel bad. It's not hopeless. I've got an idea. When I was looking for people to save the *Slash,* I found this investigative reporters' website. And it had a section with tips on getting people to talk—"

Oh, my God, Adam thought. He wanted to kill her. Another big idea from Jennifer. Like Jennifer's so-secret iPod source she couldn't even tell him. Oh, Jennifer—she would have some big-deal plan, no doubt about it, but he knew, when all was said and done, *he* would be the one who'd have to do the sneaky work, and he was sick . . .

"So one of their reporting tips," Jennifer said, "was if you can't find anyone to talk to you about problems at a company, try to find someone who's about to retire or just retired from the company. Because they're not going to be worried about pissing off their boss, no offense. They can tell the truth. What I was thinking, when you were talking with my coeditor here—if we could find a teacher . . ."

"About to retire!" said Dr. Duke. "Jennifer, that's brilliant! That's no problem at all. I can get you a list, easy. Every year, the district sends out a release on all the retirements."

"Good," said Jennifer. "And we know the ones from Harris. The *Slash* always does a little profile on each one. The boy who's writing them this year sent me the first drafts. At the middle school, I remember Mr. Bearak and Mrs. Kelleher, and in elementary, Mrs. Gross —"

"Mrs. Gross?" said Adam.

Jennifer and Dr. Duke looked at him, as if they'd forgotten he was still around.

"I had Mrs. Gross for fourth grade," he said. "I loved Mrs. Gross. She was so nice." Adam didn't say it, but what he used to love — when he answered a really hard question no one else could get, Mrs. Gross would say, "Adam, you're the complete package." He wasn't 100 percent sure what that meant, but the way her voice sounded — it had felt good, being the complete package.

"Fourth grade is perfect," said Dr. Duke. "That's one of the best examples. . . ." She made a little note. "Good," she said. "Now. You need to know one more thing. The state does not make the tests public after everyone's taken them. They say that would give away their testing secrets. They say it would make it too hard to create new tests. A lot of us think that's bull. A lot of us think they just don't want the public examining the tests, finding problems. You know how you take a Social Studies unit test, and there's a question about stuff the teacher didn't cover or a question that has more than one right answer? And you complain to your teacher? Well, the state doesn't want to deal with complaints. Talk about Top Ten bullies. The state says anyone caught giving out a copy of the test will be prosecuted to the fullest extent of the law. Maybe thrown in jail. Teachers get a copy, of course, but they're supposed to be collected in each building and destroyed afterward."

Dr. Duke stood. "That's about all I have," she said. "If you decide to write something, I'd be happy to fact-check it. Just don't call my office. Have Mrs. Quigley track me down."

She walked almost to the door, then stopped. "Adam, I'm really sorry," she said. "I know you're upset. I know you think I'm a coward, and I guess I am. But don't give up because of me. This is really important. Schools need some testing, but these state tests are taking over everything. They're squeezing the fun out of school. You know that from your science-fair story—kids used to spend months working on fun projects in school, but there's no time now because they're cramming you full of facts for the state test. When I was here in middle school—yes, I went to Harris, too—I had Mr. Brooks for World

History, and for weeks we did this game, World Domination. It was the best, but this year—"

"We know," said Jennifer. "No more World Domination. My coeditor tried to write about it last fall. Mr. Brooks asked us not to."

Dr. Duke shook her head. "I didn't know," she said. "Very sad. A great man like Mr. Brooks. Does he still make you memorize speeches?"

Adam nodded. He'd hated that assignment; he'd got an 85 on his Winston speech. He'd forgotten that stupid part about sinking into an abyss of a new Dark Age. Dr. Duke really knew how to bring up bad memories.

"Adam, you don't realize it," she continued, "but you have a very powerful gift. I hope you'll go see Mrs. Gross. Even if it doesn't work out, she'll be happy to see you. It will be a nice retirement present for her."

"Of course we will," said Jennifer.

Adam didn't answer. He hated the way adults twisted stuff around to make you feel bad. He felt like he was sinking into an abyss of a new Dark Age.

chapter 10

Don't Forget the Vomit

"You don't have to go."

"I'll go."

"Really, you don't have to. I don't mind going alone."

"I want to."

"I'm the one Mrs. Ameche called."

"You don't even like the Ameche brothers. Every time you go there, you run away. You said they're idiots."

"Mrs. Ameche's not. She's really smart and nice."

"The Ameche brothers are her sons. If she's so smart, how can she have idiot sons?"

"Your mother did."

"Oh, you are a riot, you really are."

"Can we not talk unless we have to?"

"Fine."

"Fine."

"I'll meet you there."

"Meet you there."

"Fine."

"Fine."

Mrs. Ameche was on the warpath, but it wasn't Adam and Jennifer's fault. As she led them into her kitchen, she apologized. She said she'd invited Jennifer over to talk about a big ethics problem for the *Slash,* but it was going to have to wait. "Jenny, honey, since you guys started coming, these Ameche brothers think they're Rupert Ameche-doch. They act like media moguls. They want to spend all day wheeling and dealing in their May Way West studios and forget their mother's tomatoes. You don't forget your mother's tomatoes, do you, Jenny?"

"Ma," said Don, "she's probably like a normal person, who doesn't have tomatoes."

"Come on, Ma," said Alan. "You know we work

hard on the tomatoes. It's just — the contest isn't till the end of August, Ma."

"There's lots of time, Ma," said Don. "Can you just calm down for a second?"

"Have we ever let you down, Ma?" said Alan.

Mrs. Ameche slapped her palm on her forehead. "Have you ever let me down? Am I hearing right? Do you really want me to answer that? Because I will. I just need to go upstairs and get my list. You stay put; I'm going upstairs! Stand back, I'm getting the list! You asked for it. The seven hundred thousand ways the Ameche brothers have let down their mother. Every single one of them documented. I'll be right back —"

"Ma, Ma, stop," said Don.

"Just stop, Ma," said Alan.

"We'll do your tomatoes, Ma," said Don. "I swear. Right now. We'll get out the stuff."

"We will do them, Ma," said Alan. "Just, not the list, Ma, please."

"You don't have to go upstairs, Ma," said Don. "We're on it."

Mrs. Ameche eyeballed them suspiciously, but she did stop talking about the list.

"We're happy to help," said Jennifer. "My coeditor

and I here will give the Ameche brothers a hand, so it goes faster. Then we'll talk about the *Slash*?"

"Oh, Jenny, honey, you don't have to," said Mrs. Ameche. "It's kind of . . . messy—"

"I insist," said Jennifer. "My mother's a big gardener. She belongs to the Tremble Garden Club. Her hydrangeas are pretty legendary. Sometimes I help with the planting. It's kind of fun."

Kind of fun? Right! Adam was looking forward to this. Jennifer did not have a clue what she was about to get into. This was too good to be true. He couldn't wait to see the look on her face when she realized. For once in her life, Jennifer was going to find out the true meaning of dirty work. He put on a big grin and said, "Mrs. Ameche, you're right. Jenny honey here will be a great help."

Mrs. Ameche smiled. "If you insist, that's very sweet," she said. "Come out back; I'll get you the stuff." She led them down the back stairs and across the cluttered yard. "When you're done at the rocks," she said. "I'll have a fresh batch of cannoli waiting. With the rainbow sprinkles. Then we'll talk about the *Slash*."

"The rocks?" said Jennifer.

"Oh, yeah," said Mrs. Ameche. "It's not far. Just

a block up, at the end of the street, by the river. That's where you find the best stuff. Tons of it. The birds roost on the rocks. You can't tell anyone, Jenny, but it is *the* secret ingredient that won me state champion tomato three years in a row. Did the boys tell you my tomato was nearly five pounds last year?"

Mrs. Ameche disappeared into the Ameche brothers' headquarters. They could hear her rattling around in there. When she came out, she had plastic bags, paint scrapers, old painting hats, and four pairs of surgical gloves. She handed a scraper, a trash bag, a hat, and gloves to each of them. "Uncle Louie used to work as a dental technician before he went away," Mrs. Ameche explained to Jennifer. "He'd bring us cartons of extra gloves from the dentist's office."

She told them to be sure to wear the gloves. "It's not the most sanitary stuff in the world," she said. "I don't think you can get any diseases that will kill you or anything, but it doesn't hurt to be safe."

"What's the hat for?" asked Jennifer.

"Aerial bombardment," said Mrs. Ameche. "You don't want to risk a direct hit."

The three boys were already out the gate.

Jennifer seemed frozen in place.

"Ameche brothers!" Mrs. Ameche yelled after them. "You know the drill. I need a bag full—and not just the doo. I want vomit, too."

To the east, by Adam's house in River Path, the Tremble River was lined with docks for boats and swimming, but here in the West End, the bank was covered by big boulders. The rocks—along with large chunks of cement from the demolition of old buildings—had been stacked here years ago by diesel-powered cranes to stem erosion of the river-bank. When Adam was little, he came with his dad on Saturday mornings, and they'd climb the rocks, as far as they could go, sometimes all the way to the end, where there was a chain-link fence with barbed wire, marked PRIVATE PROPERTY, that blocked off the Tremble Boat Yard.

The rocks were stacked at all angles, and it was tricky moving from rock to rock. Some were flat, some jagged, and you had to be careful where you put your foot as you jumped from one to the next. When Adam was little, he'd missed the next rock more than once and gotten some pretty good scrapes.

The Ameche brothers led the way with Adam close by and Jennifer lagging. "There." Don pointed, indicating a stretch of rocks where dozens of black birds were perched. "Can you smell it yet?"

Adam could. It was a fishy, garbagey, stinky smell that shot up your nostrils to the inside of your brain.

"When we get close," said Alan, "breathe through your mouth. It's really disgusting close up."

Adam was surprised. "I thought it was going to be seagulls," he said, staring at the flock.

"I wish," said Don.

"Cormorants," said Alan. "A nasty, ducky kind of bird."

"With vampire wings," said Don.

"Cormorants," repeated Adam. "I know them from Geography Challenge. A red fruit from a subtropical shrub found in dry parts of California, Iran, India—"

"That's pomegranates," said Jennifer. "Pome-granates."

"Right," said Adam. "I knew that."

Jennifer started to pull on the surgical gloves.

"Not yet," said Don.

"Wait till we're closer," said Alan. "If you slip on the rocks, the gloves will rip."

"And then you're touching that stuff with your raw hands," said Don.

"Try to walk on the same rocks we do," said Alan.

Don went first, Alan second, then Adam and Jennifer. The Ameche brothers moved as if they'd memorized the rocks, jumping from one to the next like mountain goats, then stopping to wait for Adam and Jennifer. When they were about fifty feet away, Adam thought he heard a thumping sound. Don stopped immediately. "I'd put on the hat," he said.

"Definitely," said Alan.

They moved closer, and Adam was sure this time he heard a thump. Jennifer must have heard, too, because she stopped. She was looking kind of ashen. "Can I ask a question here?" she said. "What exactly are we doing?"

"What do you mean?" said Alan.

"What part don't you understand?" said Don.

"All of it," said Jennifer. "I don't have a clue what we're up to." There was another thump. Adam looked around, but he still couldn't tell what the noise was.

"See that white stuff all over the rocks?" said Don, pointing. "Like they've been painted white? Well, you know what that is?"

Jennifer didn't answer.

"Bird doo," said Adam.

"That's a lot of what it is," said Don. Alan said, "There's also—" But Don interrupted him.

"I think that's all they need to understand for now, unless the other comes up," Don said.

"Very funny," said Alan. "Good pun."

"Lowest form of humor," said Don, "but thanks."

"Isn't slapstick lowest?" said Alan.

"I can never remember," said Don.

"I'm really sorry," said Jennifer, "I know you must think I'm an idiot, but I still don't get it. Why are we so interested in bird doo?"

"Oh," said Alan.

"You really don't get it?" said Don.

"Your good friend Mrs. Ameche," said Adam. "She puts bird doo in her garden for her tomato plants."

"Like fertilizer," said Don. "Normal people go to the store and buy a sack of miracle chemicals. Not Ma."

"Ma's into nature," said Alan. "Her secret ingredient. We mix the bird stuff into the soil."

"It's kind of pscyho," said Don.

"Except—" said Alan.

"It works," said Don.

They told her how Mrs. Ameche had won the state department of agriculture's contest for the biggest tomato three years in a row.

When Jennifer said she hadn't heard of it, the Ameche brothers seemed shocked.

"No?" said Don.

"It's a huge deal," said Alan. "One-thousand-dollar first prize. Plus we advertise it all over our tomato business." And here, Alan paused, changing his voice to sound deep, like a radio announcer: "Made with Mrs. Ameche's famous championship tomatoes . . ."

"Big is better and the biggest is the best," said Don.

"You try it," said Alan.

"You like it," said Don.

The Ameches explained that there were regional weigh-offs all over the state, where your tomato was matched against other large tomatoes from your area. And then the regional winners would meet at a mall somewhere in the state — it was such a big honor, the location changed every year — for a final weigh-off to crown the state champion tomato.

"Neat," said Adam. "Kind of like the NCAA

163

March Madness basketball tournament, except for tomatoes."

"Same thing," said Don.

There was another thump.

"What was that?" asked Jennifer. "I keep hearing it."

"Don't worry," said Don. "Let's just get this over with. Remember to keep your hats on." They got within thirty feet and stopped again. "You can put your gloves on," whispered Don.

"Get ready," said Alan.

"Look," said Don. "You two use your scrapers to scrape the bird doo off the rocks and into your bags."

"We'll do the rest," said Alan.

"The rest?" asked Adam.

"Not your problem," said Don.

"Our problem," said Alan.

"It's our mother," said Don.

"Lucky us," said Alan.

The cormorants were fidgeting now, moving nervously along the rocks, bending their long necks in and out of an *S* shape, and making sideways glances at their four visitors.

"Next move," whispered Don, "they'll fly."

"The dangerous part," said Alan.

"We've only been hit once," said Don. "They got Alan."

"Really nasty," said Alan.

"Here goes," said Don, and they moved forward. In an instant, the cormorants spread their wide black wings and flew off at a sideways angle, in a line, one after the other, the only sound their wings flapping.

And then there was a *thump-thump-thump-thump-thump*.

Hunks of half-digested fish — fish heads, fish tails, fish bones, fish scales, fish eyes — along with parts of eels, mud snails, crabs — fell from the sky, thumping onto the rocks.

"Oh, gross!" yelled Adam. "They're throwing up."

"I've got to sit down," said Jennifer, who looked terrible. "I think I'm going to — Oh my God . . ."

Before going back into the house, they left their plastic bags by the tomato garden, threw the gloves into the garbage, and washed their hands with the backyard hose. As Adam marched up the stairs behind the Ameches, he could smell warm cannoli. When they walked in there was a full dish on the kitchen table, and four tall glasses of milk.

Mrs. Ameche made them wash their hands again, in the sink, with soap.

"So how'd it go?" she asked as they settled in one by one around the table.

"We got your stuff, Ma," said Don, who was eating his cannoli so quickly, the custard was squirting out the far end.

Alan said something, but it was hard to tell exactly what, his mouth was so jammed with cannoli.

"Jenny, honey," said Mrs. Ameche. "Take one, don't let these gorillas eat them all."

"Not right now," said Jennifer. "I'm not very hungry, Mrs. Ameche."

Adam laughed. "I wonder why," he said, hitting the table to make a *thump-thump-thump*ing noise.

"It wasn't anything like my mother's hydrangeas," Jennifer said softly.

"I guess not," said Adam. "Jenny honey here must be part cormorant, if you get my meaning, because she —"

"She did great, Ma," said Don.

Adam tried again. "You should have seen it, just like the cormorants, she —"

"She would have made you proud, Ma," said Alan.

"Yeah," said Don. "She's tough, Ma. Didn't complain once."

"Stayed with us the whole way," said Alan.

"Breathed through her mouth like a pro, Ma," said Don.

Adam stared at the Ameche brothers. They were supposed to be *his* friends, not Jennifer's. Everything was getting twisted in favor of Jennifer.

He was sure he didn't deserve it, but for some reason, he felt like a jerk.

Jennifer, on the other hand, looked happy as a clam — a clam that had escaped the cormorants.

"I knew it," said Mrs. Ameche. "I have a nose for this. You can tell so much about people by how they work. Good for you, Jenny. You wowed the Ameche brothers. That's a tough crowd." She went over to the refrigerator, cracked a bottle of soda, put a few ice cubes in a glass with a straw, then put it in front of Jennifer.

"Ginger ale," Mrs. Ameche whispered. "Settles the stomach."

They were quiet, licking the sprinkles and choc-olate frosting off the cannoli, Jennifer sipping her drink. "Why do they do that?" she asked.

"The Ameche brothers?" asked Mrs. Ameche.

"No, the cormorants," said Jennifer. "Why do they throw up like that?"

"Ah," said Mrs. Ameche. "Well, from what I've read, no one's really sure. Scientists don't know if they're emptying their stomachs so they can fly away faster from danger, or if they vomit to scare away predators."

Jennifer nodded. "Worked on me," she said.

"Or they might just have nervous stomachs," said Mrs. Ameche. "People act like everything has an answer if they could just study it enough, but I'm not sure that's true. Animals aren't too different from humans. You can study them a ton, but you don't always know why they do what they do."

Adam nodded. He definitely agreed with that.

They'd been so busy with vomit and doo, they'd almost forgotten the *Slash*.

"So," Mrs. Ameche said, "we've got a new ethics issue with the Ameche brothers selling ads."

"Ma, we tried our best," said Don.

"We did what you said, Ma," said Alan. "Gave them the packet."

"Showed them all the great stories the *Slash* did," said Don.

"Showed them the *Slash* wasn't afraid of no Bolands," said Alan.

"Alan Ameche," said Mrs. Ameche. "Mind your double negatives. That's *any Bolands* — and I know you did. I've told you, it's not your fault. I give you all the credit in the world. We've gone from having a serious ethics shortage here, to being the Ameche Society for the Advancement of Holy Ethics. I'm very proud. If you're feeling let down, boys — we may need an Ameche family hug."

"It's OK, Ma," said Don.

"We're good," said Alan.

Adam was lost. The Ameches could really talk a lot, but if anyone had actually mentioned the problem, it had sailed right by him.

"I really appreciate this," said Jennifer.

"Well, we appreciate being appreciated," said Mrs. Ameche.

"But there's still one big problem," said Don.

"It's actually huge," said Alan.

169

Mrs. Ameche nodded. "The Ameche brothers have not sold a single ad. It appears that once people actually see the paper, they don't want to buy ads."

No one said anything, not even the Ameches. Adam felt terrible, like the time he was playing manhunt, jumped off a friend's lower roof, knocked the wind out of himself, and couldn't get his breath back.

He was sure the *Slash* was good.

Wasn't it?

"They think the *Slash* is bad?" Jennifer whispered.

"Oh, no," said Mrs. Ameche, "just the opposite. They're scared that it's too good."

She told them that people seemed scared to advertise in the newspaper that had written something so critical of the Bolands; the newspaper that prompted the state to investigate the Bolands; the newspaper that was shut down by the Bolands. People were worried that if they put an ad in the *Slash*, the Bolands would come after them, too. Mrs. Ameche talked about how the Boland companies — Bolandvision Cable, Boland Realtors, Inc., Boland Broadband, the *Citizen-Gazette-Herald-Advertiser* — provided jobs for tons of people in Tremble County.

"If a business advertised in the *Slash*," said Mrs. Ameche, "like a restaurant — and the Bolands turned against them, that business might go right out of business."

"What's amazing," she continued, "is these people know about you guys, even though most had never seen the *Slash*. They told the Ameche brothers they'd heard about this amazing newspaper that stood up to the Bolands. And it was run by kids!"

Adam understood that this was all terrible, but hearing that, he didn't feel so bad. He felt kind of mythic. People knew about him. It seemed like he really did have a shot at becoming an urban legend, if he could just move into the city.

So what Jennifer said next caught him off-guard.

"Maybe it's time to quit," she said, her voice barely audible.

They all looked at her.

"I mean, we gave it our best," she said. "There's just a few weeks of school left. We can't raise a thousand dollars that fast. Everyone's against us. If grown-ups don't care, if they're too afraid to buy a stupid ad, how can we do anything?"

Adam could hear a clock in the next room ticking.

171

"I'm sorry," Don said softly.

"We really tried," said Alan.

"We were wrong," said Don. "A newspaper's not like used golf balls."

"It's hard," said Alan.

"Jenny, honey—" said Mrs. Ameche.

"I just feel like we've done all middle-school kids can do," continued Jennifer. Though her voice was quiet, every one of her words felt to Adam like it weighed a ton.

"I feel terrible," she said. "The Ameche brothers worked so hard, and they haven't made anything for it and not a cent has been raised for the *Slash*. I just feel . . . like . . . such . . . an idiot . . . I was so stupid. A bunch of kids . . . alone . . ."

Oh, no. Adam could not stand it. Jennifer was crying. Not sniffles either. Loud sobs. He hated this. He felt sad everywhere, though mostly it pressed against his chest. Someone had to help Jennifer. She was such a good person. No one should make her cry. He wanted her to stop. She needed a hug. He felt like . . . Why did they just have to be . . . official coeditors? It was ridiculous. He hated these new rules. Who made them up, anyway? Why couldn't they go back to . . . like before . . . him and Jennifer, you know . . . That's what he really . . .

"Now wait a minute, Jenny," said Mrs. Ameche. "You stop that crying, baby doll." And she wrapped her arms around Jenny honey until the girl was totally covered in an Ameche hug. "I told you the Ameche brothers didn't sell any ads," Mrs. Ameche said. "That doesn't mean people don't want to help. They just don't want to be too public. I think they're worried that if they buy an ad, it's like sticking their fingers in the Bolands' eyes. What I started to say — what I tried to tell you before you got so worked up — was that the Ameches have collected nearly five hundred dollars in anonymous gifts from people who want to help the *Slash*."

Jennifer couldn't see it, because she was still locked up in that big Ameche hug, but Adam did: the Ameche brothers looked shocked.

"Ma!" said Don.

"Come on, Ma!" said Alan.

"Quiet, quiet," said Mrs. Ameche. "I know you wanted to tell her yourselves —"

"We did, Ma?" said Don.

"I know you did," said Mrs. Ameche. "But I just

couldn't wait. I felt Jenny needed some good news right away."

All four of them stared hard at Mrs. Ameche.

She nodded.

"Then I guess we're halfway there," said Adam.

"That's what the printer wants for a deposit," said Jennifer. "This is wonderful. . . ." And she started crying again. But before she could get re-hugged, she waved them off. "It's OK," she said. "Like Miss MacLeish used to say in kindergarten, these tears are pink, not blue. Happy tears. I don't know how to thank you, Mrs. Ameche."

"I do," said Adam. "We're going to put out the greatest *Slash* ever."

The coeditors were unlocking their bikes from the Ameches' neon-orange zebra-striped basketball hoop for the trip home.

"I'll ride with you," said Adam.

"That would be nice," said Jennifer.

"I'm glad you're not crying," Adam said.

"Thanks," said Jennifer. "I'm sorry. It's such a girl thing to do."

"No," said Adam. "That's not true. You're so —"

"Wait up!"

They turned to see Don running out from the backyard. It was an odd sight—an Ameche brother alone.

Don was carrying a jar of tomato sauce with a little bow, which he handed to Jennifer.

"You try it," said Don.

"You like it," said Jennifer, smiling. "That's very sweet, Don. Thank you."

"No, you're the sweet one," said Don.

Oh, my God. Adam couldn't believe it. What was going on now? *You're the sweet one?* He felt dizzy. Why did this Ameche have to butt in now, right at this moment? Adam finally felt like things were getting back to normal with Jennifer, maybe better than normal, and . . .

"Um, Jennifer," said Don. "I thought you might like, sometime, to you know, go to a movie, maybe, and get an ice cream or something?"

It was hard to say who looked more surprised, Jennifer or Adam. The Ameche brother looked at them both. "Oh, I'm sorry," he said. "You guys aren't . . . ?"

"Oh, no, no, no," said Jennifer.

"No, no, no, no," said Adam.

"Great," said Don. "So it's OK?"

"I'd like that, Don," said Jennifer.

"Fine," said Adam. "It's really fine." He hopped on his mom's bike. "I just remembered, I got something—" And as he raced up the street, for some idiotic reason, the houses on May Way West looked fuzzy.

chapter 11

Two Surprises, One Good

There was a knock on his bedroom door. Forget it. Adam was not going to answer. He didn't want to explain anything to anybody. He was just sick and tired of everything. He had his pillows squished down over his head and his covers pulled high over his pillows.

Another knock.

"Adam, can I come in?"

His mom. Just what he needed. A million questions.

What did his mother want? Maybe she'd think he was asleep. Probably not. She seemed to have some kind of special sleep-sniffer to know when he was faking.

"I have some mail here for you," she said.

It might be a trick to get him out of bed.

If so, it was a new trick. She'd never used the mail before. He didn't get much mail, except from his grandparents on his birthday and his aunts and uncles, and though he was ready for it to be his birthday — he was really ready for everyone to love him a lot just because of the day he happened to be born — it was still months away.

"It's a big envelope," she said.

It sounded a little true.

Maybe it was some big card from *her* apologizing for everything.

"Can I come in?"

His mother had already opened the door halfway; what was he supposed to say?

He could hear her walk over and felt the mattress sag when she sat on the edge of the bed. "You sleepy?" she said.

"Kind of," he answered.

"Well, maybe you could just pop your head out for a second so I can hand you this."

What was the use? He pulled down the covers. Before he could push aside the pillows, his Mom lifted them off his head, held them in her lap, and ran her hand gently through his hair.

She gave him the big envelope. It wasn't any kind of color that looked like it might be an apology or a funny card. It was a standard manila envelope.

"There's no return address," she said. "So I was concerned it might be — you know."

He nodded, though he didn't know exactly. Probably she meant something grown-up and nasty.

"Look Adam, I'm not trying to read your mail, but I just wanted to make sure, before I went back downstairs, it's nothing . . . you know."

He studied the envelope. His mom was right; there was no return address.

"The postmark's from Pittsburgh," his mom said. "Do you know anybody in Pittsburgh?"

He thought about that. He doubted that anyone from the Pittsburgh Pirates was writing to him.

She looked at him. "You going to open it?" she asked.

He was still lying flat and didn't move.

"Adam, is anything wrong?"

No, everything was great. Why couldn't his parents just have the decency to leave him alone to die of embarrassment in peace and quiet?

"You're not having problems at school, are you?" she asked.

He wished that was it.

"Not another in-school suspension, I hope?"

"No, Mom, school's fine, honest," he said.

"You know, Jennifer called again," she said.

He didn't say anything.

"She's such a nice girl," said his mom. "She sounded . . . I don't know . . . It's not so much what she said, but she just seemed — worried about you."

Right, Jennifer worried about him. She had plenty of sweet Ameche juicy-poohy stuff to worry about; she probably didn't even remember his name.

"Did something happen between you?" his mother asked.

"Can we please change the subject?" said Adam.

His mom shrugged. "The subject is your mail," she said. "If you open it and there's no problem, I'll put these two pillows back on your head and be gone."

Still lying down, he tore the flap open, reached in, and pulled out the papers.

There were two thin packets. He read the top of

the first page of one. Something about a covered-wagon trip. He looked through the pages. It was stuff to read and questions to answer. It was a test. A test? Why would the Pittsburgh Pirates be sending him a test?

"Holy jipes!" he said, sitting bolt upright in bed.

"What?" said his mother.

"Nothing," he said. "Really. Nothing." He had to get his mom out of there. Taking the pages, he flipped through them quickly for her. "See?" he said. "It's nothing porno."

"You're going so fast," she said, "I can't tell what it is." He didn't slow down. "It must be something big," she said. "I never heard you yell 'holy jipes' before. I don't even know what that means."

"It's just for a project at school," he said.

She eyed him, holding her hand to her face like she was a private detective peering at him through an imaginary magnifying glass. His mother really was a riot. "I can see for sure, you are up to something fishy, young man. I haven't a clue what, but I'm just happy you're sitting up." Then she held up one of the pillows. "This is yours, isn't it?" she said, and whipped the two pillows at him, then raced out of the room.

"Very funny," Adam called after her. "You're hilarious, Mom."

When he heard her footsteps heading downstairs, he got out of bed and quietly closed his door. He couldn't believe it. This definitely was not from the Pittsburgh Pirates.

Some anonymous someone had mailed Adam copies of this year's fourth-grade state reading test. And last year's test, too.

His parents had been a little psycho about the stolen bicycle. They certainly weren't going to let it go. Every week, his dad called the detective.

"Still working on it?" his dad asked.

"We are," the detective said, though it wasn't hard for Adam to imagine there could be larger things on the man's mind. His dad told the officer about Adam being sure he'd seen the bike, but it had been repainted and disguised.

"That's helpful," the detective said.

"You got a lead?" asked Adam's dad.

"No," said the detective. "But reliable information is always helpful."

Then, finally, one week, the detective had news.

They'd caught a boy doing graffiti at a Tremble school. And when they brought him home, they found a garage full of spray paints, bicycle parts, extra fenders, mud guards, and bike decals. "We charged him with graffiti," the officer told Adam's dad, "but it's just a matter of time before he tells us about the bikes. His parents seemed like decent people; they looked pretty shocked, their kid coming home in a squad car."

Adam's dad asked the boy's name and address.

"Now you didn't get this from me," said the detective.

Adam had to get to the library. He needed to do the research for his profile of Shadow for Mrs. Stanky. He needed to look up the newspaper for the day that Shadow was born — actually, the day after.

He locked his mom's bike in the rack out front, walked through the automatic doors, and headed downstairs to the research department. In the front of the room was a desk marked REFERENCE and sitting behind it was a woman at a computer who was on the phone and seemed to be answering a question about what countries had nuclear weapons.

"No, sir," she was saying. "I can only go by this list . . . No, sir, I'm not an expert on nuclear weapons. . . . Sir, according to this list from World-wide Nuclear Watch . . . Yes, they're considered the number-one source on this, sir. According to this, the Bahamas do not have nuclear weapons. . . . I see several casinos, but no nuclear weapons. . . . Yes, sir, it is possible . . . I'll check. . . . It says this website was last updated in April, so yes, sir, it is possible that the Bahamas got nuclear weapons in May, but personally, I doubt it. Yes, I do think you would have seen something in the news if that were the case. . . . No, I certainly don't know everything, sir. . . . You're right, sir, not even one-tenth of everything . . . Well, thank you, sir. . . . We try . . . and I hope you have a wonderful, nuke-free vacation."

She hung up, closed her eyes for a moment, rubbed her temples, took a deep breath, then said, "Can I help you, young man?"

Adam explained that he was in Mrs. Stanky's class and needed to look at old newspapers for their profile project.

"Oh, yes," said the librarian, and she opened her middle drawer, pulled out several papers, asked him what period he had Mrs. Stanky, then put the class list down in front of Adam. "Need you to sign this," she said. "I love this project. It's very important for you kids to see that not all research is Google." She looked down the list and said, "Let me guess — you must be Adam Canfield?"

Adam nodded.

"You're the only one left," she said. "My very last from Mrs. Stanky. Running a little late?"

Adam nodded. "Just about always," he said.

"Well you're here. That's the important thing," she said. "I'm Mrs. Miles." She asked him for the date of his subject's birthday and then told Adam to follow her.

She led him to a section of shelves in the back that had rows and rows of three-inch-square microfilm boxes. While she searched for the year and month he needed, Adam glanced at the boxes — some went back to the 1920s.

"These newspapers are really old," he said. "Very cool."

"It is," she said. "They go back to the days when Tremble had four newspapers — the *Citizen*, the *Gazette*, the *Herald*, and the *Advertiser*."

"Now there's one paper that's four times worse," said Adam.

"I didn't say that," said Mrs. Miles, but she was smiling.

She pulled out two boxes for Adam. One was the *Citizen-Gazette-Herald-Advertiser;* the other was a Tri-River Region city paper. "Next time," she said, "you should be able to find these yourself."

Adam followed her to a big metal projector with an old-fashioned crank handle that looked like something Thomas Edison invented. She flipped a switch, a light came on, and she showed him how to thread the microfilm. "Hold it by its edges," she said. "Don't smudge the film."

She cranked the handle. "This advances the film," she said, "and cranking it the other way goes back to the beginning."

There was a big opening for his head so he could look at the page images, which were projected, full size, on a screen at the base of the projector.

"Very good," Mrs. Miles said. "You should be set, though I have a question. Adam, are you Adam Canfield of the *Slash?*"

Adam nodded.

"Now, that's a great newspaper," she said. "We should have the *Slash* in our microfilm collection."

Adam stared at her. How did *she* know?

"I get it from my niece," the librarian said. "She goes to Harris."

As he cranked the handle toward Shadow's birth date, he kept stopping to read the comics and old baseball stories. He'd never heard of most of the players. Adam checked the standings. There was a baseball team in the National League called the Montreal Expos. He'd never heard of them. It made him wonder what the heck an Expo was. Scrolling through the inside pages, he saw an ad for TVs — they looked so small and fat! A story described how movie companies were complaining about illegal, pirated VCR tapes. Adam skimmed the story and wondered why there was nothing about DVDs and then remembered — DVDs weren't invented yet. And iPods weren't invented. What would Stub Keenan have done? Given out pirated VCR tapes of Blink-182 concerts, probably. It made Adam wish that he could go back in time. He'd be so smart, knowing everything that was going to happen.

It was a funny feeling reading about all this normal stuff that was going on back before you were born.

He finally reached the front page for Shadow's

birthday and then for the day after, a Saturday. Adam checked the weather report first, like Mrs. Stanky had told them. Shadow had been born on a sunny October day with temperatures in the mid-sixties and winds out of the south at twenty miles an hour. There was a small-craft warning for boating on the Tremble River.

Next, Adam read a few paragraphs of each front-page story and made notes. Angry motorists were complaining about gas prices going up to $1.50 a gallon. The president was Bill Clinton, and a story said he was fighting with Congress about — actually, as far as Adam could tell, just about everything. A three-car crash on the Beltway killed two people and snarled traffic for four hours.

But it was a piece on the bottom right of the front page that sent such a chill through him, he put down his pen and read every word.

The headline said:

NEWBORN FOUND ABANDONED IN DINER RESTROOM

It seemed like a story Adam's parents might not want him to see, and he wasn't sure he wanted to.

Every sentence he read made him nervous about the next sentence, but he could not stop himself.

The story said an abandoned newborn baby boy had been discovered alive in a trash can in the ladies' room at Big Frank's All-Nite Diner on Route 197 in West Tremble. It said a worker emptying the trash before dawn on Friday had found the baby and immediately called the police. The story credited the diner workers with doing a great job keeping the baby alive until an ambulance arrived. A Tremble detective was quoted saying that the kitchen staff used a turkey baster to suction out the baby's mouth, which was full of paper towel. The detective said that the baby had apparently been in the trash can for a couple of hours, and that's how the paper towel got in his mouth. Or there might have been other explanations, but the police didn't want to speculate. The detective said the baby was so cold, he had curled into a tight ball. To warm the infant, the grill chef had wrapped him in towels that they'd heated in the kitchen microwave.

At a press conference later in the day, the director of the Tremble County Medical Center said the six pound, six ounce baby's body temperature had dropped to eighty-five degrees and that he was

189

suffering hypothermia, but was responding to treatment. He was still listed in serious condition in the hospital's intensive care unit. The story said that when reporters asked if the baby would suffer permanent brain damage or any other problems, the medical director said it was too early to know, but "babies are tougher than we think, and I'm very hopeful."

The story finished by listing a confidential hotline number to call if anyone had any information on the whereabouts of the mother.

chapter 12

Definitely No

That night, Adam had trouble sleeping. He was squirming around so much in bed, he kept getting twisted in the covers and several times had to kick his feet loose to untangle himself. His pillows felt hot. How could anyone sleep under these conditions? He repeatedly flipped them over to the cooler side, but after a while, neither side was the cooler side. Some day, he was going to invent a microchip that would keep pillows cool all night on both sides.

He tried not to see the fluorescent numbers on the clock on his dresser, but he couldn't stop seeing them: 11:17, 12:03, 12:53, 1:18, 123:07, 1486:02 . . .

Adam was way out in front in the running club race. And he deserved to be; it really was his time. For once, nothing was distracting him and he knew, this was it, numero uno, here comes Adam Canfield, champion of the world. People were lining the street, waving and cheering him on. Dr. Duke was holding up an envelope the size of a poster board that was decorated in zebra stripes and said, GO, ADAM! Franky Cutty was there too, and he had a poster that said, BIG KIDS LOVE ADAM BEST! At checkpoints along the route, volunteers were handing out cups of water and free iPods. Adam tried to grab one, but it was just out of reach, and he wasn't going to slow down for anything; he was making his own music anyway. He was so far in front now, there were fewer people along the street—come to think of it, all the people were gone—and he could see the storefronts clearly. One, a SuperSonicSuperBuy TV superstore, was particularly interesting. Every TV was black-and-white and Adam was on all the screens, running along the race route. He waved to himself, and the boys on the screens waved back. This was fantastic—Jennifer would be so sorry she hadn't appreciated him.

As he stared at himself running across the screens, he noticed that there was a snake on his leg, which was strange, since he was positive that snakes were illegal in Tremble County. And sure enough, when he looked down to check, it wasn't a snake. The TV had it wrong. It was his To-Do list, which was unraveling out of his pocket and flapping at his side. He tried to stuff it back in, but the list just kept getting longer. If he wasn't careful, he'd trip over it, and he certainly wasn't going to give Jennifer that satisfaction. Fortunately, he was running past the West River Diner and was so far ahead, he had plenty of time, so he decided to duck in for just a second, to take care of his To-Do problem.

He dashed into the men's room, but while he was trying to stuff the list back into his running shorts, he leaned too far forward—and this was odd; he couldn't exactly explain how this next thing happened, but it definitely made sense—and he fell into the trash holder under the paper-towel machine. The trash receptacle was much deeper than you'd expect, and when he finally hit bottom and looked around, everything was dark; there were paper towels everywhere. Not a problem, he figured, but the more towels he pushed aside, the more fell on him, pressing down so much, breathing was difficult.

This really wasn't funny anymore; it was time

to stop joking around, and Adam wasn't just talk-
ing about the running club race or what Jennifer
would say. He couldn't get any air, and the more he
pushed the towels away, the more they pressed in on
him to the point where he had to conclude that this
was a lot more than a paper-towel situation. There
was someone, some human force against him. Adam
was scared, time was running out, so he screamed
for help; he didn't care what Jennifer thought. But
the towels were so dense against his face, pushing
into his mouth, no sound would come from his throat
and he gulped deep for air. This was so unfair that he
started crying. He could feel hands—he couldn't tell
whose—but somebody's were pressing against him.
Adam, Adam, Adam . . .

"Adam, wake up. Adam."

Adam opened his eyes. He was sobbing. It was
his dad. His dad was trying to kill him?

"Adam, you must have had a nightmare," said
his dad. "Are you OK? Here, drink some water."

It was a good idea. Adam sat up. His throat was
parched from all the . . . from what? He drank half a
glass, then slid back down flat.

"You want to talk about it?" asked his dad. "Seems like a really bad dream. Adam, I hope you know that you haven't a thing in the world to worry about. We wouldn't let anything happen to you. You want to come sleep with me and Mom? Like when you were little? Remember we used to put up the covers and make quilt caves?"

Adam just lay there, remembering the dream. It was so real, he couldn't imagine that it wasn't. There was such a thickness to his feelings; they seemed exactly true.

He lay quietly; it was good just to breathe.

"I'm OK now," he said. "It must have been from this TV show I was watching—"

His father raised his eyebrows. "More reason to watch less TV," he said, but he was smiling kindly, and he wasn't using his usual anti-TV, anti-computer voice. "You want me to keep the hall light on?" he asked, and he leaned down to kiss Adam on the cheek.

"That would be nice," said Adam. "Love you, Dad."

"Love you, too, Adam."

Adam knew what he had to do. He needed to go see Shadow's boss at the Rec. And not just for Mrs. Stanky's paper.

Mr. Johnny Stack must know the answer, because Adam definitely couldn't get the question out of his head:

Was that front-page baby Shadow?

"I don't talk about him," said Mr. Johnny Stack. "And his name's not Shadow. He's got a real name. And as far as that goes, how'd you get back here? They're not supposed to send anyone back unless they check with me first."

"Please, Mr. Stack," said Adam. "I have to ask— I know—" But Mr. Stack wasn't listening. He was studying some papers on his desk. It was a good thing Adam was a dogged reporter, because he was accustomed to routinely being treated like dirt. Would someone please tell him when the day would come when he'd walk up to the front desk at the Rec, say, "Hi, I'm Adam Canfield, I'd like to see Mr. Johnny Stack," and the woman behind the desk would say, "Sure, adorable sweetheart, baby doll, just go outside and around back through the double doors and he's the first big office on the right. He can't wait to see you, little honey-cakes." Yeah, right. Adam knew exactly when that would happen: when he was a hundred years old and dead. The woman had looked at him like he was going to bite her stupid tuna-fish sandwich; she said if he didn't have an appointment, it was impossible.

Fortunately, he knew where to go, since he'd visited Shadow last winter. Per usual, he had to take matters into his own hands.

"You're still here?" Mr. Stack said. "Look, I've known this young man for many years and I have never, in all that time, seen him bother anyone who didn't bother him first. You have a problemo, baby, you need to take it up directly with him. There's nothing wrong with that boy that he can't speak for himself. I've got to warn you, though, and I've told him a million times, my philosophy on this is *ignore the fools*."

And he went back to his papers.

Adam hated being treated like a fool in need of ignoring. "Listen, Mr. Stack," he said, "give a guy a chance. I just want—"

"Please go," said Mr. Stack. "I've got to finish scheduling this lacrosse tournament. The damn pairings aren't working; I've screwed something up. Team 7's playing Team 3 twice, and Team 2's not playing 7 at all . . ."

Adam glimpsed the sheet that Mr. Stack was working on. It was a tournament bracket like college basketball's NCAA March Madness championships. Or the Ameches' Big Tomato statewide championship. "There's your problem," said Adam. "That seven must be a one. It's not seven versus three; it's one versus three."

Mr. Stack lifted his head and, for the first time, peered over his glasses straight into Adam's eyes. He glanced down, checked the numbers, and looked up again. "How'd you figure that out?" Mr. Stack asked. "Especially from that side of the desk?"

"No biggie," said Adam. "I can read upside down. I've trained myself. I'm a newspaper reporter. It's a good trick to know. You go into somebody's office, you chat them up, they have secret documents on their desk — if you can read upside down, it's a big advantage."

"I bet it is," said Mr. Stack. "You trained yourself?"

"It's not that hard," said Adam. "I read the *The BFG* upside down for practice and now it just seems normal."

"*The BFG?*" said Mr. Stack. "Roald Dahl's *BFG?*"

Now Adam looked surprised.

"Good book," said Mr. Stack. "I got four sons. They're grown, but they loved that book."

"They read it upside down?" asked Adam.

"No," said Mr. Stack. "I believe right-side up. But it was even good right-side up. They loved it because . . . you know . . ."

"Whizzpoppers," said Adam.

"That's it," said Mr. Stack, looking off in the distance. "I'd forgotten. . . . My kids thought it was hilarious to read a book for school about farts. That can't have been an easy word to read upside down. . . . You're Adam Canfield of the *Slash*, aren't you?"

Adam nodded.

"I've heard about you," said Mr. Stack. "You're the one who's been so nice to Theodore — Shadow . . ."

"It's OK," said Adam. "I know he's Theodore Cox. I know you don't like his nickname. And I quote: 'Mr. Johnny Stack calls me Theodore. He says, "That's your Christian name, that's what we're going to call you. Period."'"

Finally, Mr. Stack grinned. "So that's what Mr. Johnny Stack says, is it?"

"Quotes you a lot," said Adam. "You can tell that he really thinks you're pretty great."

"He's pretty alone in the world," said Mr. Stack.

Adam told Mr. Stack about the English assignment. He explained about visiting 107A and how Mr. Willy had said to talk to him, but Adam had known that already.

"Theodore filled me in," said Mr. Stack. "He's very excited. He's never been profiled before. Christ, it's a huge deal for him just to talk to a normal kid who doesn't call him a retard. We were at the field the other day, chalking lines for Little League and he says, 'Guess who's doing a big story, and it's all about you-know-who?'"

"Hope you guessed," said Adam. "Shadow gets pretty upset if you don't guess. Boy, did he get worked up at me."

"Oh, I know," said Mr. Stack. "At the basketball courts, right? About his older brother mugging you? You probably don't realize," continued Mr. Stack, "but you're a big deal to him. When you took him on the *Slash*—my God, I think he told me about those thirteen proofreading mistakes he found about thirteen million times."

"He does repeat himself," said Adam.

"There are worse faults," said Mr. Stack. "Theodore told me the *Slash* is in trouble, said the school's not paying for it anymore because they're afraid of the Bolands. That right?"

Adam nodded.

"It would be awful if the paper fell apart," said Mr. Stack. "Theodore would die. I got to tell you — I think he considers you his best friend."

Adam nodded, but he wished Mr. Stack hadn't said that. Being best friend to a lonely person was a lot of responsibility.

Mr. Stack started telling Shadow's story, and it was surprising — Adam actually knew a lot already, from his own talks with Shadow: how Shadow had grown up without parents in foster homes; how he'd moved from home to home and now lived in a foster house in the Willows; how he didn't get along with his older brother who beat him. He was the same older brother who'd mugged Adam for his shoveling money last winter and was in jail.

"How do you know Shadow?" Adam asked.

"He found me," said Mr. Stack. "It was, I guess . . . four summers ago. I was dragging the softball field, getting ready for a night game, and I lift my head and

201

there he is, a little boy picking up trash without being asked. Never seen him before. And he just kept coming back, all summer. He was maybe ten. He'd help me mow, rake, grade; he loved hosing. After eight hours, I'd turn around—he was still working. And this was way before we paid him. Some days he'd be there at seven when I got in, and when we had night games—eleven o'clock, lights out—he was still around. He seemed to pretty much run free. There was a night I went into the Donut Shack. Had to be midnight; I was coming home from a ball game, and there he was, this little guy, sitting on a stool, twirling back and forth and talking with the doughnut man behind the counter."

"You know what he loves?" Mr. Stack continued. "Carrying around keys. I guess keys make him feel official. I got him a clip for his belt. I let him lock up the ball fields—he's in heaven." Mr. Stack waited. "What else you need?"

"The nickname?" said Adam.

"He was always on my heels, and people started asking 'Who's your shadow?,' and pretty soon, that's what everyone went by."

"So you were the original person Shadow-ed?" asked Adam.

"Nah," said Mr. Stack, "just the first time they gave a name to it.

"Adam," he said. "I don't know how you're going to say this, but his life's pretty hard. A few summers ago, the clothes he'd wear to his Rec job — we were paying him then — they were on the shaky side, so we took him out and bought him. . . ."

"We?" said Adam.

"Me and two of my sons. I figured they'd know what kind of clothes a kid would like, plus I wanted them to see how good they had it. So what happens? A few weeks later, this expensive hoodie we got and sneakers — gone. I figured he'd lost them, and it really made me mad. He said someone at his house stole them. I've never known him to lie. Unlike so-called normal people, he's too honest. So I started visiting the foster homes — I think I've been to three — and talking to his case workers. I wanted to learn his story, and I did, boy. They showed me his file folder — it was about as big as you. But the main thing was, I wanted to let these people know there was a responsible grown-up watching, so they had better take care of Theodore."

Adam got it; Mr. Johnny Stack watching over you was pretty good insurance.

"That enough?" Mr. Stack asked.

"Almost," said Adam. "When I'm not talking it's because I'm catching up with what you said—I'm always one idea behind, writing down stuff."

"You're lucky," said Mr. Stack. "I'm usually several ideas behind. We need to wrap up—I got miles to go before I sleep. Who said that?"

"Probably Abraham Lincoln," said Adam. "I always put that on tests when I don't know. He pretty much said everything."

It was time for Adam to ask the question, the one that was the whole real reason for coming.

He explained about Mrs. Stanky making them go to the library to look up old newspapers and the story he'd found about the baby dumped in the diner trash. "Since that's the day Shadow was born," said Adam. "Do you think . . . I mean could it . . . Well, was it?"

"No."

"Really?" asked Adam. "I was pretty sure."

"No."

"Do you know the story I'm talking about?" asked Adam.

"Of course," said Mr. Stack. "It was a big story back then. On all the TV news. Front page. Even national news. Big city papers sent reporters here just to write it up."

"So it was a different kid born on the same day as Shadow?"

"I guess," said Mr. Stack.

Adam searched Mr. Stack's face, but he couldn't read anything into it.

"OK," said Adam. "Just to go over this, I guess it was just a coincidence that the baby was born on the same day in Tremble and he had no parents to care for him and Shadow has no parents and the story said because that baby was left in the trash, and had towels stuffed in his mouth and was eighty-five degrees, he might be, well, damaged, and Shadow's well, you know, not exactly normal. . . ."

"Not normal?" said Mr. Stack. "He's a hard worker, he's honest, he's good and decent . . ."

"Can you at least tell me how you're so sure?" said Adam.

"No," said Mr. Stack. "It's too damn sad. We've talked enough about this. I get angry when I think about it." Adam searched Mr. Stack's eyes; he didn't believe him. He thought if he looked hard enough at Mr. Stack, he might wear him down and get him to tell the truth, but Mr. Stack just stared back.

Finally, Adam said, "OK, I guess that covers it. I guess I'm going." Adam put his notepad and pen in his backpack. "It really wasn't him?"

"No," said Mr. Stack.

Adam was just about out the door when Mr. Stack said, "If it was him—if it really was—would you put that in your report? About a boy who thinks you're his best friend? That he was born in a trash can? Jesus, Adam."

chapter 13

Dear Ask Phoebe

Everything was going wrong. Everyone was against him. He was sick of it. People said they wanted the truth, but they didn't. They were afraid of the truth; the truth was messy; the truth was painful; the truth was inconvenient; the truth was uncouth. The heck with them. Mr. Brooks, his World History teacher, had warned them at the start of the year. He'd told them that in ancient Greece, if a messenger brought bad news, they'd kill him. Ever since, people have been *shooting the messenger*. At this point, getting shot sounded like a pretty good solution to Adam.

Since he was failing left and right, since nothing was working out, he figured he might just as well keep going with his reporting and get all his failing over with at once.

His new philosophy was, "So what, right?"

He was going to report this iPod download story. A whole new group of people was about to hate him.

So what, right?

Summer vacation was coming. Just a few weeks. He could hang on. People forget everything over the summer.

He matched kids' names on the secret download list with the homeroom list and pinpointed three homerooms where a large number of kids got free downloads. One he eliminated right away because it was Stub's. How great would that be, bumping into Stub while investigating Stub?

Three mornings in a row he made secret sweeps by the two rooms to see if he could recognize kids from their yearbook photos. It was harder than he thought. The first time, he identified three kids and then wasn't completely sure it was them. But after two more pass-bys, he had eight kids he felt certain about.

It was time.

He figured if he could get two or three admitting it with their names, that would be enough to print the story.

Piece of cake.

He wished.

So what, right?

At least he had a secret plan.

Adam got to school early. He told his parents he was going in for extra help. It was true in a way—he needed all the extra help he could get. He dropped off his book bag in his locker, made sure he had his notebook, a pen, and the secret list, headed for the 300 hallway by the two homerooms and began hunting for the kids he'd identified. He tried not to look like he was looking, more like he was randomly happening by.

He spotted two boys by their lockers. And not a lot of other kids around. Perfect. He felt like racing over to get this done, but he didn't want to seem suspicious and made himself lollygag—one of their new Vocabulary Builders. *One, two, three, lollygag,* he said to himself. *And four, five, six, lollygag . . . and ready . . .*

"Finally, I got you," said a loud squeaky voice, and a chill went through Adam. He'd been found out. Stub Keenan must have spies everywhere.

"I knew it," the squeaky voice said. "I've been waiting for you."

Adam had an awful thought. That voice — it sounded familiar. Was it? Oh, no. It couldn't be. He did not want to look over his shoulder and find the world's most annoying third grader.

I don't deserve this, he thought. Please, don't let it be who I think it is.

He turned slowly. It was. And she was waving a fist full of papers at him. PHOEBE! Not Phoebe. Anyone but Phoebe. A thousand terrorists would be better than Phoebe. The entire Taliban would be better than Phoebe. He glanced around. It was a miracle. Nobody seemed to have noticed. The usual mayhem in the halls had people distracted. The two boys were still by the locker, talking. There were a couple of minutes before the bell. He could still pull this off.

"Go away," he hissed in a whisper.

"What?" said Phoebe. "Talk louder."

"Just go away. I'll talk to you later," Adam hissed again. "Please, I'm begging . . ."

"You're beginning?" asked Phoebe. "What are you beginning?"

Adam was inches from exploding. It would feel so good to scream at Phoebe with every ounce of his lung power. But that would ruin everything. The boys were still there. Hallway traffic was thinning—this was good. Fewer witnesses. All his planning. This was his moment.

"Beginning what?" repeated Phoebe. "You need to speak up; you're blurring your words."

Adam grabbed his notebook and scribbled, *I'm BEGGING! Go. Now!,* underlining the *BEGGING* four times.

"That's not how you spell *beginning,*" said Phoebe. "I'm surprised, the junior coeditor of the *Slash*—I hate to say this, but you're a terrible speller." She handed him back the paper with the correct spelling. "I love spelling words with lots of letters," she said.

The bell rang. The boys had disappeared inside their homeroom. He'd missed his chance. Phoebe!

"What are you doing here?" he asked weakly. "You're not in middle school."

"I've been looking for you for days," Phoebe said. "You're never in 306. I finished my first Ask Phoebe column. It's pretty great. Jennifer said I should go over it with you. She said you were definitely the man for the job." She wiggle-waggled the column in Adam's face.

Ever since this thing with Jennifer, Adam had been avoiding 306, but at this point he didn't care.

So what, right?

First Jennifer and that Ameche brother—"Oh, Don, I'd love to, Don. Don, that would be so nice, Don. Don, that's so sweet, Don. Don, wow, Don."

Then Mr. Stack, the kindest man ever, was mad because of Adam's question about Shadow. Then he'd missed his chance to finish the iPod story by seconds, thanks to you-know-who. And now the perfect end to his life. Editing Ask Phoebe. He knew it—this impossible, ridiculous, absurd feature was going to be the most popular thing in the newspaper. They could investigate the daylights out of everybody. They could get the Bolands thrown into prison for a hundred years. No one would notice. This would be the talk of Harris. It didn't matter that an advice column by a third grader was a human rights violation. Kids were going to love it.

Dear Ask Phoebe,

I'm outraged. My parents won't give me a cell phone. I'm in sixth grade. Isn't this against the Constitution?

Signed,

Voiceless

Dear Voiceless,

Everyone knows it's a free country, so there's no question that you're right, but suing your parents is a drag. There's a much easier way. Tell them about this little girl, Teresa. She was so beautiful, with very precious curls, and she got kidnapped on the first day of sixth grade and nearly died and it never would have happened if she had a cell phone. Good luck and don't forget to ask for unlimited texting.

Yours,

Ask Phoebe

Adam read her answer twice. "Is this true?" he asked.

"What," said Phoebe, "that it's a free country? Definitely."

"No," said Adam. "About this girl Teresa. Is this someone you know?"

"Well, kind of," said Phoebe. "I know someone named Teresa . . . but she wasn't kidnapped. Not yet, anyway."

"Well, did you hear about this Teresa person in the news?"

"Oh, come on," said Phoebe. "Haven't you ever looked at the statistics? Someone gets kidnapped in this country every three seconds. There's probably a Teresa being kidnapped at this very moment."

"Really," said Adam. "Well, then I'd suggest you go online and find the statistic, and we'll use that in the answer."

Phoebe looked outraged, but Adam did not budge. "Excuse me," she said. "This is supposed to be funny. This is supposed to help people with real problems in their real lives. People looking for a wise voice as a trusting guide through dark times. Everyone I talk to says, 'Ask Phoebe is going to be huge.' Everyone says, 'There's such a need.' You know what my grandma says? 'Phoebe, sweetheart, I can't wait.' She can't wait!"

"Well, she's going to have to," said Adam. "When

you did your stories on Eddie the janitor and the smile contest and the three-hundred-year-old tree — they were great, Phoebe, full of real people with real facts. This has to be the same. Just because it's Ask Phoebe doesn't mean there are no rules. If there's no kidnapped Teresa with precious curls, you can't say there's a kidnapped Teresa with precious curls. Now, if you want to say something like: *By having a cell phone a kid could have more protection if someone tried to kidnap or rob her,* you could say that."

"Oh, please," said Phoebe. "That doesn't have the same *oomph.* Where's the juice? People react to people; they need fellow humans to identify with. Precious little Teresa — that brings tears to my eyes. Kidnapped and gone, just because she didn't have a stinking cell phone. It makes me sick."

"Fine," said Adam. "Specific examples are great. I agree. And I'm all for tears. Tears and laughter, that's the whole writing deal. But as coeditor, I need to see some proof that there really is a precious Teresa."

"How about if we changed her name?" asked Phoebe. "Change it to Cindy, precious Cindy."

"Is there a real kidnapped Cindy?" asked Adam.

"I bet anything there is," said Phoebe. "Cindy's just the kind of name that gets kidnapped."

Adam was surprised. The other questions didn't need as much work. Someone had written in about losing his pencils and pens all the time, and Ask Phoebe actually had quite a good plan. She said she used magnetic tape on the inside of her locker door to make sure she always had a few extras on hand.

Adam thought he might give that a try. He did have a tendency to lose pretty much everything.

A boy had written in complaining that when he was at camp last summer he'd lost a tooth and the Tooth Fairy only left him a nickel. "Come on, ease up," wrote Ask Phoebe. "She's just the Camp Tooth Fairy." Phoebe advised bringing a small Tupperware container to camp, saving any lost teeth, then bringing them home at the end of the summer and resubmitting them to the regular Tooth Fairy, who paid Phoebe three dollars a tooth.

A girl wrote and said that she wanted to be an artist when she grew up, but she had two older brothers who made fun of her all the time and she was losing her confidence. Could Ask Phoebe offer any help?

Ask Phoebe answered that she had *three* older brothers, and there was no limit to how mean and stupid they could be sometimes, but other times, they were very sweet, they looked out for her, and told her not to let some big moron like the coeditor of the *Slash* discourage her. Phoebe advised tuning out any negative comments and suggested that while the girl was waiting to become an artist, she should practice her signature. "A lot of artists find themselves famous, and they don't have a good signature," Phoebe wrote. "It should be something where you can tell it's your name but looks pretty messy, like you're too busy to worry about it. And of course, all signatures must be in cursive."

All in all, Adam felt the column wasn't bad. "Do you want to say which coeditor is the moron discouraging you?" he asked, quite sure he knew the answer.

"No, it's OK," said Phoebe. "I think people will figure it out."

"No doubt," said Adam, but he wasn't angry. He'd never admit it to Phoebe, and he might not admit it to Jennifer even if they went back to, being, well, you know—but Ask Phoebe was pretty entertaining.

The thing that saved him from killing her was

that under all Phoebe's ridiculous third-graderness, she had a pretty decent heart.

"What about the letter you read out loud at the meeting?" asked Adam. "The one that had the whole *Slash* staff howling?"

"Oh, yeah," said Phoebe. "It's here. On the second sheet."

"You're going to use it," he said.

"I guess," said Phoebe.

Adam reread it.

Dear Ask Phoebe,

There's this boy in my grade; I think I might like him. He's cute and smart, he's good in sports, and we spend a lot of time together. We mostly have fun. We laugh a lot, and I think he might like me. Sometimes he even says I look good. But we just spend time together for school stuff, and the rest of the time, he treats me like I'm no one. He never gives me nice little gifts. He never asks me if I want to take a walk or go to a movie or get an ice cream. And if I get upset, he's so spacey that unless I come out and tell him, he doesn't even notice that I'm upset. I think he's the spaciest middle-school boy on the planet. Is there some way I can get him to be more mature? Or should I just give up?

> Signed,
> Confused Middle Schooler

By the time Adam got to the end, his stomach ached and his head was throbbing. How could he have not . . . ? No wonder Jennifer . . . He was such an idiot.

"An answer?" he asked softly.

Phoebe handed him a third page.

Dear Confused,

> This will be a shock to my faithful readers, but there are questions even Ask Phoebe can't answer. So Ask Phoebe went to her number-one expert—my mom. Mom said since the beginning of time, middle-school girls have been confused by middle-school boys and vice versa, so no one should take it too personally. She said while it's true that men are from Mars and women from Venus, there's a lot of good times when they meet up on Earth. She said be patient. Relax.

Don't push. Enjoy it for what it is. And never give up on anyone who makes you laugh. She said if you don't expect too much, you might be surprised. She said more stuff, but my hand was getting sore. Hope this helps.

Sincerely,

Ask Phoebe

chapter 14

On the Record

It was the first thing Adam thought of every morning: how many days left until summer vacation. As he lay in bed, under a single sheet, squinting against the morning light, his windows wide open, he could hear and feel and smell summer on the way, and it was glorious. The wind was from the south now almost every day, and it brought the moistness of the river into Adam's room, along with the sounds of tug-boat horns and gulls squawking. Last Saturday morning he'd woken to an explosion—the starting gun at the River Path Sailing Club, holding its first sailboat races of the new season. Twice Adam had been out to the civic beach — really a bunch of rafts latched together along the riverbank. But when he ducked his arm in, the Tremble still felt chilly. A couple of years ago, after a warm winter, he'd gone swimming on Memorial Day weekend, his personal early-season best, but this would not be a record-breaking year.

He thought of the next month as a running club race. Not one of his recurring running club race nightmares. Please, he didn't want any more of those. No, this was a race where he could see the finish line. He might have to punish himself to get there, he might have to dig deep to summon up every last one of his vital fluids, but once he crossed that line, he could collapse into a grassy meadow and spend his days staring up at a cloudless summer sky.

That was his goal, anyway.

"Adam, I'm really pleased," said his dad as he pulled up in front of the middle school.

"Great, Dad," said Adam. "Thanks for the ride."

"Wait, just a second," his dad said. "Do you know what I'm pleased about?"

"Yeah, sure, Dad, see you tonight." Adam tried to hop out, but his dad had him by the arm.

What was his dad pleased about? Adam's brain was used to figuring out what his parents were *dis*-pleased about. "Umm . . . you're really pleased . . . that . . . umm . . . I haven't got an in-school suspension like last semester?"

"No, Adam," said his dad, "I'm really pleased that you're going for all this before-school extra help. On your own. This is like your sixth time in six days."

"Oh, right, Dad, right. Can't get enough extra help. Bye, Dad."

"What subjects are you going for?"

What subjects? This wasn't fair. Adam wasn't in trouble; he was totally out of trouble. "Just all the big subjects," Adam said. "The usual big subjects everyone needs help in."

"Because we got a letter from school that listed all the extra-help sessions for final exams," said his dad, "and it didn't say anything about before school."

"Of course not," said Adam. "They never put it in. Everyone knows teachers are usually there early for help."

"You're not up to anything, are you, Adam?"

"Come on, Dad."

"Why do I feel like you're up to something?"

"Because you're a dad, Dad; it's your job to assume I'm up to stuff. It's OK—I don't take it personally." And he jumped out and raised his arm in a wave without looking back.

Adam had the drill down: drop off his backpack at his locker; make sure he had his notebook, his pen, and the secret list; hurry to the 300 corridor; force himself to slow down and look random (*one, two, three, lollygag, four, five, six, lollygag*); a final check to ensure he was operating in a Phoebe-free zone; then casually walk over to the locker where the two boys were talking.

"Hey, how's it going?" said Adam, holding out his notebook and pen. "I'm just checking to make sure kids got their free iPod downloads from Stub. For the election . . ."

"Oh, yeah," said the first boy.

"Definitely," said the other, and he pulled his iPod from his pocket and showed it to Adam.

"Great," said Adam. "Just checking. Can I get your names . . ."

He held his breath. He hoped they couldn't hear his heart pounding. It was so loud, it seemed to have relocated to the middle of his head, between his ears.

"No problem," said the first.

"Sure," said the other.

And they gave Adam their names. Spelled them, too.

"Great," said Adam. "Just trying to make sure. Checking people on the list." He pulled the secret list from his back pocket and flapped it in their direction.

"Cool," said one.

"This means you're voting for Stub next week?" said Adam.

"Prez Stub," said one.

"He's got great music," said the other. "Appreciate the download."

"Great," said Adam. "Thanks a lot."

"Sure," said the first boy, and he nodded down the row of lockers. "You can get him, too," he said, indicating a boy who was kneeling and pulling stuff from his locker.

"Another satisfied member of the Stub Two-Fifty Club," said the first boy.

"Another vote for Stub," said the second.

"Right," said Adam. "Thanks."

And Adam got that boy, too.

The bell was ringing. He had to hurry to homeroom. He couldn't believe it. He did it. He did it! So much worry. Arguments with Jennifer. Weeks of preparation. Getting the homeroom list from Mrs. Rose. Matching the lists. Yearbooks, YouTube, Facebook, MySpace, memorizing photographs. Practicing walk-bys. Weeks of worry.

And the actual reporting?

Just a couple of minutes.

And the key quotes?

Just seconds.

He couldn't believe it.

He did it.

He really did it.

He had to tell Jennifer.

He couldn't even be sure anymore: Was he mad at her, or was she mad at him?

It didn't matter.

He had to tell Jennifer.

He'd nailed it for the front page.

/ / / / /

A couple of times a day, Adam's mom or dad drove slowly past the house where the kid who stole the bikes lived, looking to see if they saw any sign of Adam's. This made Adam uncomfortable. "It's kind of like we're stalking him," he said.

"That's the idea," said his mom. "Let them know we know."

At dinner they were talking about it, and Adam said now that they knew the kid's name, he was going to figure out what he looked like, get the kid's homeroom number, and confront him at school.

"You think you can track him down?" said his dad.

"Sure," said Adam. "I've got a list of kids by homeroom. Last year's yearbook with everyone's photo is in the school library; just match them up and pay a visit."

"Adam," said his dad, "do you do this a lot?"

"Dad, you don't need to know all the details. Just trust me — I'm a trained reporter."

"Well, I don't want you getting in a fight over this," said his mom. "You can get in trouble at school for something that's not your fault. That's why we're talking to the police."

"Well, I think it's weird to keep driving by his house," said Adam.

His parents were quiet. They were looking at each other. Finally his dad said, "Adam's right. We need to go talk to these people."

"Really?" said Adam.

"After dinner," said his dad.

Adam was excited. He'd never seen his father get into a fistfight.

They parked in front of the house. His dad turned off the van, and Adam wondered if this was a mistake — they might need to make a quick getaway.

On the other hand, if the kid stole bikes, maybe the kid's father stole cars, and it was best not to leave it running.

Their house was nice, as nice as the Canfields', and the woman who answered the door was dressed up, like Adam's mom when she got home from work in the city. She held the screen door open while Adam's dad introduced himself and Adam.

He said he was sorry to be there, but he had reason to believe that her son had stolen Adam's bike from their front yard.

"It couldn't be my son," she said. "He wouldn't do that; he's not that kind of boy."

Adam's dad said they'd reported the theft to the police, and talked to people at school. "I have a bill for the bike," he said. "If you're willing to pay for or return the bike, I'd be happy to tell the police that we've worked this out and we wouldn't press charges."

"My son wouldn't do that," she repeated. "You're mistaken."

"Look, I know he's been in trouble," said Adam's dad. "I'm sorry. This is making me very uncomfortable. But it must be very hard living in a house with someone you can't trust. It must be a terrible thing to know your child's a liar."

And then suddenly, a kid started yelling out an upstairs bedroom window. "Leave my mother alone!" he screamed. "Stop it! And stop driving by our house! Leave us the hell alone!"

"Go back inside and shut the window!" his mother called up to him. "You're putting on a show for the whole neighborhood."

When she turned back to Adam's dad, she looked frightened.

Mr. Canfield handed the woman a business card and a copy of the bill, thanked her, and then he and Adam walked back down the path to the van.

Adam was thinking, having your bike stolen was kind of bad, but having people know you're a liar and thief seemed miserable.

Adam watched his dad put the key in the ignition. He noticed that his father's hand was shaking. He started to say something but didn't. Adam knew how nervous he got when he was reporting a story and had to accuse someone of something bad.

He hadn't realized it was the same for grown-ups.

chapter 15

A Funny Boy

Adam had become so good at avoiding Jennifer, he'd forgotten how to find her. She wasn't in any of her old places in the hallway between classes or in the cafeteria during lunch, and he felt a pang of . . . well . . . He didn't want to dwell on it, but serious missingness. And not just because he was dying to tell her about nailing the Stub Keenan story. It was a bigger kind of missingness, a more general kind of missingness, the kind of missingness that he felt in his chest, an achy kind of missingness. What was happening to him? He didn't know or care; he just needed to get back to normal.

He was worn out by being outraged just because Jennifer and that Ameche brother were—who knew what they were? Special buddy-buds, no doubt, or worse.

For the first time, he had to admit to himself that maybe they were something smoochy.

So be it. So what, right? He didn't have the energy to keep up the outrage, day in and day out, morning, noon, and night, outrage, outrage, outrage. It was exhausting. Besides, as he'd learned from Ask Phoebe—and he knew this was really a bad sign, quoting Ask Phoebe—he had messed up big time with Jennifer.

He only had himself to blame.

The truth was, this Ameche brother had shown himself to be a good Ameche, a decent Ameche, an Ameche who'd done everything aboveboard, fair and square. For that matter, it was Mrs. Ameche who was keeping any hopes for the *Slash* alive almost single-handedly.

So Adam was done with all this nonsense. What was Ask Phoebe's advice? *Enjoy it for what it is.*

He wasn't exactly sure what it is, was, or would be, but he knew he needed to go back to the way it had been, back to the time when he and Jennifer weren't only official coeditors.

He couldn't stand being just official coeditors anymore.

He needed it to be greater than official coeditors, even if it was less than something smoochy.

It was like one of those equations in math class:

Official coeditors < Adam + Jennifer < Something smoochy

Or maybe, less than or equal to something smoochy?

He knew he would see her in science, since they were in the same class, but she wasn't there either. Then he realized that Jennifer must be absent, which actually calmed him down. It was nothing personal. After class, he asked one of her friends if she was sick.

"She didn't tell you?" said the friend. "She's got seat tryouts for Blue Lake, the music camp she's going to this summer. In Michigan."

Did Adam know that she was going away? He couldn't remember.

"I guess maybe I forgot," he said.

He would have gone straight home. Clubs and sports were over for the year. But the baseball team was having an end-of-the-season pizza party. It was kind of fun. The coaches gave each player a joke award. Adam won Most Likely to Turn Up Without Several Pieces of Equipment.

When he got home, he did something he hadn't done in a long time. He sat down at the computer and messaged Jennifer.

She was there.

He asked how she'd done at the cello tryouts.

Who knows? she wrote. *Gave it my best.*

He was trying to think what to say next when she messaged again.

Nice to hear from you, she wrote.

Really, he wrote back. He meant *really,* like *really true,* but it must have come across as *really?* because she wrote back:

Yes. I've been missing you.

Oh, my God, that sounded great, but then he reread it and couldn't be sure. Did she mean *I've been missing you* in a lovey-dovey way? Or did she mean *I've been missing you* in an *I keep not bumping into you* way?

This was torture. Why did every word need to have seventeen meanings? Why wasn't English one of those good languages where each word was allowed just one single meaning and had to stick to it? They needed to talk in person. There was too much going on below the surface. Time was running out, and they had so much to go over — the Stub Keenan story, visiting Mrs. Gross about the state test, raising money for the *Slash*.

She must have read his mind.

Want to come over and work? she wrote.

Twins there? he wrote.

Sorry, she answered. *Yes.*

Jennifer's twin sisters were in third grade and were every bit as annoying as Phoebe. They wouldn't leave him alone when he went over her house: "Adam, will you be my boyfwiend?" "Adam, you look weally diesel in that shiwt."

Can you come here? he wrote.

Jennifer's mom pulled up in the Astro van. When Adam opened the screen door, one of the twins leaned out the van's sliding door, spread her arms wide toward him, and hollered, "Mawee me, baby, and we'll wide off into the sunset."

Adam gave her a weak wave; it really wasn't that bad being an only child.

Jennifer looked good. Really good. She had her hair in one of her frizzy ponytails — tight around her head and then fanning out wide in back. She was wearing a reddish sundress with skinny straps.

He'd never noticed what smooth curvy shoulders Jennifer had.

"You're dressed up," he said.

"Sorry," she said. "I had to, for cello tryouts. I was too lazy—"

"No, no, it's OK," he said. "It doesn't look bad or anything."

He asked if she wanted some food. "My mom left carrots and celery sticks and ranch dressing."

"Got any Cheez Doodles?" she asked.

"Yeah!" said Adam. "I'll get them from the garage."

"Meet you downstairs," she said, and headed to the computer in the family room.

/ / / / /

Adam was amazed. In no time, it felt like they were back to normal. Maybe slightly better than normal. Adam couldn't exactly explain it, but it felt a little exciting to be with Jennifer now.

She pulled out a legal pad that had stories listed for the June issue — if they ever raised the money for a June issue.

"I nailed the Stub Keenan story," said Adam.

"No," she said. "Really? Now, that's amazing." And they clicked Cheez Doodles, like they were making a champagne toast. "I assumed we weren't going to get it," she said. "I was ready to cross it off my list."

"Your source was right," said Adam. "The list is right, too."

"I knew it was right," said Jennifer. "The source was one-hundred percent reliable. I just didn't think it was gettable. Especially after we talked about it. You had me convinced we'd never get it into print."

"I had me convinced, too," said Adam. "To be honest, it's a little hard for me to believe." He told her the whole story — from matching up the lists, to studying the photos, to Phoebe almost ruining everything, to the three boys giving him their names.

237

"And they didn't mind talking to a reporter from the *Slash*?" Jennifer asked.

Adam didn't say anything.

"You know, you really are an amazing reporter," Jennifer said. "It's like you have special powers to get people to talk."

Adam was quiet; the only sound was him munching another Cheez Doodle. Then he said, "I didn't actually tell them I was from the *Slash*."

Jennifer made a face, started to say something, stopped. She got up and began pacing. "You didn't lie to these kids, did you, Adam?"

"No," he said. "No!"

"So how exactly—"

"I told the truth," said Adam. "I said I was checking to make sure they got their free iPod downloads from Stub."

"So they didn't know they were talking to a reporter?"

Adam shrugged.

"So *they* thought . . ."

"I don't know what they thought," said Adam. "I was telling the truth. I was checking. They saw my notebook and pen and they never asked what my

238

name was or why I wanted to know. And if they had, I would have told them."

"You would have said Adam Canfield of the *Slash*?"

"Absolutely," said Adam.

"If they asked . . ."

"Yes," said Adam. "I would have said I was a reporter with the *Slash*."

Jennifer nodded. "OK," she said. "OK . . . I think it's OK. . . . We didn't lie. . . . It's an important story, buying an election. I'll go online, check some journalism websites. See if there's any ethics stuff on this. Probably it would be good to talk to a grownup, too."

Jennifer mentioned Mrs. Quigley, the principal, whom they'd have to interview about this anyway. Adam thought of Erik Forrest, the world-famous journalist he'd written about in the last issue of the *Slash*. "I have to e-mail him one more time," said Adam. "Make sure there's nothing new on the state investigation of the Bolands."

"The Bolands are on my list, too," said Jennifer. "We have to get a comment from the Bolands."

Adam shook his head. "No way," he said. "I'm

not going back to see that woman again. One visit to Mrs. Boland's office was enough for me. You can send Phoebe."

"We don't have to," said Jennifer. "The state investigation's already been in the *New York Times*." She held up a printout of the news brief that she'd found online. "I'll get the e-mail for Mrs. Boland's assistant from Mrs. Quigley. We'll tell them we're doing a story and ask for a comment. They won't comment."

Adam liked that much better than a personal visit.

"They're going to be really surprised when they find out there's still a *Slash*," said Jennifer. "I bet Mrs. Boland turns purple again."

"Plenty of people will turn purple," said Adam. "We have to go see Stub Keenan, get a comment from him about the downloads. That won't be pleasant." In Adam's experience, when you accused an adult of doing something bad, they might yell at you, but they at least seemed to accept the need to be civilized. A kid like Stub might hit you with a chair.

Jennifer was making a final checklist.

The school election was next week; they had to see Stub in the next few days. Jennifer said she'd arrange an interview; she had a couple of classes with his campaign manager.

They needed to go see Mrs. Gross, the fourth-grade teacher, about the state test.

It turned out Adam wasn't the only one to get an anonymous envelope in the mail; Jennifer's was postmarked from Chicago.

They needed a final meeting in 306 to make sure all stories got filed on time.

Jennifer said she would call and reserve a date to have the paper printed.

"We'll have to get him the five-hundred-dollar deposit," said Adam.

"I did that already," said Jennifer. "I got the money from Don."

Don? Who was Don? Adam couldn't remember — *Don.* Don! The Ameche brother! That Don. For just a little while, he'd forgotten there was a Don, or more precisely, a Don situation. Everything had seemed so smooth and buttery up until now. Adam had to calm down. He'd promised himself. Half of him already knew this about Don and Jennifer, understood that this was coming, was perfectly clear that he should not be upset about this, that Jennifer was entitled, that it wasn't his business, that he was going to be mature about this and not let it affect his friendship with Jennifer. He just needed the half of him that understood all this to deliver the message to the other half of him, because right now that second half of him, which apparently was located in his stomach, really hurt.

He went into his pocket, pulled out his jawbreaker, and took a suck.

"After all those Cheez Doodles?" said Jennifer.

Adam nodded and took a couple more sucks. It was working. He felt calmer. He popped the jawbreaker out of his mouth and said, "The sweetness in the jawbreaker balances the salt in the Cheez Doodles. I can wash it off if you —"

"It's OK," she said. "I see your point. Look, Adam, I need to talk to you about Don. It's not —"

"No, no," said Adam. "No, it's not my business. You're right. It's none of my business. You don't owe me —"

"But I'd like —"

"No," said Adam. "We're fine. I thought this out. Honest. We have a great relationship, you and me, as coeditors, and this other stuff shouldn't affect it. We're going to put out a great newspaper and even the most powerful people in Tremble can't stop us.

We're going to say stuff the *Citizen-Gazette-Herald-Advertiser* and Bolandvision 12 would never say. We're a great editing team, the two of us." He was trying to remember — what was that advice he was supposed to be following? Oh, yes. "And I'm just happy to enjoy it for what it is," he said.

Jennifer was staring at him. She was smiling, and she looked — he wasn't sure how to describe it exactly — kind of twinkly. "Adam Canfield," she said softly, "you're a funny boy."

Adam was mixed up. Her words sounded like one thing, but the way she looked, all that twinkly business, kind of felt like something deeper.

She was staring at him really hard, but everything else about her was blurry. He felt like he was supposed to do something. Was he supposed to do something?

Finally, she looked away. "OK," she said, "So I think the first thing we need to do is go see Mrs. Ameche, tomorrow morning. Saturday, she'll be at the Busy Bee. Can you go?"

Adam's Little League game wasn't until two; he could.

"Good," said Jennifer. "We need to talk to her about getting the rest of the money for the *Slash*.

She's got so much common sense about this stuff. And then Monday, we need to call an emergency meeting in 306. Everybody has to be there. We'll tell them no excuses, it's life or death. Sound good?"

Adam nodded; it did sound good, although not as good as when she'd called him a funny boy.

chapter 16

Busy Bees

The Busy Bee Flea Market was too far to bike to, so Jennifer's mom dropped them off. Adam was surprised by what a great place it was; the Ameches never ceased to amaze him. The Busy Bee was an indoor flea market, a strange cross between a garage sale in your driveway and a very unfancy — some might say somewhat junky — indoor mall. Instead of boutique shops, there were rows of eight-by-ten foot stalls on two floors.

Adam was in paradise; he kept wanting to stop at each booth. It was like walking around the Ameches' backyard, except a little better organized.

At one booth were a father and son selling all kinds of baseball cards and memorabilia, including a Pete Rose rookie card that the boy told Adam was worth "a cool thousand." It occurred to Adam—if he just grabbed that card and ran, they could sell that one card for a cool thousand and pay for the June issue of the *Slash*. He was about to ask the price of a 1960 gold-embossed Vintage World Series Topps card of Pittsburgh Pirates immortal second baseman Bill Mazeroski when Jennifer dragged him away, leading him up the escalator to the second floor, where the Ameches had a stall in the back.

On one side of the Ameches was a booth with racks of sportswear, including big football jerseys and brightly colored sports shorts. On the other side was a woman selling nothing but ceramic cats.

Adam knew he probably should feel at least a little bit worked up about seeing Don Ameche, because of the Jennifer stuff, but the truth was, he just wasn't anymore. He was too happy to see the Ameche brothers. There was something about them—they always looked so relaxed and jolly. No matter what they were doing, it seemed to be the exact thing they should be doing. The two were sitting in folding beach chairs in front of the booth, cleaning up golf balls. Don was scrubbing the balls with a wire brush, then flipping them to Alan, who shined them up with a shammy before dumping them in a big bucket that said, GOLF BALLS! LIKE NEW! 3 FOR $2! CHEAP! Behind them, on shelves against the back wall, were a couple of model airplanes with engines they'd repaired, a set of rebuilt electric hedge-clippers, a desktop computer, and two shelves filled with jars of Mrs. Ameche's famous tomato products. Taking up most of the rest of the back of the booth was the power mower. All four wheels were back on, as was a tag that said, LIKE NEW, $324.99 CHEAP!

Last but hardly least was Mrs. Ameche, who was sitting behind an easel, painting. Beside her was a smaller easel that displayed her sign: DONATELLA AMECHE/PORTRAITS-WHILE-YOU-SHOP/SATISFACTION GUARANTEED. The sign said that portraits done in pastels started at thirty-five dollars, in oils, one hundred dollars. The sign was decorated with a painting of the Ameche brothers, and it really looked like them, even if they were wearing collared shirts.

When the Ameche brothers saw Adam and Jennifer, they gave a whoop. Alan fished two golf balls out of the clean bucket and shoved them in his mouth.

"Gwawaoooiyum," he said.

Adam looked puzzled. "What did he say?"

"Gwawaoooiyum," repeated Don.

"I think he said 'guavas and yams,'" said Jennifer.

"He wants you to guess who he is," said Don.

Alan nodded. "Gwawaoooiyum."

"You're a squirrel," guessed Adam.

Don rolled his eyes.

"He's you," said Jennifer.

"With your jawbreaker," said Don.

"Now I see it," said Adam. He pulled out his jawbreaker from the plastic bag and popped it in his mouth. "Gwawaoooiyum," said Adam.

"Alan with two golf balls?" guessed Don.

"A guava and yam?" guessed Jennifer.

Adam shook his head and popped it out. "I'm me," he said. "Anybody want a suck?"

Mrs. Ameche was so busy painting, it seemed like she hadn't noticed them.

"When Mom's painting," said Don.

"She's in a trance," said Alan.

"She knows you're here," said Don.

"She hears everything you say," said Alan.

"It's just, she puts you in the back of her brain," said Don.

"Until she's ready for a paint break," said Alan. "Or she catches you doing something nasty . . ."

"OK if we look over her shoulder?" asked Jennifer.

The Ameche brothers said that's what everybody at the Busy Bee did.

Adam and Jennifer went over behind Mrs. Ameche. She was painting a portrait of a red speed-boat. There was a photo of the boat on the easel. In the photo, the day looked gloomy, the boat was sitting in seaweedy water at a marina dock that was splattered with bird doo, and had a bunch of other boats moored nearby.

In Mrs. Ameche's portrait, the exact same boat was tied to an old-fashioned wooden dock by a thick rope, on a crystal-clear lake, under a blue sky with one and a half puffy white clouds floating by. Mrs. Ameche was just finishing up the second cloud.

"It's a twenty-one-footer," whispered Don.

"Five-point-oh two-seventy-horsepower Volvo GXi EF Inboard/Outboard," said Alan.

"Good engine," said Don.

"Mom could've put the owners in," said Alan.

"Costs extra," said Don.

"Lady was on a budget," said Alan.

A man came up to them.

"Oh, hi," said Don.

"You're back," said Alan.

The man said he'd decided to buy the lawn mower. "You want to start it up again?" said Don. "Just to make sure?"

"No, that's fine," said the man, "Engine's good. I did want to know—would you take two-seventy-five?"

The Ameche brothers looked over to Mrs. Ameche, who kept her eye on the canvas but scratched her ear with the end of the paintbrush before getting back to the cloud.

"Three hundred," said Don.

"OK," said the man, "deal." And the Ameche brothers led him over to the mower to finish up the sale.

"So, how are you, Jenny?" asked Mrs. Ameche.

"The painting's beautiful," said Jennifer.

"Thank you, sweetie," said Mrs. Ameche, who'd finished the second cloud and was now dabbing in a row of birds in a *V* formation flying off in the distant sky.

"Yeah," said Adam. "But no offense, it doesn't look like the photo."

"Adam!" said Jennifer.

"Oh, Adam," said Mrs. Ameche. "Of course it doesn't. You're such a hotsy-totsy reporter, but honest to buzzbee, I don't think you have a lick of business sense. People at Busy Bee, they're putting out hard-earned dollars, they don't want some boring real-life portrait. They want better than real life. This woman—she's giving this painting to her husband. It's his boat. They're married forty-five years, God bless. Money must be tight—she can't afford the extra fifty dollars to put him in the boat. After forty-five years, you think he needs to see seaweed? This is what he wants to see when he goes fishing."

Adam nodded. Mrs. Ameche was always getting so worked up. She really had a weird way of thinking about stuff.

"We're in two different businesses," said Mrs. Ameche. "You reporters, you're after truth. Nothing wrong with that. Especially reporters brave enough to tell the truth to people like the Bolands. My customers, they get enough truth every day. They've got the bitter truth coming out of their ears. They need a truth break . . ." Mrs. Ameche opened up a worn appointment book that was stacked with photos and note cards. She grabbed a wedding photo from the top. "See this couple? Notice how short he is? When I paint their portrait, I'm going to make him taller than her. Nicer for them . . . Hold on . . ."

A woman and two young kids had stopped to watch Mrs. Ameche paint. "You should preserve their faces," Mrs. Ameche said to the mother. "They won't look the same in a year."

"Oh, I know it," said the mother, who started to walk away.

"I can do it in twenty minutes," said Mrs. Ameche.

"We're just visiting from New York," said the mother as she headed off.

Adam watched them disappear down the hallway. He didn't know if he could take being turned down like that. It was funny — he didn't mind asking strangers to do stuff for him for one of his stories, because it really wasn't for him personally, it was more like part of this noble quest for truth. But trying to sell someone something just so you could get money? He felt embarrassed for Mrs. Ameche.

"Did that hurt?" asked Jennifer.

"Did what, Jenny?"

"Being turned down like that?"

"Oh, my gosh, no," Mrs. Ameche said. "I figure I get about fifty turn-downs for every yes. So when someone says no, I'm just getting closer to my yes."

Don handed his mother the cash from the lawn mower, and Mrs. Ameche tucked it away under her painter's smock.

Several people came by and bought jars of tomato products. They seemed to be repeat customers. They asked for specific products: Mrs. Ameche's famous championship tomato paste. Mrs. Ameche's famous championship stewed tomatoes. Mrs. Ameche's famous championship green pickled tomatoes. A security guard bought two jars of sauce and six golf balls.

An old man who didn't buy anything but just seemed to want to talk asked the Ameche brothers how the new crop of tomatoes was looking; he asked if they were going to win a fourth straight championship.

"Growing big, I bet," said the old man.

"Hard to say," answered Don.

"Too early," said Alan.

"Have to ask Mom," said Don.

"Right now, she's not taking questions," said Alan.

"Tight deadline," said Don.

"Wedding portrait," said Alan.

"Oh, I know how it is," said the old man. "When she rises from her coma, you tell her Red Tony said hello."

"We will, Red Tony," said Don.

"Thanks, Red Tony," said Alan.

When he'd gone, Mrs. Ameche looked around her canvas and said, "That man is a public nuisance. For twenty years, he's been trying to figure out the secret ingredient in my fertilizer. Every year he enters the state championship, and I don't think he's ever grown a tomato over two pounds. It's a terrible thing to say, but sometimes I just can't help judging people by the size of their tomato."

"You're a snob, Ma," said Don.

"I bet a lot of good people have small tomatoes," said Alan.

"You're right," said Mrs. Ameche, who kept on painting. "You are right. I plead guilty to being a genius when it comes to tomatoes. We all have our faults. Except these two —" and she wagged her paintbrush at Adam and Jennifer. "So, what are you doing here? If you came to buy the lawn mower, it's sold."

They told her they had enough stories to put out another great issue of the *Slash*. They quickly described how the reporting was going. When they got to the story about the state test getting easier, Mrs. Ameche actually stopped painting, stood up, thrust both her fists in the air, let out a loud whoop, and then started doing a strange dance that looked like jumping up and down on a pogo stick while pumping her arms in and out like a boxer.

"Ma, please," said Don.

"Mom, not in public, come on," said Alan.

"Ma, this can't be good for business," said Don.

"You're going to get security up here," said Alan.

Mrs. Ameche stopped dancing. She looked disappointed. "Jenny, the Ameche brothers are turning into teenagers," she said. "They're afraid of what other people think. I used to do my Ha-Ha, I Told You So, Ha-Ha dance — the Ameche brothers would dance right along. Am I right, boys? You used to love doing the Ha-Ha."

"Cut it out, Ma," said Don.

"Can we just get back to regular here?" said Alan.

Mrs. Ameche sat back down and resumed painting.

"So," said Adam, "we need your help, Mrs. Ameche. We have ten days to get the paper to the printer. That's ten days to raise another five hundred dollars to get it printed."

"We know how hard the Ameche brothers tried," said Jennifer. "And we feel terrible. We may not even be able to pay them."

Mrs. Ameche didn't say anything; she just kept working on the wedding portrait.

"Is she in her painting trance?" whispered Jennifer.

"No," said Don, "she's thinking."

"How can you tell?" whispered Adam.

"The eyes," said Alan.

"They're more darty," said Don.

Adam was staring at the wedding portrait. The man *was* taller than his wife now, but the funny thing was, it didn't look as ridiculous as it sounded. Mrs. Ameche had drawn the couple from a slighty different angle from the photo, sort of off to the left looking downward into the picture from the husband's side, and somehow from that angle, it seemed he really could be taller, that the photo might have been wrong.

"OK," said Mrs. Ameche. "When I'm in a tight spot like this, I always try to think of a similar moment in a great movie and how the good guys got out of that. And right now I'm thinking of *The Wizard of Oz* and how that lovely Dorothy — and I have to tell you, Jenny, you remind me a little of her; you've got that same sunniness — how she just wanted to get back to Kansas. And after she's been through everything, she goes to that good witch and the good witch tells her —"

"Ma," said Don, "they don't want to go home."

"They don't live in Kansas, Ma," said Alan. "They need five hundred bucks."

"Oh, shush. What the good witch says is Dorothy had it in her power the whole time to go home any-time she wanted; she just needed to click her ruby slippers a bunch and say she wanted to go, and she was out of there."

Adam looked at Jennifer's feet. She was wearing sneakers. They didn't look that clickable.

"You have the ability to raise that money; you just have to tell people you need it," said Mrs. Ameche.

"We did this all wrong. We were trying to sell ads like a regular paper. You have to explain your situation. You're a great newspaper, and the Bolands and the school board shut you down. And you've got more truth to tell. You've got to go to all the people who believe in you and the ones you've helped. This is America, and Americans may bellyache about the media, but they love freedom of speech. It's a country of blabbermouths. They will help. Like that woman you wrote about, with the wooden cow that got stolen. She sounded like a rich lady—lived out on Breckenridge, right? Well, I bet she'd be happy to donate a couple bucks to help the *Slash*—you got her cow back—"

"Whoa," said Jennifer. "She wanted to buy a mail subscription—I bet you're right."

"Yes," said Adam. "That secretary for the lawyers who saved the basketball hoops—she said the same thing."

"I knew it!" yelled Mrs. Ameche. "I knew it—" and she rose like she might do her Ha-Ha dance again, but stopped when Jennifer said, "Hold on."

Mrs. Ameche glanced at the Busy Bee ceiling. "Don't tell me, Jenny. Now you're embarrassed by the Ha-Ha."

"No, no," said Jennifer. "It's not that."

"Ma, she wouldn't say if she was," said Don.

"She's got too nice manners, Ma," said Alan.

"No, no," repeated Jennifer. "It's not the Ha-Ha I'm worried about—it's ethics."

Ethics! thought Adam. Oh, no. It seemed like they were about to get out of this, and there was that stupid word again. *Ethics.* It was always getting in the way of everything. He hated ethics; he wished they'd just dry up and die.

The Ameche brothers looked stricken.

"It's not our fault," said Don.

"We've been one-hundred percent good ethics since you yelled at us, Ma," said Alan.

Jennifer waved them off. She said the same thing to Mrs. Ameche now that she'd said to the *Slash* staff several weeks before: She was worried that if she and Adam and others on the *Slash* were asking for money from people who'd been sources for their news stories, it would be like they were asking them to pay for being written about in the *Slash*. And then everyone would start thinking only people who gave money would get their names in the paper. "That's not what we're doing," Jennifer said. "But it might look like that."

Adam mentioned how he'd turned down money from Mrs. Quigley. "Jennifer gave us this huge talk about the wall separating the business side from the news side," he said.

"The wall!" said Don.

"Not the wall!" moaned Alan, and the two looked at each other, put their hands to their chests, spun around like corkscrews, then fell to the mall floor like deceased Ameches.

Mrs. Ameche ignored them. She told Jennifer and Adam she didn't see anything wrong with asking people like the wooden-cow lady for money if there were no plans to write about them again. Mrs. Ameche said that she could see how the principal was different, since there would probably be something about her in every issue. And she said if it turned out that they *did* need to write about someone who gave them money in some future issue, they would just have to mention that in the story. "You just say, 'Full Disclosure,' and you tell the truth. I got to tell you—the *Slash* is fighting for its life here. I don't think you can worry too far ahead. You've got to get this issue out."

"Full disclosure," Jennifer repeated softly. "Sounds all right."

"Full disclosure!" said Adam, grinning; he felt like kissing Mrs. Ameche for making their ethics problem go away.

"Full disclosure, Ma," said Don.

"We're not really dead, Ma," said Alan.

The coeditors had to go. Adam had baseball; Jennifer, a cello lesson.

They said bye to the Ameche brothers, giving them double knucks, and thanked Mrs. Ameche. She walked them along the hallway to the down escalator. She promised she'd have the Ameche brothers send out a fundraising message for the *Slash* on their *Talk Till You Drop, All-Live Except the Recorded Parts* webcast. "You know the viewership of that webcast," Mrs. Ameche said. "They might raise ten bucks if you're lucky. For once," she continued, "this is not a job for the Ameche brothers. You two have it in your power to do this. Just click those ruby slippers . . ."

She gave Adam a friendly rub on the head and squeezed Jennifer in a big Ameche hug.

Adam hopped on the down escalator, but when he turned to say something to Jennifer, she wasn't there; she was still at the top. Mrs. Ameche was holding her arm, and Don had joined them — Don?! — and Adam heard Mrs. Ameche say, "You're all right about this?" Then Jennifer was saying something back, and Mrs. Ameche was saying something else back, and then Mrs. Ameche was kissing Jennifer on the cheek! What was that? Though he tried with all his might, Adam couldn't hear what they were saying — a girl in front of him was on her cell phone describing her new ceramic cat — and the escalator just kept rolling along, carrying Adam down and out.

chapter 17

Room 306

"Can everyone please sit down and listen up?" Jennifer called. "Come on, guys. . . . We've got a lot to do. Please . . . It's a week to get the paper to the printer. . . . Come on. . . ."

It was tough; everyone was thinking about the end of school. Summer vacation. Kids just wanted to be free. Adam was watching two boys on a nearby couch, both sports reporters. They were talking right through Jennifer, totally oblivious. One of the boys was holding his arm out, and the two were studying the black ink spots on his hand. The boy with the spots was saying how you could make a fortune if you could just invent a kind of permanent marker that could wash off. And the other boy was saying how stupid this was, since if it could wash off, it wasn't a permanent marker.

As coeditor of the *Slash*, Adam knew he should have told them to shut up and listen to Jennifer. There was so much to do. But he didn't have it in him. These two boys were exactly like Adam, last year, when he was just a star reporter for the *Slash*, before Jennifer had tricked him into becoming her coeditor. These two completely oblivious idiots were having so much fun, debating how permanent permanent marker had to be, to be washable and still be permanent marker. That's what Adam wanted to be talking about.

Not tracking down Stub Keenan.

Not investigating the state test.

Not raising money for the *Slash*.

The permanence of permanent marker. That was a mull-able topic with infinite possibilities for a middle-school boy.

But before he could mull, he was distracted by the quiet. Jennifer had on her supersonic coeditor meltdown glare.

She'd silenced them.

"OK, Adam," she said. "Tell everyone about Stub."

A few more weeks and they'd be done. Swimming in the Tremble. Jumping on the trampoline at his grandma's cottage. Learning to surf at the beach. Wakeboarding 180s. Lying on the dock at Lake Ameche, looking up at the sky and watching Mrs. Ameche's two clouds float by.

He could do this.

They loved the Stub story.

Several asked where to get a free download.

Someone suggested doing a music review of Stub's Top 250 Hits.

"If his music's kind of shaky," said a girl. "It could backfire. He might lose."

A lot of them had heard little things, but none had put the whole story together. A few said there'd been a rumor about getting free downloads, but they'd assumed maybe a skateboard or cell-phone company was doing it. A boy had gone online trying to track it down, but didn't get any hits for Harris or even Tremble. One girl had been asked if she wanted a free download but didn't realize what they were talking about and didn't have her iPod with her, anyway.

Adam asked if she remembered who it was.

She said it was a boy, but she didn't know his name.

"Was it Stub?" asked Adam. "Do you remember what he looked like?"

"I don't know," she said. "Kind of cute."

Adam didn't say anything, but he was thinking he might be the last true reporter left on the continent.

"What did Stub say when you told him you knew?" asked Sammy.

Adam said they hadn't talked to Stub yet.

"Ouch," said Sammy. "That could be messy, Ad-man. You want some of us to go with you? We'd do it. You might need a posse."

A third-grade hand in the back was waving wildly. "I volunteer, I'll do it! Pick me!" squeaked who else — Phoebe! Just what he needed. It wasn't bad enough that they had a third grader writing the paper's advice column. Now she was going to be his bodyguard. He'd kill her.

"We'll be all right," said Jennifer.

Adam looked at her. "We will?" he said. He was

quite sure that if Stub and his goons punched some-one in the face, it wouldn't be Jennifer.

"Trust me," said Jennifer. "The coeditors can handle it."

The sports reporters had finished their stories, but Jennifer wanted them to include the final season win-loss records for each team. "That's important," she said. "I hate reading about how the girls' lacrosse team had this great season blah, blah, and there's no record."

"When we finished our stories," said the boy with permanent marker, "the season wasn't over. You're the one who wanted us to get them in early."

"OK, so now you have to go back to the coaches and find out," said Jennifer. "And we'll insert the final records."

The boys moaned.

"Right, Adam?" said Jennifer.

Adam was quiet. It was easy for Jennifer to say; the girls' tennis team was undefeated. The boys baseball team was 3–9. He wondered if the base-ball coach had told the *Slash* reporters about Adam Canfield's double that had won the game against

Broad Meadows Middle. That was the kind of nice little fact that could really spice up a sports story.

The reporters who'd done the bike-theft story were up next. Adam might not have gotten his back, but the story was turning out to be really interesting. The reporters found fourteen kids who'd had their bikes stolen, and none had gotten them back. They talked to a community relations spokesman for the Tremble Police Department, who said it appeared there were two bike rings operating in town. One, he said, seemed to be some kid walking home from school who just grabbed bikes he saw lying around. That, of course, was what had happened to Adam's bike. The other seemed to strike at night. The thief would find a bike left on the side of a house or on a patio or in an unlocked garage, grab it, and leave a crappier bike in its place. "So they cruise the neighborhoods on a bad old bike, see a better one, and then just ride off with nobody noticing," explained one of the reporters. "How you know you've been hit—there's a crappy bike lying on your lawn when you wake up in the morning. You see that crappy bike, it's like the kiss of death."

Sammy had found the perfect chocolate milk at

a new restaurant in town. He gave it a top mark of 4.5 yummy-yummies, plus an extra half-yummy for perfection. The milk was cold. It was served in a tall glass-glass, not a plastic-glass. The glass was seven inches high—Sammy had measured it. He liked to be precise. There was no chocolate syrup visible at the bottom of the glass—meaning all the chocolate had been stirred in. The drink was served with a straw and was not filled to the top—there were one and a half inches of space, so if you blew bubbles, they wouldn't spill over and mess up the table—not to mention wasting perfectly good chocolate milk.

"I just want everyone to know," Sammy said, "that I went back three times on three different days to make sure it wasn't some freak, one-shot perfect thing, and it wasn't. I mean, I wanted to be fair. . . . I think that's important . . ." He seemed to be waiting for someone to say something, but when nobody did, he said, "Thank you very much," and sat down.

Everyone was still. They were amazed at how much thought Sammy had put into writing about a glass of chocolate milk. They felt like they were in the presence of greatness.

Jennifer called him back up.

"That's only half," Jennifer said. "Tell them the rest. Come on, Sammy."

Sammy looked puzzled.

"The other story you did."

Sammy shrugged. "The restaurant?" It turned out that the new restaurant with the perfect chocolate milk was called Only Kids Only, and just like the name said, it was really just for kids. Sammy had written a whole separate story, calling it "a revolutionary breakthrough in kids' dining." Parents could drop off kids or sit in a waiting room, but only kids were allowed to eat there. The menu featured kid food — peanut butter and jam, grilled cheese, chicken nuggets, tuna fish with nothing in it, quesadillas with chicken and cheese only — no onions or relishy nonsense. And they only served top-of-the-line desserts, like Mrs. Radin's Famous Homemade Super-Chunk Buckets O' Chocolate Moisty Deluxe chocolate-chip cookies.

"It's pretty great," Sammy said. "You can order like twenty different types of PB&Js. I got strawberry jam with double crunchy peanut butter on whole wheat, and they'll take the fat berry parts out of the jam if you ask. . . ."

"Gross," said a girl. "I hate those berry boogers."

270

"And you can order all these good side dishes. I got it with Cheez Doodles and carrot sticks. The whole thing came to five dollars."

Everyone was talking at once; they all wanted to go to Only Kids Only.

Adam shot to his feet. "Quiet!" he called. "Quiet. I think there's an important lesson here. This is all about excellence. Sammy had a dream: to find the perfect chocolate milk. A lot of us, including me, thought it wasn't important enough to make a story, but Sammy stuck to his principles. And he sacrificed— I guarantee you, he drank a lot of bad chocolate milk on the way to that 5.0. He did not give up. A lot of people might say, 'Oh, fine, this chocolate milk is good enough for our readers.' Not Sammy. No way. He searched until he found a glass of milk that met his standard."

They were on their feet now, clapping and whistling and banging the tables.

Sammy turned a bright pink, but he was beaming. He raised his hand and kept saying, "Thank you, thank you. . . . I know every one of you would have done the same thing."

It was time to talk money. Adam and Jennifer brought them up to date. The coeditors told the staff

271

they needed to raise another $750; Jennifer wanted to make sure they had a little extra in case there were any unexpected, last-minute costs from the printer. Plus they were hoping to have some money left over to pay the Ameche brothers.

They repeated almost everything Mrs. Ameche had said, including the part about the *Slash* being a great newspaper that had more truth to tell. They talked about the importance of going to every single person who'd believed in them. About the only part of Mrs. Ameche's speech they left out was the *Wizard of Oz* stuff — the last thing they needed was a room full of news hounds clicking their heels and chanting that they wanted to go home.

Jennifer explained that the money must come with no strings attached. Just because someone gave didn't mean the *Slash* was going to write some nice, puff-job story about them. "And anyone who does ask for favors, just say never mind and don't take their money," said Jennifer.

"We're making a list," she continued, lifting her pen high and wiggling it at them. "And we need to know now — right now — how much each of you can raise. And I must have it by the end of the week. I'm not talking what you'd like to raise, or what you might possibly raise, what could be or what may be . . . I'm talking five days from now."

"Cold, hard cash," said Adam.

The coeditors didn't know what kind of reaction they'd get, but in the few seconds it took Jennifer to look up from the legal pad where she was making notes, practically every hand in the room had shot up.

They were all talking at once. People mentioned several teachers and coaches and librarians who they knew would give. Adam wrote down the Tremble children's librarian who'd helped him on his Shadow report—the one who had told Adam how much she'd liked the *Slash*.

"That's good," said Jennifer. "Librarians, I didn't think of that—librarians seem quiet, but they're kind of surprising people."

Adam wrote down Mrs. Rose, and Danny, his grown-up friend from the animal shelter, and Erik Forrest, the world-famous journalist, and his favorite teacher, Mr. Brooks.

"I bet I know a thousand people, cinchy-easy, who'd give," said Phoebe. "There's Eddie the janitor and Mrs. Eddie, his nice wife, who made us the cookies and calls me Little Sweet Potato, and his grown-up children, who loved my stories best of any stories . . . and —"

Adam had to give Phoebe credit: even when she was doing good, even when she was helping her fellow man, she still somehow managed to find a way to be really annoying.

"We're getting there," said Jennifer. "But —"

"I'm not done!" squeaked Phoebe. "I pledge the twenty-eight dollars and seventy-eight cents that I made selling my bead necklaces and ankle bracelets at the Riverfront Crafts Fair last weekend —" She took a deep bow. "Thank you, thank you," she said. "I bet I collect the most of everyone. Thank you, thank you."

"I pledge one hundred dollars and zero cents," said Shadow. "From my job at the Rec, working for Mr. Johnny Stack and doing what needs doing. And I'm going to get money from Mr. Johnny Stack, too. He likes the *Slash*. Mr. Johnny Stack says it's good for a person like me to mix with kids like that. So, I think he will give a lot, which is not an exact amount, but it will be."

Shadow never ceased to amaze Adam — he didn't even have his own house to live in or parents to live with.

"Shadow," said Jennifer, "that's so nice, but it's too much. I know how hard you work—"

"Work's not hard for me," said Shadow. "Mr. Johnny Stack says work is my middle name. It's not my really middle name. It's just a figure of speech. My really middle name—"

"Nobody cares what your really middle name is," said Phoebe. "We're trying to collect money to save the *Slash*. No offense or anything, but like Mr. Adams, my Language Arts teacher, says, you need to focus . . ."

"Focus-pocus!" said Shadow. "Mr. Johnny Stack says when it comes to work, no one can focus on a job like Theodore Robert Cox, which is my real name, including my real middle name and my first real name and my last real name and not Shadow, my real nickname—"

"Excuse me," said Phoebe. "Can I say one word here?"

"*Excuse me. Can I say one word here?* is eight words, not one word," said Shadow. "Even *one word* is two words. You're just saying everything because twenty-eight dollars and seventy-eight cents is not the most of everyone, thank you, thank you. One hundred dollars and no cents is. And I can prove it."

"Stop," said Jennifer. "Stop, stop, stop. You two,

you have to learn to get along better. Come on. It's great what both of you are doing. Everyone is doing the best they can, and that's wonderful—"

"That's right," said Shadow. "I'm just doing better than her."

"Oh, we'll see about that," said Phoebe. "There's still five days to go. I'm going to ask special permission to set up a table at lunch in the cafeteria to sell my necklaces so I can rack up the bucks."

Adam's head was pounding. "Stop," he said quietly. "Please stop. Please." Phoebe started to open her mouth, but Adam screamed, *"No!"* and it seemed like she heard him this time, because she sat down, pulled out a purse full of beads, and started stringing an ankle bracelet.

Watching Phoebe, it occurred to Adam that maybe she was the perfect reporter. She was exuberantly and irrationally self-confident, it was impossible to wear her down, she never took anything bad you said about her personally if she even noticed at all, and whatever ridiculousness she was up to, she always seemed to be able to twist it into something useful. Her shameless pledge war with Shadow set off a whole new round of pledges from the staff. Kids pledged to donate their babysitting money, mother's-helper money, snow-shoveling money, leaf-raking money, yardwork money, car-washing money, returned-bottle money.

When Jennifer finally lifted her head, having caught up with all the names and pledges people had given her, she said, "If everyone comes through, looks to me like we'll have more than we need — as long as everyone means what they said." She paused; it seemed like she was trying to decide whether or not to say something.

"You know what's funny," she said. "I'm looking over this list — no one mentioned parents."

They were quiet. It was true: they — Adam included — hadn't even thought about their parents, but it made sense to him. Room 306 was their place. The *Slash* was theirs. Of all the activities in their overprogrammed lives, it was the one thing they did where they were the ones who decided where to go and whom to talk to and whom to listen to and whom to trust and whom not to trust — certainly they weren't about to trust Mrs. Boland, or Dr. Bleepin, or their old principal, Mrs. Marris, or Stub Keenan. They still needed help from grown-ups. Lots of grown-ups. But they chose which ones — like Mr. Brooks and Mrs. Rose and Erik Forrest and Mrs. Willard and Reverend Shorty and their acting principal, Mrs. Quigley, and Mrs. Ameche. Mrs. Ameche was a perfect example. Adam and Jennifer had found Mrs. Ameche all by themselves, which made her seem better. She was theirs.

For everything else, their parents made all the decisions. Their parents took them to baritone and cello and choir and ballet and Irish-step lessons. Their parents signed them up for baseball and tennis and lacrosse and soccer teams. And when their parents dropped them off at the field, other grown-ups, who were picked out by their parents, told them where to stand and when to run and when to stop running and when to swing their bats and when to take a pitch — even if it was right down the middle and Adam was dying to clobber it.

In Room 306, if Adam felt like swinging, he swung away.

"I might ask my parents," Adam said softly. "If we're really desperate."

Jennifer nodded. "Me, too," she said. "If we're really desperate."

It was time to go. Adam and Jennifer were hoping to catch Mrs. Gross after the meeting to interview her about the state test. Every last one of them had people to visit, phone calls to make, e-mails to send, money to raise. Not since last winter, since they'd all used Adam's 100 percent foolproof middle-of-the-night wake-up method and e-mailed out the story on Mrs. Marris stealing money, had the entire *Slash* staff been so unified in a single cause. The atmosphere in 306 was positively tingly.

"Before we go," said Jennifer, "listen up. Before we head out on this mission, I just want to say how proud I am. We're going to do this. We're going to put out this paper. We're going to show the school board and the Bolands and everyone else that they can't stop the *Slash* from being published. They shut us down, but they did not shut us up. So . . . wait, wait . . . Hold on, everyone — Adam, you want to make a little speech? Any final words to motivate the troops?"

A speech? Adam thought. A speech? Adam could talk well enough when he needed to, but he wasn't sure it would turn into an actual speech. He felt a little too disorganized to make a speech. A speech was more like a bunch of words you thought up ahead of time and repeated back in the proper order.

Then something occurred to him.

"Yes," he said. "I know a speech. An actual

279

speech . . . Give me a second. . . . OK, I'm ready. It's pretty historic." He raised both arms, as if he was an orchestra conductor.

"June 18, 1940," he began. "The Bolands and the school board know that they will have to break us here in 306, or lose the war. If we can stand up to them, all Harris Elementary/Middle may be free and the life of the world may move forward into broad, sunlit uplands. But if we fail, then the whole world, including the United States, including all that we have known and cared for, will sink into the abyss of a new Dark Age."

Adam climbed up on the picnic table in the middle of the room. "Let us therefore brace ourselves to our duties and so bear ourselves that if the *Slash* and Harris Elementary/Middle School last for a thousand years, men will still say, 'This was their finest hour.'"

The staff of the Slash had witnessed a lot of good talking in 306, but what Adam said was the most speechy that any had ever heard from a fellow kid. They didn't know exactly what it meant, but it sounded great. They stood and cheered, and then they grabbed their backpacks and went marching out the door. Even the oldest among them, the eighth graders, were excited about having a finest hour.

chapter 18

Mrs. Gross Doesn't Know

They were rushing down one of the hallways at the elementary school toward Mrs. Gross's room. Harris Elementary dismissed a half hour after the middle school, but the *Slash* meeting had gone longer than expected. Hopefully, Mrs. Gross would still be around.

Lots of kids were in the corridor by their lockers, gathered in little groups, talking and dillydallying. No one could dillydally like an elementary school kid, and Adam felt a pang of jealousy for their less-programmed lives. As he and Jennifer hurried by, kids looked up, stared, then cleared the way. Adam knew what they were thinking:

Stand back—middle-school kids passing.

It was fun to be big.

Mrs. Gross's door was closed, but when he peeked through the window, he could see that she was still in there, talking to a parent.

He and Jennifer pulled off their knapsacks, flopped onto the floor, and sat with their backs against the lockers to wait. Jennifer took out a strawberry granola bar, breaking off half for Adam.

"That was some speech," she said.

"Yeah," said Adam. "I pulled that one out of my butt."

"It's funny," she said. "When we practiced in the lunch room—I didn't remember anything about Harris or the *Slash* or 306 being in there. Winston went to Harris?"

"Don't think so," said Adam. "I had to twist around a few things to make it fit."

Jennifer nodded. "Poetic license," she said. "I like poetic license. From what I can tell, if you're a famous writer, you can make grammar mistakes and it's OK, because you've got poetic license."

"Typical," said Adam. "They give it to grown-ups, but they'd never give it to a kid. Kids are the ones who need poetic licenses."

Adam finished the last bite of granola bar. It tasted great, but that reminded him of how hungry he was. He thought about pulling out his jawbreaker and having a big suck, but it always attracted attention at school. He was afraid it might get taken away. He was hoping to suck it down until it disappeared, even if it took two or three years.

"I need to talk to you about something," said Jennifer.

"Uh-oh," said Adam. "What did I do now?"

"No, nothing like that," said Jennifer. "About me. Me and Don."

God, why did she keep wanting to talk about this? Did she like to torture him? All Jennifer had to do was mention the Ameche brother's name, and Adam could feel his face get hot. It wasn't fair. He was working so hard at not getting worked up about this. It was definitely all straightened out; they were done with this, finished, squared away, concluded, resolved, wrapped up. He knew this and his brain knew this, but for some stupid reason, the rest of his body wasn't paying attention. At that moment, he would have given a million-dollar reward to any person alive who could invent a cure for blushing.

"Adam," said Jennifer, "I want you to—"

"It's OK," said Adam, "You don't—"

"I do," said Jennifer. "I want to explain. I want to."

They heard the click of a knob turning. Mrs. Gross's door was opening. She was saying good-bye to the parent.

"Darn," said Jennifer. "Every time . . ." Before Adam could stand, she grabbed his sleeve, pulled him toward her, put her lips right against his ear, and whispered, "We will finish this afterward, Winston Canfield."

He hated this. Why did everything have to be so mixed up? Even her whisper felt nice.

"Oh my, my, my, my, my, is that you, Adam Canfield? Look at you. You're so grown-up. And handsome. My, my, my, my, my."

"Hi, Mrs. Gross," said Adam. "Yeah, it is me."

"Let me look at you," she said. "Oh, my, my, my. I mean it. My, my, my, my, my. Come with me for a second." She put her arm around Adam's shoulders and ushered him to the back of the room, where there was a door leading to the adjoining classroom. "Miss Iannoni!" Mrs. Gross cried. "Look who I have here! Adam Canfield!"

"Oh, my gosh," said Miss Iannoni. "The complete

package. He's arrived, and just in the nick of time, too."

"This is a wonderful surprise," she said, and waved to Miss Iannoni, leading Adam back to her room. "Are you coming to say good-bye? You know, I'm retiring."

Adam nodded. "Sort of," he said. "Ah, Mrs. Gross, this is Jennifer. We're coeditors of the *Slash*. . . ."

"That's right. I knew that," said Mrs. Gross. "I'm sorry I pulled him away like that, Jennifer. It's just been a long time. Thirty years teaching, you don't get that many complete packages. I've heard a lot about you, Jennifer, but I never was lucky enough to have you. I tried. I requested you — you wouldn't know that. But they accused me of trying to steal all the superstars. I think you had Mrs. Deane for fourth?"

"I did," said Jennifer.

"And if I'm not mistaken, you have twin sisters coming up to fourth next year?"

Jennifer nodded. "If they ever let them out of third."

"Well, if they're anything like their big sister, that shouldn't be a problem," said Mrs. Gross. "So are you the ones responsible for sending the reporter to interview me? About retiring? He was so nervous. His name was Stevie, wasn't it? A fifth grader, I think. He never looked up from his list of questions. I had to write down my answers for him. Shyest reporter I've ever seen."

"We didn't know that," said Jennifer. "But the story actually turned out fine. I liked the part when you said you were inspired to be a teacher by your second-grade teacher's kind personality. And the reporter wrote, 'Many say the same about Mrs. Gross.'"

"Really?" said Mrs. Gross. "I'll have to show that to my husband."

Adam was caught off-guard. He didn't think of Mrs. Gross as having a husband, at least not one she'd mention out loud to a kid. It seemed a little personal. "Um, Mrs. Gross," he said. "Do you mind if we close the door? We have something private to talk to you about."

They got right to it. They told her they'd heard the state test scores had gone way up this year because the test was so easy. They didn't name Dr. Duke but explained that they had an actual grown-up secret source.

Then Adam pulled out the manila envelope from Pittsburgh and showed Mrs. Gross the copies of the fourth-grade state tests from this year and last year.

"Oh, my," said Mrs. Gross. "My, my, my, my, my. You're not supposed to have those. That's against the law. Where did you—? Actually, no, don't tell me. I don't want to know."

"We don't know either," said Adam.

"They just showed up in the mail one day," said Jennifer. "I got a set, too."

"My, my, my, my," said Mrs. Gross. "My, my, my, my."

"I know what you mean," said Adam. "That's how I felt, too—incredibly my, my, my. Look, Mrs. Gross, I need to ask you something right away, before we go over all this stuff. We were hoping you might look at the two tests with us and tell us if you think this year's was easier. But—"

"Oh, Adam," said Mrs. Gross. "I don't have to look to tell you that. No question, it was easier. The teachers have talked about it for months, since we gave the test. We talked about it so much, we talked ourselves out. Last year I had kids crying during the first reading passage. They had stomachaches. One wet himself—tinkle, tinkle, little star. A girl threw up—all over the answer sheet. Some got so worked up, they could barely concentrate for the rest of the test. You know fourth graders; they're still like Jell-O. Now, this year—oh, my. This year, they're taking the test, they open the booklet, they look at the first reading passage—they're humming 'Ode to Joy.' *Bum-bum-bum-bum, we adore thee.*"

Adam noticed that Jennifer was taking notes like crazy. Normally, he'd do the same, but he'd made up his mind. He wasn't going to have another situation like Dr. Duke, where someone told him her deepest secrets, then said, "Oh, by the way— *offthe-record!* Ha, ha, got you!*" That Dr. Duke—he was still angry. *"Didn't Mrs. Quigley tell you? I can't be quoted."* The brave, jokey Dr. Duke. Not again, he swore it. Mrs. Gross was supposedly going to let them use her name—emphasis on supposedly, as far as Adam was concerned. He would not break his arm taking notes, just to have her pull a Dr. Duke.

"Mrs. Gross, I have to ask," he said. "Do you mind if we quote you on this stuff? We really need someone who's willing to use her name."

"No problem," said Mrs. Gross.

"I mean, a lot of times, people tell us stuff, they're all outraged and everything and they want us to do a big investigation and then—"

"It's fine, Adam."

"They say, 'Oh sorry, you can't use my name with that,'" said Adam. "We had a situation—"

"You can use it," said Mrs. Gross.

"This person," said Adam, "acted so high and mighty and jokey—"

"*Adam Canfield!*" yelled Jennifer. "She said yes. Listen up, you dodo! Hello!"

Adam stopped talking. "Really?" he said.

"Yes," said Mrs. Gross. "As long as you make clear that I wasn't the one who gave you the tests. I'm planning to spend my retirement in Florida, not Sing Sing."

"Really?" said Adam.

"That's great," said Jennifer.

"I've had plenty of time to think it over," said Mrs. Gross. "Carolyn called me. She said you might visit."

"Carolyn?" repeated Adam.

"Said we might visit?" asked Jennifer.

"Who's Carolyn?" asked Adam.

"Why, Carolyn Duke," said Mrs. Gross. "She and I taught together for years. Her classroom used to be right through that door."

"Dr. Duke?" said Adam.

"Oh, yes," said Mrs. Gross. "Dr. Duke. One of the bravest educators I know."

DEAR LEVI
Letters from the Overland Trail
By Elvira Woodruff

April 3, 1851

Dear Levi,

I am writing to you from the state of Ohio, and even though it is only a week's drive from home in Sudbury, I feel as if I'm already a long way from Pennsylvania. I wonder what I will feel like after travelling almost three thousand miles to Oregon? Tired, I reckon, after all that walking!

None of the men or older boys ride in the wagons, as that would be cowardly, seeing how the oxen have such heavy loads to pull. Many of the women and children walk also. Some of the younger boys do nothing but hunt for firewood and frogs (the frogs being for their own amusement), but since I am twelve years old, I work right alongside the men most of the time.

My day starts at about four thirty in the morning when I have to cut out the oxen from the herd and drive them to the wagon for yoking and hitching. Then I help Mr. Morrison check over the running gear. We have breakfast and are ready to travel by seven o'clock. We're on the road till noon. Then we unhitch the oxen and set the stock to graze before taking our lunch. After an hour or so we hitch up again and go on for another four or five hours. I can tell you that walking fifteen to twenty miles a day can tire the strongest legs. I have much to write you about, but the fire is getting low and I need to rest up for tomorrow's drive.

Your brother,
Austin

Dear Levi,

We now have twenty-four wagons in our train, as two new parties joined us yesterday. Everyone is in good spirits, and there is much talk among the men about the gold mines at Butler's Mill in California, though some of the families in this party have Oregon fever and are looking to settle along the shores of the Columbia River.

I surely hated leaving you behind in Pennsylvania, but you know I couldn't pass the opportunity to go out in Oregon and see about Pa's claim. He staked everything he owned in this world on a new start for us. In his last letter he told Miss Ameila that should any accident befall him we should seek out Mr. Ezra Zikes, for he had promised Pa to look after his affairs and protect his claim for us.

Now that Pa is gone I am hoping that Mr. Zikes will help me to get work and lodging at the lumber camp where Pa worked. Once you're old enough, Levi, you can come, too. Till then, mind Miss Amelia and don't go chasing after her chickens too much.

Your brother,
Austin

The River Otter

By Janeen R. Adil

A river otter is at home in ponds, lakes and rivers. Her thick brown fur is waterproof. It keeps her warm and dry, even when she swims in cold winter waters.

The river otter is a great swimmer. Her long body is shaped for swimming, and her big back feet help her move quickly through the water. She can swim on her stomach or dive deep into the water. Sometimes, though, she just likes to float on her back.

Her dinner might be fish or frogs she catches. Crayfish are a favorite meal. She eats in careful little bites.

River otters love to play in the deep snow. They play hide and seek. Another fun game is to slide down a slippery hill, splash! right into the water. Sometimes a river otter will dive for rocks. Then she will juggle a rock in her paws. Balancing a leaf on her nose and chasing her own tail is a lot of fun, too!

The river otter sleeps on a bed of dry leaves. After a rest, it's time to eat, swim and play some more.

Mrs. Gross was great. She went through both tests with the coeditors and pointed out differences. She had them count words. The reading excerpt in the hard test from last year had 453 words. It was about a family traveling west on the Oregon Trail. There were six characters to keep track of, and most had old-fashioned names: Levi, Austin, Pa, Mr. Morrison, Miss Amelia, Mr. Ezra Zikes. The story was written in 1850s Western style with phrases like "Cut out the oxen from the herd and drive them to the wagon for yoking and hitching," "Check over the running gear," and "Set the stock to graze."

"Kids today don't talk like that," said Mrs. Gross. "The passage mentions a train and they mean wagon train. Our kids hear train, they think of their moms and dads taking the train into the city. Just compare the titles," said Mrs. Gross.

Last year's story was "Dear Levi: Letters from the Overland Trail."

This year's reading passage was "The River Otter."

"The River Otter!" said Adam.

"The River Otter!" said Jennifer.

"So easy," said Mrs. Gross. They counted this year's passage — a measly 184 words. "And it's just a basic description of an animal they've all heard of and may have seen swimming in the Tremble River. Or at the zoo. The sentences are much more simply structured. Pick any one."

"'The river otter is a great swimmer,'" read Adam.

"'Her dinner might be fish or frogs,'" read Jennifer.

"Oh, my God," said Adam. "That's baby stuff. Listen to this sentence." It was from the hard passage: "'In his last letter he told Miss Amelia that should any accident befall him we should seek out Mr. Ezra Zikes, for he had promised Pa to look after his affairs and protect his claim for us.'"

"'Should any accident befall him,'" repeated Adam. "No one talks like that."

"Big difference," said Mrs. Gross. "Big. We teach our kids to make a personal connection to what they read. The Oregon Trail—that's foreign to them. It's not that they can't do it—they can. It's just a lot harder than a story about an otter eating frogs."

They were nearly finished.

"I kind of know the answer to this last question," said Adam, "but I just need to hear you say it. Mrs.

Gross, you're the teacher. Do you think you had anything to do with scores going up?"

"I got a cash bonus," said Mrs. Gross. "Teachers, principals, deputy superintendents — we all get extra pay if the test scores go up."

"So, do you think they went up because of you?" Adam repeated. "You're the one who sees the kids most. It must have something to do with you. I thought you were pretty great, Mrs. Gross."

"That's nice, Adam, but I was the same teacher last year, when the scores went down. It can be so many things, and not just how hard the test is. It can be the group of kids I get in my class that year. Sometimes the kids I get are a little sharper; sometimes they have more challenges. That's not me; it's who they send me. You know how I said I tried to get Jennifer? Well, suppose one year they give me three extra Jennifers. My test scores go up. Is that me? Or is that three Jennifers?"

Adam was quiet. His brain felt clogged. He felt as if someone had told him water might not be wet. "So when they print stories about scores going up in the paper — does it have anything to do with kids getting smarter and teachers teaching better?" he asked.

"I don't know," said Mrs. Gross.

"But you're the teacher," said Adam.

"I don't know," said Mrs. Gross.

The hallway was empty now as they headed out a back exit, walking toward the elementary-school playground. They had a half hour to kill before the late buses arrived.

Two mothers and their little kids — none looked older than kindergarten — were racing around from the slides to the swings to the monkey bars. The air was warm, the sun still strong, so the coeditors headed for a big oak and sat on the grass in the shade.

"I'm starved," said Adam. "Got anything else to eat?"

She didn't.

"Mind if I take a couple of quick sucks?" He pulled out his jawbreaker. "I know it kind of grosses you out."

"Not anymore," she said. "You can pretty much get used to anything."

From his pocket, he pulled out the plastic bag, which was getting really stretched from all the use, then popped in the jawbreaker.

"Anyone ever suck one down to nothing?" Jennifer asked.

Adam held up his hand to get in a few more slurps, then put it away. "Supposedly this kid in Australia got one down to marble size in nine days, then swallowed it. They claim it's a world record, but I don't know. I saw it on a blog—hard to know if you could trust it."

Jennifer nodded. "I guess if you worked on it sixteen hours a day for nine straight days—it's possible, maybe."

They were watching the little kids. One boy was flying along the monkey bars, grabbing a bar with his right hand, the next with his left until he reached the end, vaulted off, ran back, and did it again.

"That kid's good," said Jennifer. "I always had to hold on with both hands. . . ."

"You know who was great?" said Adam. "In kindergarten—Stub Keenan. You think this little guy will grow up to rig an election?" Adam felt funny, like he was watching the actual former Stub. "People change," he said softly.

"Stub got a lot bigger," said Jennifer.

"He's not that big," said Adam.

"He is," said Jennifer. "He's like the football

297

team's star linebacker. I bet he weighs forty pounds more than you."

"Great," said Adam. One of the things Adam really didn't like about Stub — he always called Adam *Big* Adam. Hilarious. Adam intended to be good and ready when they went to interview Stub about the election.

"I'm packing a weapon," said Adam.

"No," said Jennifer. "You have me."

"Right," said Adam. "I'll clobber him over the head with a coeditor."

"So here's what I started to say," said Jennifer.

Adam opened his mouth to stop her, but Jennifer grabbed his lips with her fingertips and mooshed them together. "I'm not going to let go," she said, "unless you promise to listen. . . . You promise? You have to."

"Eebyeebywooby," said Adam. It was impossible to talk when someone had your lips mooshed together. For a second, Adam thought of jerking back. Even though Jennifer had surprisingly strong fingertips — it must be all the tennis and cello — he could've gotten out of it easy.

The truth was, he didn't mind.

"I don't know," said Jennifer. "That didn't sound like 'I promise, dear wonderful Jennifer.' Is that what you were saying?'"

Adam gave her a thumbs-up and she let go.

"Don Ameche is not my boyfriend," she said.

Holy cripes. For once, Adam was at a loss for words. He'd been so sure. It seemed like that Ameche brother knew all the right moves — take girls to movies, give them tomato sauce, and stuff. Don had so much going on — all those business projects, sneaking onto the golf course at midnight, putting the wheels back on power mowers, and making big bucks. He was a pretty exciting individual. He just seemed more action-packed than Adam. The Ameche brothers and Adam all went to middle school, yet when Adam was around them, he felt so — he hated to admit this — so *young*.

"I mean, I thought we might be," said Jennifer. "And there was a little . . . you know . . . nice personal stuff. . . . But I learned something. . . ." She looked at him.

Was she waiting for him to talk? Adam didn't know what to say. It couldn't be his turn yet; she'd only said a couple of sentences. Having this talk was

Jennifer's big idea. He was just planning on saying a few words at the end and then they could get back to normal.

"It's nice when a boy takes you to a movie and asks you out for a Sunday afternoon and holds your hand . . ."

Oh gross, *gross,* why was she telling him this? He did not want to hear it. He did not want that picture in his head.

"But that doesn't mean it's going to work. You can take someone to a movie and give them nice little gifts and spend Sunday afternoon together, but it still might not add up to something special. I was wrong."

Adam had been on the verge of standing up and running home, but then he heard Jennifer say those three little words. He didn't ever remember hearing those words from her.

"I was wrong," she repeated.

"You don't want to go to movies?" asked Adam.

"Oh, I do," said Jennifer. "But not *Blood Zingers of the Purple Sage.*"

Adam had wanted to see that; he'd heard the special effects were really amazing. But he got Jennifer's point. "Too many people getting their heads cut off?" he asked.

"Pretty much the whole hour and forty-five minutes," she said.

"Sunday afternoons?" he asked.

"Great in theory," she said. "But Don wanted to go to Tooky Berry's Billiards and Paintball Emporium. He had coupons for a semiautomatic rental gun, full goggle system, and safety orientation. A three-hundred-dollar value."

Adam nodded.

"So," said Jennifer, "I just wanted you to know . . . that me and Don . . . we're still . . . but we're not . . ."

Adam nodded.

"So, that's about it," she said. "I just felt I had to say . . ."

Adam nodded.

"Not really *had* to," Jennifer said. "Wanted to say. I wanted you to know."

Adam nodded.

"Is there anything you want to say?" asked Jennifer.

She was looking at him really hard again. There was definitely something; he just wasn't sure he could. It felt a little dangerous.

"Sorry," he said.

"Sorry?" she repeated. "Sorry? You're sorry it

didn't work out with Don Ameche? Oh, God, Adam, you *are* sorry."

She stood and pulled on her backpack.

The late buses were coming up the driveway.

He ran to catch her.

"I'm not sorry," he said.

She kept walking.

"I'm not the least bit sorry," he said. "I'm glad."

She stopped.

"You are?" she said.

"I am," he said.

He was smiling.

"You are," she said. "I can tell."

He was beaming; he couldn't help it.

"Come here," she said, and she put one hand on each of his shoulders, leaned toward him, and pressing her lips against his right ear, whispered, "I'm glad you're glad." Then she yelled, "Yipes!", bolted off, and looking back over her shoulder called, "Last one's a rotten egg."

For once, he did not chase her. He did not want to lose the feel of her whisper.

chapter 19

A Boy and His Bike

Money was pouring in — everything from hundred-dollar checks donated by grown-ups to quarters, dimes, and nickels from Phoebe's daily cafeteria bead sales. Jennifer didn't have an official count yet; there were still two days until the Friday deadline, and a lot of people hadn't reported back. When she saw Adam before science class, she told him it looked like there was going to be enough to print the *Slash*, plus pay the Ameche brothers, and maybe even have a little left over.

"We can start a bank account for the *Slash* for next year," said Jennifer.

"We're having a party," said Adam.

"Adam Canfield," said Jennifer, "these people gave this money because they believe in the *Slash*. Free speech. The First Amendment, all that Constitution stuff."

"Come on," said Adam. "I remember for a fact — the unit we did on the Constitution — the right to have parties is guaranteed. Swear it is."

"Political parties," said Jennifer. "Democrats. Republicans. Not birthday parties. Not surprise parties. Not *Slash* staff parties."

"Oh, my God, you are a killer," said Adam. "Everyone works so hard — reporters have got to have a little fun. That's in the Constitution."

"Sure," said Jennifer. "Right beside birthday parties."

"Oh, yeah?" said Adam. "How about life, liberty, and the pursuit of happiness — fun, fun, fun!" He raised his hand in a *V* for *victory* sign, then dashed into class before Jennifer could appeal to the Supreme Court.

/ / / / /

Between studying for finals and goofing off when they should have been studying for finals, the *Slash* reporters finished their stories.

The coeditors read them to make sure all the big questions had been answered and the right people had been interviewed. Then they passed them on to the copy editors, who looked for problems with grammar, spelling, and sentence structure, and sent them back to Jennifer and Adam for one more read.

The last kid to see stories was Shadow, who was fond of explaining, "I find any mistakes that no one else found because these mistakes were so tricky or sometimes not so tricky." Shadow loved describing the mistakes he found to Adam. It was Shadow who noticed that Sammy had spelled Nesquik wrong. "N-e-s-q-u-i-k is chocolate milk," said Shadow. "N-e-s-q-u-i-c-k is chocolate milk in a hurry."

"Good job," said Adam.

"I know," said Shadow. "I found nine mistakes so far. The boys' lacrosse team was seven wins and six losses, not eight wins and six losses. You can't count scrimmages as wins. Scrimmages are practice games. Practice games aren't real games. Scrimmage wins aren't real wins."

"Are scrimmage losses real losses?" asked Adam.

"Good question," said Shadow. "No."

"Good job," said Adam.

"I know," said Shadow. "That's nine so far and we don't even have your story on the student-council election yet. Probably a lot of mistakes in that, too."

"Thanks," said Adam. "I appreciate the vote of confidence."

"I know," said Shadow. "Probably I'll find eleven mistakes or even twelve by the time I finish."

"Good job," said Adam.

"Maybe thirteen or maybe fourteen mistakes," said Shadow. "That's just maybe but it could be probably."

After all the stories were edited and the pages laid out, the paper would go to the printer, who would make up one copy—the proof. They planned to show that to Mrs. Quigley to be sure there were no big problems they'd missed. They didn't have to—the *Slash* was a true, independent, kid-financed paper now—but Jennifer felt they should pick one grown-up they trusted to see the paper before it went off into the world. "I don't want the Bolands suing us for a billion dollars," said Jennifer.

"How long do you think it would take Phoebe to make a billion dollars' worth of ankle bracelets?" asked Adam.

"Under a week," said Jennifer.

"She is pretty high-energy," Adam agreed.

And then, hopefully, they'd roll the presses, five hundred copies of the *Slash*, plus the new *Slash* website designed by the Ameche brothers.

From Mrs. Quigley, Jennifer got the e-mail address for Mrs. Boland's assistant. The principal did not look overjoyed. "You're investigating the Bolands again?" she asked. "Another Boland story? I'm going to have to buy us all bulletproof vests. I may have to reopen Mrs. Marris's old bomb-shelter bunker downstairs."

But she seemed calmer when Jennifer explained there was no new investigation; they were just following up on the last story.

Jennifer shot off an e-mail to the Bolands with a few questions, basically asking if they had any comment on the state investigation into buying up the Willows.

To take a little of the sting out of it, Jennifer

mentioned that they knew the state's investigation had already been reported in the *New York Times* and they were just following the *Times* story. She asked them to please let her know when they had received her e-mail.

The coeditors didn't want the Bolands complaining that the *Slash* hadn't given them a fair chance to comment.

Jennifer was surprised.

That same afternoon, Mrs. Boland's assistant, Clarence, responded, verifying that he had her questions and would get back to her. Jennifer told Adam it was a pretty normal e-mail — nothing too mean-spirited.

Adam wasn't nervous about his finals. He was a good test-taker and could usually bluff his way through any black holes in his memory.

He *was* nervous about the meeting they had coming up with Stub Keenan. The more he thought about it, the more he was certain that Stub was going to pound him out.

He and Jennifer had talked about going to Mrs.

Quigley first and telling her what their reporting had turned up. That way Mrs. Quigley might stop the election and the *Slash* editors wouldn't have to break the news to Stub.

Let Mrs. Quigley do the dirty.

Stub probably wouldn't hit Mrs. Quigley.

If he did, that really wasn't Adam's problem.

But the coeditors decided that would not be fair. What if Stub had some reasonable explanation? What if he said he was only giving the iPod downloads to kids who were his closest friends and would have voted for him anyway?

Maybe Stub did have 143 closest friends. Who knew?

They felt that going to the principal before seeing Stub would be like finding him guilty before he could give his side.

So they were going to meet with him — right after school.

Adam intended to be prepared.

In case things got violent.

He wasn't going to get caught off-guard and smacked like the time he'd been mugged for his shoveling money without fighting back.

If Stub came at him, Adam would be armed and dangerous.

He wasn't kidding.

Writing the profile on Shadow for Mrs. Stanky was turning into a nightmare. The research paper counted for half their fourth-quarter grade.

Partly he was stalled because he had too much info — he knew Shadow too well. Shadow seemed so complicated, Adam was afraid he couldn't fit everything in, didn't know what to leave out, and feared he wouldn't get it right when he put it down on paper.

Even worse: Could he do the paper without knowing the answer to what might be the biggest question in Shadow's life?

Was Shadow the baby in the diner trash?

Is that why Shadow was the way he was?

Had Mr. Johnny Stack told Adam the truth?

Adam didn't think so.

But he didn't know.

Adam kept trying to get started. He'd gone over his notes and used colored marker to underline the most important ideas and quotes. The problem was, practically every word out of Shadow's mouth was a great quote; Shadow didn't say anything the regular way. Picking the best was hard.

In big letters, at the top of the screen he'd written: THEODORE ROBERT "SHADOW" COX.

So far, that was it.

Adam would sit in front of the computer, mull, go upstairs, see what was in the refrigerator, come back down, and stare at the screen. Fifteen minutes later, he'd do it again, looking a little harder in the fridge to see if he'd missed anything.

By the fifth visit, the leftover tuna fish didn't look that bad.

His problem was not Mrs. Stanky. He was almost sure that Mrs. Stanky would never know if he left out the story of the baby in the trash. No way she had time to check every front page her students looked up at the library.

This was about writing truth. It was what Erik Forrest, the world-famous war correspondent had told Adam: don't stop until you get to the bottom of things.

Adam was sure he hadn't hit bottom yet.

How do you write a profile when you can't answer the most important question in a person's life?

He thought about going back to the fridge, but he really couldn't bear looking at that bowl of tuna again.

He slipped into the garage and took out his new bike. His dad had surprised him — it wasn't his birthday or Christmas or anything.

His dad said they'd waited long enough.

He said Adam wouldn't be a boy forever.

It was a brand-new, creamy turquoise, Kelly Byrne cruiser with thick whitewall tires and a big, tan-brown seat. Adam loved just looking at it. He loved running his hands over the wide fenders. The curve of the handlebars was perfect. He liked feeling the thickness of the leather seat; no matter how far he rode, his butt never got sore.

When he pedaled hard, the cruiser made a soft whirring noise and he knew no one would ever catch him.

He rode to the back path, turning and heading east along the river, racing past the civic association boathouse where the *Slash* staff had held their secret late-night meeting last fall.

He passed the dock where Jennifer had kicked

312

him really hard for no good reason and the sand dune where the two of them had lain side by side looking at the stars.

That was nice.

As he biked by people, he glanced away. He didn't want anyone saying hi to him, and pulled his baseball cap low. He wished he could ride forever across this great nation. He wished that everywhere he went, people would know about him, but not know who he was.

The world's most famous unknown biker.

He kept riding, past where the houses stopped, past the docks and beaches, to where the riverbanks changed from sand dunes and dune grass that rattled in the wind to bright green swampy marsh where sea-gulls and terns and egrets lived. He could see the tall poles and wooden platforms that the conservation center had built to give the ospreys a place to nest so they'd lay their eggs and wouldn't become extinct.

He stopped to pick a cattail, ripping apart the fat pod on top and blowing the wispy filaments into the wind.

Then he picked another cattail and, holding it upside down by the fat pod, turned it into a sword.

Biking on, he was unafraid, whipping the cattail

through the air and slaying every type of foul beast known to man, including Stub Keenan, demonstrating martial arts moves that Jennifer never even knew existed.

He loved his bike.

And that made him think of his old bike being stolen.

And that made him think of the story the *Slash* had done on bike thieves.

And all at once he knew exactly what he had to do to finish his profile of Shadow, and he raised his cattail high and let out a mighty war whoop.

chapter 20

Hitting Bottom

On Thursday, they had a half day of school. In the afternoon, instead of regular classes, there were extra-help sessions for final exams.

Adam told his parents he planned to go, and technically this was true.

He did *plan* to go. He definitely had the evidence of *planning* to go; it was there in black and white, right on his To-Do list. At breakfast, he just happened to leave the list out on the kitchen table while having a bowl of that cereal with the dried strawberries that brighten up when you pour milk on them.

And his dad just happened to notice the list while Adam was hurrying to get his stuff together for the bike ride to school:

Thurs. Ext Help: LA, WH, M, Sci.

"Adam, you forgot this," said his dad, who was standing by the front door to say good-bye. "You know, you're really growing up. I'm very proud of you. We used to have to remind you of everything. Come here, big guy."

"I have to go, Dad," Adam said. "I'm biking. It's getting late."

"Oh, Adam," said his dad. "Life is short. There is always time for a hug." He grabbed Adam and gave him a real big squisher.

"Have a great day," his father said.

"Right, Dad."

Adam loved his dad, he really did, and he probably should have just told him the truth. There was nothing terrible. It was just — the truth took so much time, there were so many factual pieces to it, and you really could wear yourself out making sure everything got in there where it was supposed to go. Plus, if you didn't say it exactly right, if you forgot one little stupid fact, your parents could start yelling and ordering you around, and then you were in actual trouble for no good reason.

He got home around noon.

It was fun being alone in the house so early in the day.

He got the phone number off the calendar in the kitchen. His dad had written it down and circled it in marker; he must have called two dozen times since the bike was stolen.

It took Adam three tries.

Twice, the man was on the other line. Adam left messages with his phone number. But Adam wasn't going to wait forever. He couldn't. He had to get this paper done. It was due tomorrow.

The third time, Adam asked if he could just hold until the other call was finished.

He kept watching the clock. It was more than five minutes; he worried that he had been hung up on, but the dial tone did not come on.

"Yeah," a voice said finally. "Detective Cole."

Adam explained that he was the one whose bike had been stolen.

"Listen, kid, you got any idea how many—?"

"By the grafitti boy," said Adam. "My dad talked to you—"

"Oh right, right," said the detective. "That's . . . let me see, I got the file . . . Canfield. I was at your house. River Path, right? Your dad and I talk a couple times a week. We're getting to be great old buds. Very persistent, your father. Like I told him, I really got nada until we go to court. That's about a month—"

"No," said Adam. "That's not why I'm calling. I've got a problem and I didn't really know—actually I thought you might know."

"Kid, if this ain't an open case, I really don't got time. I'm on the clock."

"It's just—I remember you said, like, twenty-five years you're a detective," said Adam. "And it's this old case, I think it was pretty famous—I need to know what happened."

"Hell, kid, you going to ask me about a bike stolen twenty-five years ago?"

"No, no," said Adam. "It's not a bike. It's a baby. Well, it was a baby. A baby left in the trash at a diner . . . Big Frank's—"

There was quiet on the line, and for an instant, Adam feared they'd been disconnected. "Third precinct," the detective said at last. "Out Route 197. Big Frank's All-Nite. That was a huge stink. Lot of heat. Big stories. That's a long time ago, kid — you probably wasn't even born."

"Yeah," said Adam, "just about."

"So what's the deal here?" asked the detective. "You know something?"

"I might," said Adam.

"You might?" said the detective.

"Uh-huh," said Adam.

"This isn't some joke?"

"No," said Adam.

"Hold on, kid," said the detective. "Just hold on a second. . . ." The phone went quiet again, then the detective asked, "You mind if I tape this, kid? Our conversation? You don't care, do you?"

Adam didn't. But this was weird. Why would anyone want to tape him?

He asked Adam to state his first and last names slowly and spell them, just so they'd have it for the record.

"OK, Canfield, what do you know?"

Adam explained he had this school project to do a profile. And he had to go to the library and read the microfilm, and he'd gone back to that date —

319

"Look, Canfield, can we get to the point?" said the detective. "You know something about this case?"

"I might," said Adam.

"You might?" said the detective.

"I might," said Adam. "I'm not sure."

"You going to tell me?" asked the detective. "This ain't a guessing game, Canfield. We ain't playing twenty questions. I deal in information. Solid information. I think I mentioned I'm on the clock. You got a name for the mother?"

"It might be Cox," said Adam. "See, there's this kid—"

"That's C-o-x?" asked the detective. "OK, good. This is unbelievable. Now we're getting someplace. So how do you know this?"

"Well," said Adam. "I know the birth date of the kid. And this kid has the same birth date."

"Wait now, Canfield. So this Cox lady had a baby on the same date that the baby was found in the diner bathroom? At the All-Nite?"

"Exactly," said Adam. "That's why I think it's him."

"Geez," said the detective. "My God. This could be it. Well, where do we find this Cox woman? We'd love to . . . you know . . . talk to her. . . ."

"Oh, I don't have a clue," said Adam.

"OK," said the detective. "Let's see—do you know someone who does?"

"I thought *you* might," said Adam. "That's why I was calling. I thought maybe you found her. Not you exactly. The police. And you'd know about it. And might be able to tell me."

"Oh, no, Canfield," said the detective. "Why do you think I'm asking you all these questions? We'd love to find her. So, how do you know it's her? Who told you?"

"No one told me," said Adam. "I just figured it out myself."

"Geez, kid . . . you figured it out yourself? But no one told you? . . . You're not hearing voices or nothing are you, Canfield? Look, I seen your house, I met your folks. They seemed pretty stable. Didn't seem like they'd have a wack-job kid."

"Not me," said Adam. "I'm not the wack job. It's Shadow—Theodore Cox. Actually, he's not a wack job, either. He's just . . . kind of different, you know? I don't know exactly what it is, but he's in Special Ed classes, 107A, like he might be a little developmentally disabled . . ."

"Canfield, I'm thinking of coming over there and

arresting you for harassing a police officer — namely me," said the detective. "This ain't no joke. This case has been in our cold case file — it's one of the biggest unsolved crimes in Tremble history. You better not be making this stuff up."

"No," said Adam. "I swear. I'd never do that — did you say unsolved?"

"I did," said the detective. "Unsolved. We never found the woman who left that baby. You didn't know that?"

"Never found her?" asked Adam.

"No," said the detective. "Why do you think I'm asking her name?"

"You're asking me?" said Adam. "I was asking you. I know the kid. Not the mother."

Adam heard a loud bang and without thinking screamed, "Don't shoot!"

The detective laughed. "That's funny," he said. "I was just testing to see how hard I could bang the phone on the desk and not break it — they make 'em pretty good. Look, Canfield, I'm at the point, I don't have a freakin' clue what we're talking about anymore. Why don't you back up and tell me exactly what you know about this case and why you're calling. Go ahead. Nice and slow. I promise not to get upset."

"Should I go back to the school project part?" asked Adam.

"You go back to wherever you need to go," said the detective.

So he did. Adam explained about Mrs. Stanky's project profiling a kid, about the microfilm, and about seeing the page-one story on the baby found in the diner bathroom. "The story said a baby left like that could suffer brain damage and stuff," said Adam. "And this boy I'm writing about — Theodore Cox — his nickname is Shadow, that's what everyone calls him — like I explained, he's in Special Ed. And he lives in foster care. He doesn't have any parents. And I figured, if a mother did that to her baby, they'd take the baby away and put him in foster care. So I thought maybe that baby had grown up to be Shadow — born on the same day and everything. And really, that's what I wanted to know. Is that baby in the story my friend Shadow? That's all. I'm sorry, I wasn't trying to bother anybody. I just wanted to . . . you know . . . find the truth . . . I didn't mean to upset you, especially when you're on the clock and everything."

The line was quiet.

"Detective Cole," Adam said. "Is it him?"

"No, it's not," said the detective.

Adam waited, but the detective was quiet.

"How do you know?" asked Adam.

"I just know. Your friend is not that baby."

"I'm really sorry," said Adam. "Someone else told me the same thing—I'd just like to know, for my own mind, how you know? Please."

"It's just not," said the detective.

"Do you know the real kid?" asked Adam. "I'm not asking his name. I just kind of wonder—you know, what he's like. Did he turn out to be normal and everything?"

"No, he didn't," said the detective.

"Well, what's he like?" asked Adam.

"He's not like anything," said the detective. "That baby died."

chapter 21

Armed and Dangerous

"They want to meet us by the boys' baseball field," said Jennifer.

"Way over there?" said Adam. "That's where they want to do the interview? Great."

"It's not like that," said Jennifer.

"Oh, yes, it is," said Adam. "They must know. They have to know. Otherwise why would they? Have you ever done an interview for the *Slash* out in back of the school?"

"Sure," said Jennifer, "when I interviewed the seventh-grade softball coach —"

"When you weren't covering sports?" Adam asked.

Jennifer seemed to be racking her brain, but Adam wasn't buying it.

"You meet someone out back if you're going to fight," said Adam. "Not when you're looking for a friendly exchange of ideas."

"We're going to be fine," said Jennifer. "Give me a little credit."

"Fine," said Adam.

"Fine," repeated Jennifer. "Really."

Adam nodded, but he didn't mean it. Jennifer didn't get how vicious boys could be. Most girls didn't. She'd never been punched in the nose hard by someone who really meant it. The hurting wasn't the worst part. It was feeling like you were going to throw up and the tears coming into your eyes and you couldn't even see straight to smack the jerk back.

They'd been waiting by the backstop about ten minutes when they saw two boys walking across the fields.

"Who's the other one?" asked Adam. "Billy Cutty? The campaign manager?"

Jennifer nodded.

This was great. He was bigger, too.

"So, Big Adam," said Stub, "how's it going? Ever get your bike back? I've been keeping my eyes open."

"Not yet," said Adam, "but thanks." Adam felt uneasy; he hadn't expected Stub to be nice.

"Heard you wanted to see us," said Stub. "Something about a story on the election. That right, Billy?"

"That's it, Stub," said Billy. "That's what Jennifer told me."

"Hey, I don't know you," Stub said to Jennifer, and he held out his hand to shake hers. "Wow. I always thought kids on the student paper, were, you know, kind of nerdy — no offense, but boy, I was wrong. You'll want one of these." He motioned for Billy to give Jennifer a Prez Stub button.

Oh, God, Adam could feel it; he was blushing again. Why wouldn't his body just do the normal stuff and leave him alone? Why was his blood in such a hurry to rush to his face? Why couldn't it stay under his neck where it belonged, slosh around in his chest like everyone else's?

He had a terrible thought — if he got a bloody nose, would the extra blood make it bloodier?

"You OK, Big Adam?" said Stub. "You're looking a little tomatoey over there. You two aren't . . . Hey, I'm sorry . . . I'm certainly not . . ."

"Stub's just friendly with everybody," said Billy Cutty. "It's nothing personal. Just turning on his campaign face."

"That's it," said Stub. "Got to shine it on everyone. Everyone's a vote. Tuesday's the biggie."

They all nodded.

There was an awkward quiet.

"You know, I've got a question," said Stub. "A little confusion is what it is. Billy tells me you're doing a story—I thought the *Sash*—"

"*Slash*," said Jennifer.

"Right, right, the *Slatch*—I thought it got shut down or something. By the principal? Quigs did the dirty I heard. That right? You guys got in some trouble or some deal?"

"Something like that," said Jennifer. "But we figured how to keep it going. It's definitely coming out. Last week of school."

"Cool," said Stub. "When I win, I'll give you guys a nice interview. Fill you in on my plans for next year. Ice-cream parlor in the cafeteria. McDonald's for lunch. New skateboard park. Make a nice front-page story. 'PREZ STUB SAYS BIG CHANGES COMING!'"

"That's great," said Jennifer. "It's good to have all that in the paper, for the record, so when we

328

really do get the stuff, people will know whose idea it was."

"Prez Stub," said Stub.

Right, thought Adam.

Adam was especially looking forward to the roller coaster in the boys' bathroom.

"That cover it?" asked Stub. "We got stuff to do. Election's coming fast. Can't let up. Never can get enough votes, hey, Billy?"

Billy Cutty nodded.

"We're trying for a shutout," said Stub. "Heh, heh. Anyway, nice talking. Don't forget, Prez Stub!"

"Ah, Stub," said Jennifer. "We have a few questions—"

"Sorry, Jan," Stub said. "GTG. We'll do it after the election. Date?" And he turned to leave.

"Stub," called Jennifer, but he kept walking.

"Ah, Stub," said Billy Cutty, "I told Jennifer we'd do this. I think she has something else."

Stub looked at Billy. "You think she has something else?" said Stub. "Did I hear that? You think she has something else? You're telling me? If I remember, I'm the one running for president. Do I have that right?"

"Stub, take it easy," said Billy. "Jennifer's cool. She's in my math class. I just told her—"

"Ahhhh," said Stub. "Well, maybe you should have told me before you told her."

"What are you talking about?" said Billy. "You're acting crazy."

"Oh, I'm acting crazy?" said Stub. "This isn't even a school paper anymore. They got shut down. Lying or stealing or something, for all I know. None of this counts. I don't got to talk to them."

He turned to walk off, and Billy grabbed his arm.

"Drop dead, asshole," said Stub, and he pushed Billy hard to the ground.

Adam stood frozen in place while Jennifer bent over to help Billy. "Are you all right?" she asked him. "Are you bleeding? You are. Your hand."

"I'm sorry," Billy said.

This was weird, thought Adam — there was definitely something big going on here, but he did not have time to sort it out. He had worked too hard on this story. He had planned everything down to the last second. He had figured how to get those kids to talk to him and tell him the truth about the downloads. Who else would have pulled that off? And the funny thing was — he didn't even care about the stupid election. It wouldn't make one bit of difference who was president — the grown-ups ran the school.

The only way they were getting McDonald's for lunch was if they skipped school and went to the drive-through.

On the other hand, the principle of it pissed him off. Buying the stupid election? What a jerk.

Adam ran after him. He was sure Stub knew what they were up to, but they hadn't asked him a single question. They had to at least tell him what they were up to. They had to tell him what their investigation was about. They had to give him a chance to answer — those were the rules.

Adam knew what was going to happen. He knew exactly what Stub's answer would be. It didn't matter.

"Stub," he said, catching up, "wait."

Stub kept walking fast.

Adam fell into step beside him.

Adam was sure of it: everything was about to explode. But in that last calm moment, he had the strangest thought. He knew Stub was about to beat the crap out of him, but for some ridiculous reason, he felt sorry for Stub. Walking straight ahead, pretending nothing was going on, when Stub knew full well that he was about to be called out for what he did. He couldn't control it, and he was hoping he

331

could make it all disappear by just walking fast and looking straight ahead.

"We got evidence that you gave kids free iPod downloads to vote for you!" yelled Adam.

Stub stopped, then turned to face Adam. "Oh, you got evidence, huh? I can't give friends downloads? Big Adam got a problem with that?"

"We got a list — 143 kids. They all friends?" asked Adam. "That your answer?"

"Really?" said Stub. "Can I see that list, or am I supposed to trust you?"

Adam nodded. That was fair. Stub was entitled. Adam pulled a copy of the list from his back pocket and handed it to Stub. He had his notebook and pen ready to get a comment.

Stub ripped the paper into several pieces. "Sorry," said Stub. "My fingers slipped."

"Right," said Adam, making a note. "So that's your answer? Anything else?"

"This," said Stub, and he knocked the notebook and pen out of Adam's hand and, raising his arms, lunged toward Adam. Stub was trying to get him in a headlock, and his right arm brushed Adam's head, but Adam twisted, ducked, and just squirmed loose.

Stub pivoted back toward him.

"Stop it!" someone screamed. Was that Jennifer? She sounded so far away.

Adam's hand was in his pocket. He'd had enough. He was sick and tired of being pushed around. He'd stood there like an idiot when those high-school kids had mugged him last winter and taken his shoveling money. He'd let some jerk steal his bike right from in front of the house. Not again. No way. He pulled out the plastic bag. He gave it one quick, hard, tight twirl high over his head. And then, just as Stub straightened up and raised his arms to lunge again, Adam leaned toward him and whipped that plastic bag with the hard white sphere inside as if it were a lead ball and chain wielded by a gladiator in ancient times — smacking it straight into Stub's stomach.

There was a gasp.

The next thing Adam knew, Stub was on the ground, on his back, sucking air.

"Was that a slingshot?" asked a boy.

"Jawbreaker," said Adam. He looked around. There was a crowd gathering; kids had built-in radar for finding fights.

Adam leaned over Stub and said, "Is he OK?"

"Yeah," said another kid. "Looks like he just got the wind knocked out of him. He'll be on his feet in a minute."

"I didn't start it," Adam said.

Someone had his arm and was pulling him away. It was Jennifer. "Come on," she said. "We have to go. Before any grown-ups show up." She turned to Billy and said, "You'll make sure Stub's OK?"

Billy nodded. "I really am sorry," he said. "I didn't think this . . ."

"I know," said Jennifer.

She had Adam by the arm and was leading him toward the street on the far side of the school.

"I didn't start it," said Adam.

"Shhhh," said Jennifer. "Let's just get out of here."

"Is he OK?" asked Adam.

chapter 22

The Acting Principal's Office

"So tell me again," said Mrs. Quigley. "You're saying Stub Keenan has rigged the election? And how exactly do you know this?"

"We know it one-hundred-percent exactly," said Adam. "It's definitely exactly."

"That's not what she means. . . ." said Jennifer.

"It's completely exactly," said Adam.

"Adam," said Jennifer, "would you . . ."

"I would say one hundred percent, completely and totally exactly, no question about it, really totally, definitely exactly to the max, right up to the tippity top of everything. We know it. We do."

Jennifer had her head in her hands.

"Are you OK?" Adam asked.

"Jennifer, be patient. He's a great reporter," said Mrs. Quigley. "Just a bit literal—it's part of the greatness; he expects people to mean what they say."

"What?" said Adam. "What did I do?"

Jennifer tried again. "Mrs. Quigley doesn't mean 'How sure are you that the election is rigged.' She means, 'Tell me how you know it's rigged.'"

"Tell you?" said Adam. "Why would I tell you? You know as much as I do. Jennifer, get a grip."

"Tell *her*," said Jennifer, pointing to Mrs. Quigley, who gave Adam a little wave for emphasis.

"Oh," said Adam. "Why didn't—?"

They told Mrs. Quigley about the secret list of downloads Jennifer had obtained, about the three kids who admitted to Adam with their names that they got free downloads for their votes, and about what Stub had said when Adam confronted him—although Adam left out the part about the interview being done under tense conditions in deep center field.

Mrs. Quigley wanted every detail; she examined the list of 143 students and asked how they got it.

"Can't tell you," Jennifer said. "I'm not being

336

impolite, Mrs. Quigley, but it was given to me by a secret source."

"Not a bad source," said Mrs. Quigley. "That's quite a list. Sounds like Brutus did Stub in. Poor Stub."

Brutus? Adam was trying to think; he couldn't remember any kid at Harris named Brutus. The name was familiar though. Brutus . . . Brutus . . . Something in World History with Mr. Brooks last fall?

"And what did Stub say when you asked him?" said Mrs. Quigley.

"I can give you the exact words," said Adam. He pulled out his notebook and flipped the pages.

"Oh, my gosh," said Mrs. Quigley. "What is that all over your notebook?"

"Just a little mud," said Adam.

"A little mud?" said Mrs. Quigley. "You could plant corn in that notebook."

Adam scraped off a chunk of hard mud and read Stub's words from his notes: "'I can't give friends downloads? Big Adam got a problem with that?'"

Mrs. Quigley nodded. "That is an admission of sorts," she said. "I assume you're Big Adam?" She was quiet. "And I assume he didn't attempt to claim these were his 143 best friends?" Again she was quiet.

Finally, she said, "OK, I'll have to get Stub in here and listen to his side, but assuming your reporting holds up and he's as guilty as he sounds, I'm going to put off this election until the new school year. There isn't enough time left this year. It's going to be the new principal's problem."

She took down Jennifer's e-mail address. "I'll send you my official decision and a quote for the story after I talk to the Keenan boy," she said. "I don't know what I'm going to do with him. Twenty-five years I'm a principal and I think I've seen everything, but I haven't. Anyway, I guess that's it."

Adam couldn't believe it. He'd done it. He was seconds away from being free and clear. Not one word from Mrs. Quigley about the fight. He'd been so worried. Every time the phone had rung at home Thursday night, he'd been sure it was the school, calling to tell his parents he'd been suspended. His parents would kill him. Especially his mom. And especially his dad, too.

At school on Friday, every time his class was interrupted by a call from the office, he was sure they were summoning him to his holy grave.

By the time Jennifer had led Adam away from the

338

ball field, a lot of kids had seen it, and each would tell his hundred closest friends.

He felt so lucky. It seemed impossible: Not one kid had said anything that leaked into the grown-up world.

Adam wanted to dance out of Mrs. Quigley's office. Correction: he wanted to fly out of that office. He felt like summer was on the other side of that door, and here he came.

But if there was one thing his many years as a reporter had taught him, it was to hold it all in until you were free and clear. Never tip your hand. Patience.

The coeditors thanked the acting principal and said they'd get her a copy of the *Slash* to read after the proof came back from the printer.

They were standing. Adam was playing it cool now; he was in no rush. What did he have to hide? Slow-and-steady Eddie, that was him.

He let Jennifer go in front of him. Mr. Manners. What was the rush? She was out the door and so was —

"Adam."

Did she mean him?

She couldn't; it was too late. Time had run out.

"Yes, you. Could I speak to you for a minute?"

"Do you want me to . . ." Adam said, and motioned toward Jennifer out in the main office, by Mrs. Rose at the front counter, safe from all harm.

"No," said Mrs. Quigley. "Just you. Please close the door."

Adam sat back down. The room felt so big and empty without Jennifer. Until that moment, he hadn't realized how hard the seats were in the acting principal's office. He couldn't get his butt comfortable, which made him remember how great his butt felt on his new bike and the thick, soft tan leather seat, which made him remember how wonderful it was to be on that bike, free, riding along the river, which reminded him how unfree he was at this very moment and how his unfreedom was only likely to increase.

"Young man, you know that fighting is a very serious offense," said Mrs. Quigley.

Adam nodded.

"Do you have anything to say?"

Adam didn't. He thought of saying this was unfair, the buzzer had gone off, the game was over, they were out the door, time had expired—but he was sure Mrs. Quigley would not buy it. He figured his best strategy was to say as little as possible and try to figure out what Mrs. Quigley knew. Maybe she was talking about another fight. Maybe she was talking about fighting in general, not any special case of fighting on the baseball field, just everyday normal fighting. Maybe she just wanted to give him a story for the *Slash* about the dangers of fighting for anyone, anywhere, at any time, not just the kind of fighting that happened Thursday afternoon with Stub Keenan.

Adam would be delighted to write that story.

"Did you start it?" she asked.

This was really going badly.

Adam shook his head no.

"That's what I heard," she said. "However, it seems that you finished it."

Mrs. Quigley stared at him, but when he didn't say anything, she stood and began pacing. "Adam, I want to tell you a story," she said. She told him about her oldest son, and how when he was in third grade, there was a bigger kid on the school bus who always sat beside him, a supposed friend, and every day, when the bus went around this same curve on this same street in this same neighborhood, the kid would lean into the curve and slam her son against the inside wall of the bus. She figured this out because she noticed him in the bathtub one night with big black-and-blues on his right arm and right thigh. She wanted her son to tell the bus driver, but he wouldn't, and she offered to call the school herself, but he begged her not to. "So I told him that sometimes the only way you can get a creep like that to stop is to whack him back."

Until that moment, the honest truth was that Adam had only been half listening. But suddenly he was all ears. Whack him back? Yes! What a great principal! What a great principle!

Mrs. Quigley said, "I see I got your attention."

"Did he whack him back?" asked Adam.

"He didn't," she said. "He liked that option. He was like you, no 'fraidy cat, but he worried that if he whacked him back, he'd get in trouble at school. And I told him he probably would, but I said that when the school called, I wouldn't be mad, that I'd tell them the truth and that he'd take his punishment, and we'd move on."

"He didn't whack him?" asked Adam. "So what happened?"

"You know," said Mrs. Quigley, "I don't know how they worked it out, but eventually, when the two got older, they were pretty good friends, even though I couldn't stand the sight of that boy, and I wanted to whack him myself, even after he grew up and became a doctor. A real jerk."

Adam couldn't tell if this story was good news or bad news. Was the point to whack or not to whack?

"So, you're saying I should *not* have whacked Stub back when he hit me?" asked Adam.

"No," said Mrs. Quigley. "I'm saying even if it's right to whack, you have to expect consequences. And for better or worse, you're sitting with me, Harris Middle School's consequences chairperson. I'll be honest, Adam, what worries me most—I heard you used a slingshot. That's a weapon. That's assault."

"No slingshot," said Adam.

"Some kind of nunchucky thing," Mrs. Quigley said.

Adam shook his head. He pulled out his jaw-breaker.

"Oh, my God," she said, "how does that work?"

Adam untwisted the bag and popped the jaw-breaker into his mouth. He took several slurps before popping it back out. It felt good to get a mid-day sugar upload. "It's pretty simple," he said. "You just pop it in and suck."

Mrs. Quigley was sitting again. She was doodling on a piece of paper. Adam took a peek — it looked like daisies with human faces in the middle. He hadn't realized that principals doodled.

"This one's definitely not in the principal's manual," she said. "Let me feel that thing." Adam handed over the plastic bag and Mrs. Quigley squeezed it. "It's hard," she said.

Adam nodded. "That's why I was careful," he said. "I had to get the exact spot."

"The exact spot?"

"Want me to show you?" said Adam, standing and heading toward Mrs. Quigley. "Everyone's stomach—"

"Adam," said Mrs. Quigley. "Show me on you."

"But then you won't be able to feel it," said Adam.

"It's OK," said Mrs. Quigley. "I'll just follow along."

Adam took his right hand and pushed it into the middle of his stomach. When he found the right spot, his mouth popped open. "That's it," he said.

"It's the exact spot where you get the wind knocked out of you."

"Really?" she said.

He watched Mrs. Quigley push in her own stomach in several places.

"Higher up," said Adam. "It's kind of in the middle, halfway between your belly button and ribs."

Finally, Mrs. Quigley's mouth popped open.

"That's it," Adam said. "You got it. Good job."

"How do you know that?" asked Mrs. Quigley.

"I just figured it out one day, feeling around my stomach," said Adam.

Mrs. Quigley was doodling again. "What am I going to do with you?" she asked without looking up.

Adam shrugged. He didn't care much anymore. He was getting too worn out. He just wanted to be finished. It was a lot of pressure, sitting so long, alone, in the principal's office. His head was pounding, and his brain juices were dried up. What was the worst she could do to him? Throw him in prison? At least he'd get a rest.

"Look, Mrs. Quigley, I got to tell you, whatever you have to do, it's OK. I'm ready to be punished.

All I can say is, I really was afraid Stub was going to beat the crap out of me. I tried to figure a way to stop him, so I could just get out alive. I wasn't going to hit him in the head with a jawbreaker. I didn't want to give him brain damage. I didn't want to break his kneecaps, so I thought I'd take a chance and try to knock the wind out of him. . . ."

"Do you knock the wind out of a lot of people?" Mrs. Quigley asked. "You seem pretty good at it."

"First time," said Adam.

Mrs. Quigley was smiling. He took a peek; her daisies had little smiley faces, too.

"Plus the other thing—" said Adam, but he stopped.

"Plus what?" asked Mrs. Quigley.

"Plus nothing, Mrs. Quigley. That's pretty much it."

"Plus what, Adam?"

He hesitated; he didn't know if he could trust those smiling daisies.

"Plus, those kids mugged me for my shoveling money last winter," he finally said, "and I got my bike stolen. If I got beat up again—that's pretty much it. Every kid would think I was a wuss. They go after you. Like you said. In that story about your son."

346

The acting principal pulled a tissue out of the box on her desk and blew her nose. It seemed like she was going to ask him something else.

But then she just thanked him and said he could go.

He got up. "Mrs. Quigley," he said, "what are you going to do to me?"

"Adam, I haven't a clue. But don't you worry about it. Nothing too bad. You just finish up that newspaper. Show everybody." And she pressed in her stomach and smiled at him.

chapter 23

Finished

The coeditors worked right up to the last minute finishing the paper. They'd get what they thought was a final comment from someone for a story, and then, because that supposedly final comment turned out to be not final enough, they had to get an even more final comment, or they needed to find someone to explain the supposedly final comment or the comment about the supposedly final comment.

Good reporting was way too much work. Sometimes, Adam fantasized about giving it all up and doing a blog where he could spend his time shooting out opinions based on other people's reporting. That would be the easy life, merrily blogging his days away right along with everyone else in America.

Unfortunately, he couldn't do it.

That wasn't him.

For better or stinking worse, he was a reporter, destined to roam the earth uncovering cold, hard facts.

They decided to play the lead story *huge*, at the top, stretching across two-thirds of the front page, with the biggest headline since they'd been coeditors of the *Slash:*

WE'RE STILL HERE!!!
STAFF RAISES MONEY TO PRINT *SLASH*!
STATE INVESTIGATES BOLANDS!

Adam and Jennifer had argued about how many exclamation points to put after *We're Still Here.* Adam wanted at least a dozen. Jennifer said one was plenty. She went online, found the *New York Times* stylebook, and e-mailed the entry on exclamation points to Adam: "In news writing the exclamation point is rarely needed," the stylebook said. "When overused the exclamation point loses impact."

See? she e-mailed him.

Adam wrote back:

That's ridiculous!!!!!
This is big news!!!!!!!!!!!!
A bunch of kids put out our own newspaper all by
ourselves!!
!!
!!

In the end, Jennifer negotiated him down to what Adam kept calling "three measly exclamation points."

The student council non-election was the off-lead of the paper, running on the top left of the front page.

ELECTION OFF
VOTES FOR TUNES?
IPOD SCANDAL ROCKS HARRIS

The statement Mrs. Quigley had e-mailed to Jennifer was very carefully worded and much longer than they'd expected. Even though their story named Stub, Mrs. Quigley did not. The acting principal said that for privacy reasons she couldn't identify the student involved, but for short, she'd refer to "him/her" as student 916154. Mrs. Quigley said that when questioned, 916154 admitted having given many fellow students free iPod downloads, and Mrs. Quigley had concluded there were so many involved—at least 143—they couldn't possibly all be 916154's friends. Mrs. Quigley noted that 916154 claimed that no one had to vote for him/her, it was a free country, and 916154 said he/she didn't think he/she had done anything wrong.

The acting principal wrote that since middle-school students were at an age when they were still learning to make ethical choices, still figuring out right from wrong, she was going to use this as a teaching opportunity rather than a disciplinary matter. And then she said in her twenty-five years as a principal, this wasn't the first time she'd seen a case of kids trying to win votes by doing improper favors. Many, many years ago, she said, there had been a candidate for recording secretary who let younger girls sit in the back of the school bus with her in exchange for their votes. Mrs. Quigley said this girl had gone on to be a very successful pharmacist, filling many prescriptions that helped sick people get well, and so it was clear that middle-school students could learn from their mistakes.

At the end of Mrs. Quigley's note was a paragraph marked, "Off the record/Not for publication/Private correspondence."

Mrs. Quigley wrote: *Coeditors: I told 916154 that I was cutting him/her a big break by not suspending him/her and that if I heard that he/she bothered you/ you in any way because of your/your story, I myself would personally come out of retirement to deal with him/her in this matter. He/she assured me that he/ she understood and would stay away from you/you.*

Jennifer felt better after reading Mrs. Quigley's note, but not Adam. "Doesn't mean a thing," he said. "He'll come at me again. A kid like Stub is not going to forget getting knocked down in front of the whole school."

"I don't know," said Jennifer. "I was talking to Billy — he said Stub was pretty shook up from his meeting with Mrs. Quigley."

"You seem awfully buddy-buddy with Billy Cutty," said Adam.

"We're in math together," said Jennifer.

"No," said Adam. "It's more than that. He was

your secret source, wasn't he? He gave you that list of free iPod downloads."

"Oh, come on," said Jennifer. "That's ridiculous. Billy was Stub's campaign manager. He'd be the last—"

"No, he wouldn't," Adam said. "The way I figure it, Billy and Stub have been buddies forever, play the same sports. Stub decides to take over the school, Billy's a good guy, he agrees to help, and then, when he's in it up to his ears, he realizes what a jerk Stub is and feels guilty. It was Billy, wasn't it? He gave you the list."

"Adam Canfield," said Jennifer, "even if it were true, and it's not, you know reporters can't give up their secret sources. You're the one who always says that before revealing a source, you'd walk through fire, wrestle with alligators, swallow a tub of poison."

"I never said that," said Adam.

"Well, you should have," said Jennifer.

The story on the state test getting easier was going to run across the middle of the front page, but they were having lots of problems with it.

Jennifer had sent an e-mail to the state education department, describing the results of the *Slash* investigation and asking for a response.

She got an e-mail back that was twelve long paragraphs, single-spaced.

The last paragraph said, *Bottom line: The same scale score always represents the same achievement level of the State Learning Standards per state education law, statute 324.67 section 2(d) revised 279.12 (t).*

Adam could not believe it. "That's the bottom line?" he said to Jennifer. "That's the worst bottom line I ever heard of. A bottom line is three words: 'We screwed up.' Or, 'I killed him.' This is way too many lines for a bottom line. Do we even know for a fact this is English?"

"It is," said Jennifer. "I checked every word online, and it's definitely English."

"Just because every word is English doesn't mean the sentence is," said Adam.

Jennifer nodded. "True bagels evergreen," she said.

They were dying to be done, but agreed they needed to go back to Dr. Duke for a translation. Once again, Mrs. Quigley helped set it up. They met during lunch Monday on the school tennis courts, which were empty at that hour and were surrounded by a fence with green mesh, so no one could look inside.

Adam could not remember seeing very many adults as happy as Dr. Duke after they showed her the response from the state. It was like watching Mrs. Ameche's Ha-Ha dance. Dr. Duke kept saying, "You did it, you did it."

"We did what?" asked Jennifer.

"They admitted it!" yelled Dr. Duke.

"They admitted it?" asked Jennifer.

"Where?" asked Adam. "You mean the part about 324.67 section 2(d)?" Adam thought maybe that was some secret code of surrender under the Geneva Convention.

"No, no, no," said Dr. Duke. She showed them. There, buried ten paragraphs in, was this sentence: "'Because of varying levels of difficulty of the questions on the two exams, students had to answer a few more questions correctly in this year's test than last year's test and get more raw points to get the same scaled score.'"

Dr. Duke looked up triumphantly, but the coeditors still were lost. "Don't you see?" she said. "Oh, my God, I have been doing this too long. I actually understand the state education department. But it's good news for you, my dear *Slash*ingtons, very good news. They have surrendered to the *Slash*. They are admitting that this year's test is easier! And they're claiming they scaled this year's scores tougher to make this year's scores and last year's scores comparable. Bottom line: they obviously scaled them way too easy this year, since everyone did ten percentage points better than last year. Get it?"

Adam sort of did, but he certainly didn't feel good enough to do the Ha-Ha. This was way too complicated. "Dr. Duke," he said, "no offense, but any chance you could give us a bottom line that's little enough to actually fit on one single line? These fat bottom lines are really wearing us out."

Dr. Duke was quiet, then said, "State secret to better test scores: easier tests."

Adam ran that through his head a few times and liked it. So did Jennifer. Dr. Duke had given them their headline. It wasn't three words, but it was a respectable bottom line. Still, he didn't feel like doing the Ha-Ha. "How are we ever going to explain this in a story?" he asked her.

"You're going to quote Dr. Duke," said Dr. Duke.

"But I thought you couldn't be quoted," said Adam.

"I couldn't," she said. "But that was before you did all this great reporting and got the state to admit it."

"But didn't you say they shoot the messenger?" said Adam.

"They do," said Dr. Duke. "But I'm not the messenger now; I'm the translator. You're going to tell your readers you asked Dr. Duke to explain the state's response."

"They don't shoot the translator?" asked Adam.

"Not to the best of my knowledge," said Dr. Duke.

The other two articles on the front page were the bike-theft story and Ask Phoebe. The coeditors debated long and hard over whether they should put Ask Phoebe out front. They went through a whole bag of Cheez Doodles arguing it out. Whenever it came time to put the paper together, Front-Page Phoebe would reemerge, like some monster from the deep, noodging mercilessly, noodling, hinting, pleading, cajoling, doing everything in her annoying third-grade power to once again get her story on page one. It actually made it hard for the coeditors to decide fairly, since they wanted to stick her articles on the last page, under the bowling-team results, just to spite her.

That week she bombarded them with daily e-mails:

People keep asking if my front-page streak is still alive—any idea what I should tell them?????

Heard you're working on page one—need anything
from me?

A nice feature—like Ask Phoebe, for example—
could lighten up a serious front page, don't you
think?

My grandma was asking if I'd be front page
again—she's kind of old, so I was wondering what
to tell her. She has heart problems.

In the end they decided to put it on page one
because it would give readers a few laughs and a
break from all the seriousness in the other stories.

Despite Phoebe.

However, they did continue the column on the
back page, under the bowling-team results.

At the end of the column, they printed the Ask
Phoebe link to the new *Slash* website. As the world's
greatest third-grade reporter explained to her readers:
"In case you have questions during summer vacation
and need Ask Phoebe to solve your problems right
away."

They had included the letter from Confused
Middle Schooler. Adam wanted to apologize to

358

Jennifer for being so stupid but didn't know how. She had never admitted writing it, and he didn't want to embarrass her; things were going too well.

So he would have let it go, except when the two of them were making a final check for errors, Jennifer said, "I wonder if readers will think this letter is as hilarious as the *Slash* staff did."

"The boy in the letter sounds like a total idiot," Adam said.

"He's not that bad," said Jennifer. "The girl's the bigger idiot."

"No, no, she's not," said Adam. "It took courage to write that. You know what I don't get, though — why such a neat girl would write a nincompoop like Phoebe."

"Maybe this girl thought it was a safe way to get the boy's attention," said Jennifer. "They say middle-school boys aren't really good at talking about feelings."

"Makes sense," said Adam.

"Just a theory," said Jennifer.

They were done.

They were actually done.

They couldn't wait to get that golden CD to the printer. After school Tuesday, the two of them were going to ride their bikes to the print shop and drop it off. They were so excited about everyone finally seeing the paper. Jennifer had looked up Mrs. Boland's mailing address at the Tremble County office building. They were going to use twenty dollars from the extra money they'd raised to express-mail her one of the first copies hot off the presses.

Adam wanted to include a note: *Dear Mrs. Boland, Thought you might be interested, heh-heh-heh. PSYCHE!*

Jennifer nixed the note part.

The printer wouldn't print the paper.

At first he said the shop had a big summer rush. "June weddings coming out of our ears," he said. "Holy Communions, brisses, the auto show, Tooky Berry's Paint Ball Emporium annual summer shoot-out."

The coeditors could not believe what they were hearing. It was too shocking to understand at first. "You have stuff like that every June," said Jennifer. "We always do a June *Slash*. We never had a problem before."

The printer said there were other factors, like he was having trouble with one of the presses, and they were running behind.

"How far behind?" Jennifer asked.

"When do you need it?" he asked.

School was almost over. The eighth-grade moving-up ceremony was in three days.

Jennifer told him by the start of the fourth week of June at the latest.

"Oh, no," said the printer. "It would be July at best."

July, thought Adam. Everyone would be gone by July. He'd be gone. Surfing at his grandma's cottage. Wakeboarding. Picking wild blueberries. Lying in those open fields staring up at Mrs. Ameche's two perfect clouds. This wasn't fair. They'd killed themselves to get this done, and now this guy was telling them they couldn't have it until July?

"Mid-July at earliest," the printer said.

Jennifer was smoking mad, Adam could see it. She pulled out the receipt for the five-hundred-dollar deposit for getting the *Slash* printed and waved it in his face.

"You'll get your money back—don't worry," he said.

"It says right here that we could get the *Slash* to you anytime this week," Jennifer said. "We made our deadline."

"Well, you barely made it," the printer said.

"You've got to be kidding," said Adam. "You guys have been printing the *Slash* forever."

"It's different," said the man. "My understanding is that you're not the school paper anymore. That right?"

"So what?" said Adam. "We're still paying the same money."

"So it's not the same relationship," said the man. "Look, kid, I got things to do. Wait here. I'll get your money."

Jennifer and Adam looked at each other. Something rotten was up. They could smell it. They were pissed. Adam started pacing the room. Everywhere were glossy publications, brochures, piles of freshly printed wedding invitations, confirmations, bar mitzvahs, recreation schedules with the summer hours for the county parks, flyers for Tremble's July Fourth fireworks display and stacks and stacks of the latest *Citizen-Gazette-Herald-Advertiser*.

The *Citizen-Gazette-Herald-Advertiser*? Adam

froze. The Bolands' *Citizen-Gazette-Herald-Advertiser*? Oh, my God, that was it. This guy printed the Bolands' newspaper. Mrs. Boland must have ordered him not to print the *Slash*. "What a coward!" Adam blurted out.

"Who?" said Jennifer.

Before Adam could say another word, the man came back in and handed Jennifer an envelope with the deposit money.

"Count it," Adam said to Jennifer. "Make sure it's all there."

She did, got to the end, made a funny face, and started counting again.

"I knew it," said Adam, looking at the printer, "You should be ashamed. We may not be the high and mighty Bolands, but we are kids."

"Adam," said Jennifer softly. "Stop. It's not what you think. There's two hundred dollars extra."

"I'm sorry," said the printer. "I really am."

chapter 24

And the Living Is Easy

The thing about the United States of America — even before there was a country, even before there was a Congress and a Supreme Court and a president and a White House and a First Lady and interstate highways, even when this great continent was still mostly bears, beavers, trees, and fruited plains, there were already lots of guys with printing presses. Adam and Jennifer had no problem finding another printer to do the *Slash*. The Bolands might have scared and bullied and threatened the citizenry of Tremble County. But as big a media conglomerate as Bolandvision Cable was — with monopolies in forty-eight television markets across the nation—the farther you went from Tremble, the more their bulliness shrunk. The coeditors asked several adults—Mrs. Ameche, Mrs. Quigley, Mr. Brooks, Adam's grown-up friend Danny—for names of print shops and put together a list of more than a half dozen, mostly in the Tri-River Region's three cities.

The first one they called said yes.

They decided to use the two hundred extra dollars to print a hundred additional copies of the *Slash*.

And they now planned to express-mail *ten* copies to Mrs. Boland just for the pure joy of it.

The days that followed were sweet for Adam. While the coeditors waited to get the *Slash* back from the new printer, they took final exams. This wasn't nearly as bad as it sounded. School was a half day during exam week, and even if they went for extra help, they were done by noon. With sports and clubs over, they had the rest of the day free. Adam finally got to go swimming in the Tremble River. He put together a big basketball game at the Rec courts and organized his friends into a game of manhunt on the streets of River Path.

Wherever he went, he rode his new bike.

It was like a dress rehearsal for summer vacation, and it felt great.

After the English final, Mrs. Stanky handed back their profiles. Adam got an A+. She wrote that in all her years teaching, she'd never read a better profile. She liked Adam's ending best.

Adam had written:

> The thing that makes Shadow such an enjoyable friend is that you can tell him the exact truth even if it's not that good, and he doesn't get all worked up. I apologized to him for thinking that he was the baby in the trash, and he said he was happy he wasn't, since that baby died. Shadow told me he wasn't the way he was because of the trash; he was the way he was because a certain condition in his brain he was born with makes him different, but still just as good as everybody else. Shadow said some kids have the same thing as him, but they might have it worse because he's fighting to work hard in school without needing an aide. Next year, he will not be in 107A; he

will not be at Harris. He will be going to a school full of big kids, and you have to get up at 6 a.m. and take a bus to learn to be a carpenter. He told me, "To get in, I had to do a lot of stuff which I'm doing right now. Take a test. Complete homework on my own. Study real hard. Work without an aide and ask for help when I don't understand, definitely the right thing to do." When I told Shadow I'd miss him next year, he said he'd miss me too, since he likes to work for the *Slash* and find all the mistakes I make.

Early Tuesday morning, the entire *Slash* staff gathered in the alley behind the West River Diner. Adam and Jennifer had six big bundles of the June issue, tied with wire. Everyone was tingly with excitement. The coeditors gave each staff member twenty-five copies to hand out. Jennifer had already put aside papers for Mrs. Quigley and for Mr. Brooks, who would get them to all the teachers. In case there were any problems, they had safely stashed away twenty-five copies at Jennifer's house.

The staff was so worked up, it was hard for the

coeditors to get their attention. Finally, Adam lost patience and slammed half of his bacon-egg-and-cheese sandwich on the sidewalk. It didn't make much of a sound — just a little scraping of tinfoil against the concrete — but the sight of a middle-school boy wasting perfectly good food was a shock and silenced them.

He and Jennifer explained that they didn't expect any trouble. They said that they had talked to Mrs. Quigley, she'd given them the go-ahead, she knew today was the day, and no teachers or security guards would cause them any problems. But she'd also warned that she couldn't control anyone from the central office who might happen by or heaven forbid, the police. "At the first sign of trouble," Adam said, "make a single, high, loud caw like a crow — that's our official warning signal." He demonstrated for them and it came out pretty good; he'd been practicing for the past week in the shower. "You hear that caw," he continued, "stick whatever newspapers you have left in your backpack and get into the school as fast as possible."

Jennifer said she needed five volunteers for a recovery committee. They would go around the school and be responsible for grabbing any papers that had been tossed out and were still in good enough shape to reuse. "We don't want to waste a single issue," she said, and they understood. They'd raised every penny to print that paper themselves. It hadn't been easy.

"Any questions?" asked Adam, and the moment he did, he knew it was a mistake. Phoebe was wiggling her hand wildly.

"What?" he said. "Please, we've got to get over to the school. Make it fast."

Phoebe pulled a plastic bag from her pocket. "In case any of Stub's boys give us a problem, they're going down," squeaked Phoebe, who started twirling a jawbreaker high over her head.

Adam looked at Jennifer. Phoebe really was out of her mind. And what was worse — this was the person they were allowing to give advice to a whole school full of impressionable children.

"Phoebe, no," said Jennifer. "Put that thing away. No violence. If there are any problems, I want you going right into the school. Please tell me nobody else has one of those ridiculous things."

And then, one by one, the entire staff, every last one of them, pulled jawbreakers out of their pockets and twirled them high overhead.

Including Jennifer.

They were howling.

They were cawing like crows.

Everywhere Adam looked, he saw those hard white spheres, orbiting past his head.

What idiots. What divine jerks. What perfect nincompoops. He loved them, every last one of their ridiculous birdbrain selves.

Finally, Sammy raised his hands for quiet. "Adman," he said, "just wanted you to know we appreciate all you do."

And then they holstered their jawbreakers, grabbed their piles of newspapers, and, falling in formation behind Jennifer, marched down the street to spread the news.

Spread it, they did. In the past, people had to read the stories to figure out what the big deal was. This time, just being handed a copy of the *Slash* seemed like a miracle.

"Isn't this shut down?" kids kept asking.

"Not anymore," squeaked Phoebe. "By the way, you might want to check out the Ask Phoebe column. On the front page. It's me, in case you were wondering."

While geographically they couldn't be urban legends, they were rapidly becoming the next best thing: suburban superheroes, a band of kids who single-handedly stood up to the school board and the superintendent and all the deputy super-dupers *and* the most powerful family in Tremble County, and all by their lonesome selves printed a newspaper that was as true as true could be.

At least that was the superhero myth. In reality, no one knew better than Adam and Jennifer that they never could have done it without all the good grown-ups who'd helped. Adam thought of it like that scientific principle they had to memorize in Mr. Devillio's class, the Law of Conservation of Matter: for every sworn enemy who tried to destroy them, like Deputy Super-Duper Bleepin, there was an equally powerful friend to the bitter end, like Deputy Super-Duper Duke.

Thanks to the Ameches' online edition, their stories spread well beyond Tremble.

Someone had e-mailed a copy of the *Slash* story on the state tests to the *Capital Times*, the biggest newspaper in the state. And that paper's education reporter had called both Dr. Duke and Mrs. Gross to interview them for a story on how everyone was now saying the state test was easier this year.

Jennifer received more than three dozen e-mails from people who'd read the "WE'RE STILL HERE!!!" story and wanted to donate. Person after person wrote, *Finally, someone willing to stand up to the Bolands.*

She also got three e-mails from people complaining about their cable bills and one from a woman in Nome, Alaska, upset about her HD reception.

They didn't know if it was a coincidence, but two days after the *Slash* came out with its story on all the unsolved bike thefts in the county, the boy who'd stolen Adam's bike was arrested.

Of course, not all the reaction was positive. Stub Keenan was a very popular fellow. Lots of kids said that the real reason the election was called off was that Adolf Quigley had been scared that Stub was about to get everyone McDonald's for lunch and couldn't stand to see kids having fun.

And when the *Capital Times* did its story, the state education commissioner himself came out of a very important meeting of the state's high commission on standards to be quoted saying that this whole ridiculous rumor about the test getting easier was started by a gang of troublemaking punks in

372

Tremble County who ran an underground paper and were too lazy to study.

Many parents of Harris students were upset, too. Some worked for Bolandvision and some worked for companies that depended on Bolandvision. Others just admired the Bolands for being so successful. They liked the idea of bulldozing the last poor neighborhood in the county and putting up mini-estates for successful people exactly like themselves.

At a garden-club meeting, a woman told Jennifer's mom that her son Roderick knew for a fact that the Harris principal allowed the banned newspaper to meet at the school, and they were going to demand an investigation.

Friday at 11:15, the final bell rang. Classroom doors burst open and kids flooded the hallways. They were loud and boisterous and happy. Nothing could stop them now, and no one tried.

Summer was upon them.

That night, the *Slash* staff gathered at Only Kids Only to celebrate. Everyone came except three staff members who'd already left for overnight camp. The boys looked like their usual selves, in sports shorts and

T-shirts, but most of the girls wore dresses. Jennifer had on her red summer dress with the little straps that had made Adam notice her curvy shoulders.

She had arranged to get the private banquet room in the back of the restaurant. The manager wanted to charge them half the regular price because of Sammy's great stories, but Jennifer explained that was impossible — they had to pay the full banquet-room cost because of journalism ethics. The manager kept insisting until Jennifer said they'd have to go somewhere else. Finally he agreed, saying he'd never had anyone bargain up the price before.

What a party! Food was served buffet style with one whole section of the table set aside to make your own PB&J. There was a blue neon sign they could switch on whenever they wanted that said ONLY KIDS ONLY, and when they did, the room got dark, except for the sign, and even the waiters and waitresses had to leave. It really was Only Kids Only.

All night they made chocolate-milk toasts until they were giddy, and then the Ameche brothers taught everyone to Ha-Ha. Both Don and Alan danced with Phoebe, who asked for their autographs when the music stopped.

Jennifer announced a contest to see who could

suck down their jawbreaker most by the end of the summer. And since Adam had a head start on everyone, she presented him with a brand-new, unsucked jawbreaker on the condition that he promised not to use it to knock the wind out of anybody. Then she kissed him on the cheek, he turned redder than one of Mrs. Ameche's championship tomatoes, and they all started cawing like crows.

Things got so rowdy, Shadow had to go around opening every window to let out all the noise.

They partied full-out until after ten.

Adam and Jennifer were the last to leave. They had to pay the bill and figure out a 20 percent tip.

"Great party," she said.

"I was thinking," said Adam, "just kind of . . . you know . . . wondering if you might like to come over to my house tomorrow, take a swim at the civic beach, get an ice cream at Marvel, maybe go to a movie."

Jennifer put down her calculator. "Ice cream?" she said. "A movie?"

"*Gossip Girls 7* is playing at the Tremble 10," said Adam.

"You want to see *Gossip Girls 7*?" said Jennifer.

"Well, not exactly," said Adam. "But I read this advice column in the newspaper about a really stupid middle-school boy . . ."

"Ahhh." She nodded. "I wouldn't believe everything you read in the paper."

"I know," he said.

She stared at him. "I can't," she said.

"Really?" said Adam. He felt like an idiot. Why had he ever . . . He was sorry he even . . . Forget everything. From now on . . . "No big deal," he said. "I've got to get going anyway." He jumped up.

She grabbed his arm and yanked him back. "You are such a funny boy," she said. "I'd love to go with you, Adam. It's just, we're leaving for the airport at, like, seven in the morning. Music camp. In Michigan."

"Oh," he said, nodding.

"Stay here," she said. "Don't move." She went over to the wall and flipped the switch, so the room got dark and the blue Only Kids Only sign came on.

She was back. "Where were we?" she asked. She was looking very soft and melty in the blue neon light.

"I think we were at the part where I'm a funny boy," he said.

Adam knew what he had to do, though he wasn't

sure he could do it. He leaned toward her, so close he could smell her fruity apricot shampoo. She closed her eyes, and so he did, too. He pushed out his lips, and then leaned forward a little more and then . . . he bumped into something bony and pointy—oh, my God, it had to be her chin. He'd missed. He felt like an idiot. He wanted to . . . But as he opened his eyes, her long fingers were on his cheeks. They were steering him to her lips. Their lips touched.

It didn't feel like too much, and Adam wondered if maybe he was making his lips too tight. Then her fingertip was on his lower lip, and it was going back and forth slowly, just barely touching, like when he was little and his mother put sunscreen on his lips, except this didn't feel one bit like his mother. Then it was just her soft lips brushing his soft lips and he couldn't tell where his stopped and hers started or where he was or why anyone would care about anything else.

"I'll write," she said.

That would be nice, Adam thought, but he forgot to say it aloud; he just waved as she walked out.

He sat there for a while in the neon-blue dark, he didn't know how long, just trying to hold on to the feeling. And then he had the weirdest thought— where had Jennifer learned to kiss like that?

Author's Note

The two reading passages included in Chapter 18 are actual excerpts from the New York State Education Department's fourth-grade reading test. "Dear Levi: Letters from the Overland Trail" was from the 2004 state test. "The River Otter" was on the 2005 test. Do you agree with Adam and Jennifer about which is easier?